A CRYSTAL

"Mimsey, what did yo▮▮▮▮▮▮▮▮▮▮▮▮▮-
tically whispered. We▮▮▮▮▮▮▮▮▮▮▮▮ ▮
bakery unless there were no customers to overhear us.

"Well, my stars!" Mimsey kept her voice low, though it trilled with excitement. We all leaned closer. "It appeared to be an emergency, though of what kind I simply can't pretend to know. My dear little pink stone only indicated that you needed help, darlin'." She looked around at the others.

I pressed my lips together. "Your crystal ball is nothing more than a gossip, then."

Her face fell, and Bianca gave me a stern look. I backpedaled. "I mean, yes, Declan and I discovered a body under a rhododendron bush in the square, but that doesn't have anything to do with us. Long term, I mean."

"What!" Ben exclaimed.

Heads all over the bakery turned toward us, and I felt my face redden. I scooted closer to Lucy and motioned Ben to the cushion next to me. "Shh."

He ducked his head. "Sorry." He sat down and whispered, "A body? What happened?"

Praise for
Brownies and Broomsticks

"Katie is a charming amateur sleuth, baking her way through murder and magic set against the enchanting backdrop of Savannah, Georgia. With an intriguing plot and an amusing cast of characters, *Brownies and Broomsticks* is an attention-grabbing read that I couldn't put down."

—Jenn McKinlay, national bestselling author of *Death by the Dozen*

Also Available from Bailey Cates

THE MAGICAL BAKERY MYSTERIES

Brownies and Broomsticks

Bewitched, Bothered, and Biscotti

A Magical Bakery Mystery

Bailey Cates

AN OBSIDIAN MYSTERY

OBSIDIAN
Published by New American Library, a division of
Penguin Group (USA) Inc., 375 Hudson Street,
New York, New York 10014, USA
Penguin Group (Canada), 90 Eglinton Avenue East, Suite 700, Toronto,
Ontario M4P 2Y3, Canada (a division of Pearson Penguin Canada Inc.)
Penguin Books Ltd., 80 Strand, London WC2R 0RL, England
Penguin Ireland, 25 St. Stephen's Green, Dublin 2,
Ireland (a division of Penguin Books Ltd.)
Penguin Group (Australia), 250 Camberwell Road, Camberwell, Victoria 3124,
Australia (a division of Pearson Australia Group Pty. Ltd.)
Penguin Books India Pvt. Ltd., 11 Community Centre, Panchsheel Park,
New Delhi - 110 017, India
Penguin Group (NZ), 67 Apollo Drive, Rosedale, Auckland 0632,
New Zealand (a division of Pearson New Zealand Ltd.)
Penguin Books (South Africa) (Pty.) Ltd., 24 Sturdee Avenue,
Rosebank, Johannesburg 2196, South Africa

Penguin Books Ltd., Registered Offices:
80 Strand, London WC2R 0RL, England

First published by Obsidian, an imprint of New American Library,
a division of Penguin Group (USA) Inc.

First Printing, January 2013
10 9 8 7 6 5 4 3 2 1

PUBLISHER'S NOTE
This is a work of fiction. Names, characters, places, and incidents either are the
product of the author's imagination or are used fictitiously, and any resem-
blance to actual persons, living or dead, business establishments, events, or
locales is entirely coincidental.
    The publisher does not have any control over and does not assume any re-
sponsibility for author or third-party Web sites or their content.

ALWAYS LEARNING   PEARSON

Acknowledgments

It takes so many people to create a book and get it into the hands of readers. I'm grateful for the opportunity to work with Kim Lionetti, and so many thanks go to the hardworking team at Penguin/NAL: Jessica Wade, Jesse Feldman, Kathleen Cook, Kayleigh Clark, and all the others who contributed their talent and dedication to this project. My writing buddies, Bob and Mark, provided tons of useful feedback. The inspiring ladies of the Old Town Writing Group gave me unfailing encouragement. And Kevin Brookfield was—and is—my anchor.

Chapter 1

"Mmm, that was delicious." Declan McCarthy leaned back on his elbows and looked up through the branches of the live oak arching overhead. His eyes reflected the electric blue of the clear October sky.

"Even if you do say so yourself," I said.

He blinked slowly. "I could take a nap right now."

Mungo, my Cairn terrier, sighed his agreement.

I slapped my human companion lightly on the knee. "It's only nine a.m., lazybones."

"Not my fault you insisted on a breakfast picnic, Katie."

"Well, it's your fault for bringing so much food."

Declan did all of the cooking for the crew when he was on duty at the firehouse. Right now he was on days off, and when he'd offered to put together a Saturday-morning nosh for the two of us, I leaped at the chance. I spent so much time in the kitchen of the Honeybee Bakery that a morning off was pure heaven. Not that I didn't love my work.

Declan had packed up a culinary extravaganza of Low Country breakfast shrimp, Tasso ham and cheese grits, flaky buttermilk biscuits slathered with butter and peach jam, and a thermos of freshly squeezed orange juice. Mungo had sampled all but the last with the verve of the canine gourmet that he was. On my way to meet Declan in the parklike setting of Johnson Square, I'd stopped by the Honeybee and grabbed a couple of dark-roast coffees and some pumpkin spice cookies for, God help me, dessert.

Now, stuffed to the gills, I stretched out on the quilt. "It's been hot for this time of year, don't you think?" Not that I'd lived in Savannah the previous October, but it seemed like the sticky heat was going to go on forever.

The previous April I'd driven my Volkswagen Beetle from Akron, Ohio, to Savannah to open the bakery with my aunt Lucy and uncle Ben. It was a fresh start after a broken engagement and years at an unpleasant job. Six months later I was the proud owner of a tiny carriage house in Midtown and part owner of the bakery, and I felt a sense of belonging with my new friends that I'd never known before.

Declan—one of those new friends—looked down at me with a smile. "Ah. But not here. There's always a breeze in Johnson Square. Don't you know the story?" He indicated the marble obelisk towering nearby.

I shook my head.

His sweeping gesture took in the whole historic square. "Nathanael Greene, the Savior of the South himself, absolutely despised fair Savannah. He hated the heat, and for some reason he especially hated all the Spanish moss."

"Because of the chiggers?" The elegantly draping

plant wasn't really a moss at all, and it deceptively housed a teeming population of tiny red biting insects.

"I daresay that didn't help." He pointed to the towering white monument. "Ol' Nathan is buried right there, and he keeps the air-conditioning on for everyone who comes here."

I snorted.

"It makes a certain amount of sense," he said. "I believe he ultimately died of heatstroke. Notice anything else?"

My gaze followed his upward. Then it dawned on me. "There isn't any Spanish moss on these trees!"

"That's right. Nathan forbids it to grow."

My eyes narrowed. Normally I would have poohpoohed the notion, but since I had discovered six months previously that I was a hereditary witch, my willingness to believe in magic of all sorts had expanded exponentially.

Declan shrugged and sat up. "That's the story, anyway." He was a big guy, but sitting there grinning at me he looked all of fourteen years old. I couldn't help but grin back, and had to resist the urge to ruffle his dark curls.

Then he looked over my shoulder, and his smile faded. "Poor guy. Must be sleeping it off."

I turned to look where he pointed. It took a few moments, but then the dark outline of a figure lying under a mature rhododendron bush became clear in the morning shadows. Stripes of buttery sunshine cut obliquely across the bricks of the walkway and the small expanse of grass, which made it even harder to see.

Squinting helped. It was a man. A large man. His

blue shirttail had come untucked from a pair of khaki slacks. I made out a worn brown boot, caked with mud. A shiver ran down my back, and I Knew.

I pushed up to my feet. "I don't think so, Deck."

"Katie . . ."

Ignoring him, I walked swiftly toward the prone figure, Mungo at my heels.

"Katie!" He scrambled up. "What are you doing?"

Other than a woman reading the *Savannah Morning News* on a bench in front of the Coastal Bank on Bryan Street, no one was near the square. The pathways were curiously empty. Silent, even. My steps slowed as I neared the five-foot-tall rhododendron's mottled shadow.

I stopped, reeling at the sight. The man lay half under the bush, but I could see that dirt smeared the faded chambray fabric of his shirt. His slacks were dirty and had a hole in the knee, and the one visible boot was heavily scuffed under its coating of mud. His worn shirtsleeve brushed the edge of a tattoo on his left bicep, and below that a sturdy black-and-silver watch hugged his wrist above a dirt-encrusted hand devoid of rings. I leaned forward enough to make out the words *TAG Heuer* on the timepiece.

When I dared to look at the man's face, I saw tanned skin, full lips, a hooked nose, and bushy eyebrows sprouting beneath a high forehead. Thick white hair spread around his head in an exaggerated halo. One side was streaked with deep red beginning to dry to brown.

Almost against my will, my attention returned to the tattoo. It appeared to be some kind of wreath, with three equidistant pairs of lines extending from it. There was nothing the least bit threatening about it. So why did the telltale shiver begin at the base of my neck, work its way down my spine, and then make the return journey?

Mungo sniffed at the boot, then saw the tattoo. He made a little sound in the back of his throat and jumped back, then blinked up at me with eyes full of doubt.

I nodded down at my familiar. "Yeah. I know."

Just to make sure, I nudged the boot with the toe of my trail runner as Declan reached my side. His fingers closed on my arm, ready to pull me away.

"Careful," he whispered.

"No need." I shuddered. "He's dead."

"How exactly is it that you happened on this guy?" Detective Peter Quinn asked me, running his fingers through his thick gray hair.

"Declan and I were having a picnic and saw him lying there." I tried not to sound defensive.

Quinn was a regular Honeybee customer, and had known Uncle Ben Savannah's former fire chief—in a professional capacity for years. Unfortunately, I'd first met Quinn in a professional capacity as well—his profession, not mine. He still brought up how I'd barged into his murder investigation, though at least he usually smiled about it.

He wasn't smiling now. "So you spread a cozy blanket out on the grass and unpack your little picnic, and then—*boom!*—you just happen to glance under a bush and there's a dead man."

"Well, we ate first," Declan said.

The thought made all that lovely food in my stomach do a slow flip-flop. Mungo poked his head up from the tote bag slung from my shoulder and glared at

Quinn. Around us, crime scene specialists poked and prodded the foliage, took pictures, and dropped bits and pieces of who-knew-what into evidence bags. The whole square was cordoned off, but the three of us stood inside one corner, off the street but out of the way of the technicians trying to do their jobs.

The detective sighed. "Well, at least you don't have to worry about solving this crime for me, Katie. I'm pretty sure the Savannah Police Department can handle the death of a homeless man all by ourselves."

"Homeless man? Did you see his watch?"

A short, slightly rotund man with an unfortunate comb-over broke loose from the knot of people surrounding the rhododendron and its grisly guest and stomped toward us. I watched him approach and tried to ignore the alarm bells ringing in the back of my mind. When Quinn saw me looking over his shoulder, he stood and waited for the other man to reach us.

"Katie Lightfoot, Declan McCarthy, this is my new partner, Detective Franklin Taite." Quinn smiled when he said it, but the smile didn't quite reach his eyes.

I turned to the newcomer. "Nice to meet you, Detective."

"So you know these two?" Taite said to Quinn by way of greeting. A New York tang rode under his words, tight and abrupt.

But Quinn smiled easily. "Katie and her aunt and uncle have the Honeybee Bakery down on Broughton Street. Declan is a firefighter with Five House."

"So what's the story?" Taite demanded.

Declan and I repeated what we'd already told Detective Quinn. I ended with, "Do you know who the victim is?"

Taite spoke to me with exaggerated patience. "Victim? Of what? There's no official determination of cause of death yet."

I frowned. "Maybe not official, but he was assaulted. I saw the blood."

Taite snorted. "I'm sure you like to watch those detective shows on television, Ms. Lightfoot. But let's try not to be sensational. Especially if the press starts asking questions, all right? Wouldn't want to get yourself in any trouble for speaking out of turn, now, would you?"

Declan frowned at the mention of the press, and I knew he was thinking of my friendship with crime-reporter-turned-columnist Steve Dawes—a friendship he heartily disapproved of. A long-ago family tragedy had made enemies of those two, and my fondness for both of them didn't help matters a bit. I didn't know if I would ever tell Declan I was a witch, but I trusted him with my life. Steve, though—he knew I practiced magic because he was also a witch. A sexy, intriguing male witch who made me crazy in more ways than I liked to admit.

My thoughts came up short as I realized this balding jerk of a detective had just threatened me. The heat of the day had increased and suddenly felt oppressive. The cooling breeze from earlier had given way to a dank stillness. The ghost of Nathanael Greene had abandoned us all.

Taite stepped closer. Mungo leaned out of my tote bag and bared his teeth at him. I smoothed the hair between the dog's ears with my fingertips. The growl died in his throat, but I could still feel him quivering beneath my hand.

Ignoring my canine companion, the detective patted me on the shoulder. "I'm sure it was horrible finding a dead man like that. You probably didn't take a very close look, and that's for the best, honey. You just go home and forget all about the whole sad situation."

I sensed Declan bristling beside me. "Listen, Katie's not some delicate . . ." He trailed off when I put my other hand on his arm.

"'Horrible' is one way of putting it, Detective," I said with heartfelt emphasis. "I imagine I did miss a few details."

Quinn watched me with a wry expression.

"There you go," Taite said. "But don't you worry about it. We've got everything under control. Your friend Detective Quinn here will check in with you if we have any more questions, or perhaps I will. After you've had a chance to settle down a little, of course." With another dismissive pat, he directed what was intended to be an encouraging smile at me, nodded at Declan, and made his way back to one of the many minions of officialdom already investigating the suspicious death.

"Why, that—," Declan spluttered.

I shook my head. "It's okay."

"But he was so condescending!"

I was watching Quinn, who suddenly wouldn't meet my eye. "Since when do you work with a partner?" I asked.

He sighed. "Since the new captain doesn't approve of lone wolves."

A smile crept onto my face. Quinn struck me as more of a lone dachshund than a lone wolf. "You must have really made him mad for him to saddle you with Mr. Charm."

"Eh, he's a Yankee, and a little obsessive, but he seems smart enough."

"Really? Is he the one who suggested the *victim* was homeless?"

Quinn shrugged. "You're right. It does look like someone hit the poor guy, but it could have been an accident. And he's certainly filthy."

"I think you should take another look, Peter. Because that man is wearing a TAG Heuer chronograph watch. Those are spendy—I was going to buy my dad one for his birthday a couple years ago until I realized there was no way I could afford it. Unless the dead man stole it, he's anything but homeless. Eccentric, maybe, but there are plenty of people in Savannah who fit that description."

"Katie's right," Declan said. "His clothes are pretty scruffy and dirty, but not living-on-the-street dirty. He's clean shaven and looks pretty fit."

Peter Quinn distributed a scowl between us before finally nodding. "Noted."

"You didn't answer my question about who the poor guy is," I said.

"No wallet." His words were clipped. "But we have all we need from you on this case. Understood, Katie?"

"Of course."

After clearing my uncle Ben's name the previous April, I had sworn off murder investigations. For the last six months I'd been having the best time of my life, living in a city I loved, doing the kind of work I enjoyed most at the Honeybee Bakery, learning about spell work

10 Bailey Cates

and my magical abilities from my new coven, and spending time with Aunt Lucy, Uncle Ben, Declan . . . and Steve Dawes. Why would I want to jeopardize that by interfering in a police matter?

Never mind that the image of the dead man's tattoo felt like a brand on my inner vision.

Chapter 2

Pausing inside the front door of the Honeybee Bakery, I breathed in the aroma of freshly baked goodies and listened to the murmur of voices in conversation. The espresso machine came to life as Uncle Ben brewed a coffee confection for a waiting customer. Mungo, knowing he had to stay hidden when we were inside the bakery, snuggled deeper into the bottom of my tote bag.

Light amber walls rose to the high ceiling on three sides, while the vertical expanse behind the cash register blazed a rich burnt orange. The tall chalkboard menu mounted there listed coffee drinks and sweet and savory items from the kitchen. Garlands of candy corn were draped from the chalkboard's corners as well as from the stereo speakers and the glass display case next to the register, full of scones and cookies, biscotti and cupcakes and muffins. The bottom shelf was packed with loaves of the house sourdough bread, which was beginning to gain a reputation among Savannahians who appreciated such things. Each day we also offered something special that wasn't on our regular menu. Today it was salted caramel apples, a crispy-salty-sweet concoction that I also planned to serve at the Honeybee Halloween party coming up in less than a week. My mouth watered at the thought of them.

Of course, the candy corn garlands were some of the not-so-spooky decorations we'd been putting in place as we geared up for the party. On the windows facing Broughton Street we'd painted ghosts cavorting between cartoon headstones. Velvet spiders nestled among the vases of flowers on the blue bistro tables, and black paper silhouettes of mice crawled along the baseboards.

At the far end of the room soft brocade sofas invited people to settle in and sample from the overflowing bookshelf nearby. The Honeybee Halloween tree sat in the corner. Uncle Ben had sprayed a fake Christmas fir glossy black. Strings of tiny green fairy lights and more garlands of candy corn looped around it, and orange glass balls painted with jack-o'-lantern faces hung from the branches.

Light jazz drifted through the spice-and-coffee-scented air at low volume. Customers sat in the blue-and-chrome chairs in small groups or accompanied by their trusty laptops. The stainless-steel appliances visible in the mostly open kitchen echoed the silvery tones and let people know they were in a working bakery, not just a storefront. The most recent addition to the bakery staff, Cookie Rios, moved into view carrying a sheet pan of cookies just out of the oven.

Aunt Lucy chatted with a woman who was picking up one of her custom-decorated cakes while Ben handed the steaming coffee mug to his customer. As I watched, a familiar contentment crept over me, and the muscles along the back of my neck relaxed. I loved this place. After pastry school in Cincinnati and a few years as assistant manager of a bakery in Akron, I finally had what I'd always dreamed of: a place where I had free rein to create my own recipes and bake to my heart's content. Not to mention working with two of my favorite people in the world.

Though in one respect starting the Honeybee hadn't turned out quite the way I'd imagined while packing and planning back in Ohio. I smiled, remembering a day before the Honeybee grand opening. Lucy had been stirring dried sage from her herb garden into a batch of scone dough, muttering all the while. I'd thought it odd, but soon forgot about it. Not long after that, she revealed that the muttering was an incantation, a *spell*, and told me that I, like her, came from a long line of hereditary hedgewitches—green witches with a special affinity for herbal craft and cooking. The idea had certainly taken some getting used to, but now I was eagerly learning about the Craft.

Ben turned, reaching for the day's mail, and saw me standing by the door. His eyes lit up in greeting behind his rimless glasses. Shaking his head, he put down the envelopes and came out from behind the counter.

"What are you doing back here on your day off, sweetie? I thought you were meeting Deck for a date."

"I guess you could call it that." I didn't like to think of our platonic picnic as a date, but I could see how Ben would. Steve probably would, too—if he knew about it. And for that matter, I couldn't have guaranteed it would have stayed quite so innocent if a dead body hadn't intruded on our morning. Declan was so easy to be with that I sometimes let my guard down. "Something happened, though. I thought I should tell you before Peter Quinn does."

Ben's eyebrows shot up at that, but before I could say anything more, laughter erupted from the far end of the Honeybee. Recognizing it, I leaned around my uncle to see. Sure enough, Jaida and Bianca had stopped by for their usual Saturday lattes and were sitting in the reading area by the big bookshelf. They were both members of the book club my aunt and I belonged to.

The spellbook club—that was what my coven called itself.

The door opened behind me, and Mimsey Carmichael hurried in from Broughton Street. Two steps into the bakery she saw me and paused, a grin crinkling the crow's-feet at the corners of her eyes. "Oh, good. I hoped you'd be working today." Her indigo slacks brushed the tops of alligator shoes dyed to match. A long vest in a lighter shade of the same color hung gracefully over a crisp blouse as bright white as her smooth pageboy.

"Actually, I just stopped in for a few minutes," I said. "Did you need me for something?"

Mimsey peered up at me, her blue eyes twinkling. "Did anything interesting happen to you this morning?" She was also a member of the spellbook club and a frequent visitor to the Honeybee. Among other specialties, she favored color magic, and her attire invariably reflected that. From my lessons with her I knew indigo was the color of intuition.

I looked at Ben, and he raised his eyebrows in question. He wasn't a witch, but since he was married to my aunt he knew about our magical antics.

"I guess you could say that," I said to Mimsey.

"I knew it!" Satisfaction spread across her face. "Or at least my shew stone did. And Jaida and Bianca are still here? Good. Let's get Lucy and Cookie, and you can tell us all about it." Cookie was not only the newest Honeybee employee; she was also the youngest member of the spellbook club.

My uncle smiled. "Drop your stuff in the back and then come tell us all what happened. That way you won't have to do it twice."

Mungo shifted against my hip.

"Right." I headed for the small office at the rear of the bakery, wondering what Mimsey had seen in the sphere of pink quartz—literally a crystal ball—that she called her shew stone. Divination was an iffy business and open to plenty of interpretation.

I had to admire Ben's ability to put his curiosity on hold. It was amazing, really, how much he'd mellowed since retiring as Savannah's fire chief and starting up the bakery. I'd wondered whether he might find running a business a bit tame after so many years of saving lives and property, but when I asked him about it he told me his position as chief had become so much about administration and politics that he'd welcomed the change.

With Mungo deposited out of sight, I returned to find that Lucy had finished with her cake customer and was sitting with the others by the bookshelves. She beckoned Ben and me over. As we made our way through the tables he greeted many of the customers by name, briefly asking after one man's family. Yes, this was the perfect venue for his particular social talents. Even tourists who stopped in for a snack ended up feeling like my uncle was an old friend before they left.

"I do believe Cookie's nearly finished with her duties in the kitchen for a while and will be able to join us momentarily," Mimsey said. "Sit down and take a load off while we wait for her."

"Hi, everyone." I sank gratefully onto the sofa next to Lucy. Ben remained standing where he could keep an eye on the register and the front door.

My aunt, sweeter than was sometimes good for her, looked like a throwback to the sixties with her batik print skirt and mane of blond hair streaked with gray. She was shorter than me by several inches, and now patted my bare knee with a calm smile. "Glad you could join us."

The others murmured greetings. Mimsey took a seat on the sofa opposite Lucy and me. On her left sat elegant Bianca Devereaux, a fortysomething single mom and practicing Wiccan with an affinity for moon spells and making piles of money in the stock market. She smiled now and said, "Mimsey has made us all quite curious about your morning, Katie."

In the chair next to the sofa, Jaida French cocked her head to one side. "Did something happen when you were out with Declan?"

"We weren't 'out,'" I protested. It sounded weak, though, and she rolled her eyes.

"Where were you *not out*, then?" She might be wearing jeans and a Bob Marley T-shirt right now, but Jaida was a lawyer by profession. Interrogation came as naturally to her as the tarot magic she practiced.

"Johnson Square," I said. "Now wait until Cookie gets here, and I'll tell you everything."

Cookie Rios was the reason I was able to take this Saturday off in the first place. Four months before, she'd given up her job as an apartment manager and, out of the blue, asked to work at the bakery. Lucy, Ben, and I had jumped at the offer. Business was going great guns, and we desperately needed the help. Her addition to our staff freed up more time for me to learn the Craft.

Each of the spellbook club members had been schooling me in her own magical specialty, and I'd been attending the spellbook club meetings; for the most part our gatherings really were about studying spells and spellbooks. I added to my personal grimoire— a kind of magical journal where I recorded my spell work—every day, but I knew I still had a long way to go. Gradually, I was getting a handle on some of the specifics about practicing magic. It was really all about different ways to focus intention in order to manifest change in the real world. Witches are naturally better at it, but magic exists for anyone who wants to reach for it. The spellbook club practiced a gentle, subtle magic.

Well, for the most part. A couple of things had surprised me during my relatively short journey. Things like being able to direct energy to healing, or infusing my voice with a Command. But we all believed in the Rule of Three: All actions and intentions came back to you threefold—so it paid to be careful with your abilities.

"Ah, what is this all about, then?" Cookie's slight Haitian accent lilted from above and behind me.

I tilted my head and watched her come around to sit on Mimsey's right. Her teensy apron barely covered her miniskirt, but with those lanky legs and her graceful manner Cookie could pull off the skirt-and-tank-top combo with an oddly tasteful sexiness. She regarded me with jade eyes that were a little too wise and a little too willing to break the rules. Her lips curved into a smile.

"Mimsey, what did you see in your shew stone?" I practically whispered. We didn't usually talk magic in the bakery unless there were no customers to over-hear us.

"Well, my stars!" Mimsey kept her voice low, though it trilled with excitement. We all leaned closer. "It ap-peared to be an emergency, though of what kind I sim-ply can't pretend to know. My dear little pink stone only indicated that you needed help, darlin'." She looked around at the others.

I pressed my lips together. "Your crystal ball is noth-ing more than a gossip, then."

Her face fell, and Bianca gave me a stern look. I back-pedaled. "I mean, yes, Declan and I discovered a body under a rhododendron bush in the square, but that doesn't have anything to do with us. Long term, I mean."

"What!" Ben exclaimed.

Heads all over the bakery turned toward us, and I felt my face redden. I scooted closer to Lucy and mo-tioned Ben to the cushion next to me. "Shh."

He ducked his head. "Sorry." He sat down and whispered, "A body? What happened?"

Glancing behind me to make sure no one was too close, I said, "Peter Quinn says it's a homeless man, but I don't think so. Quinn has a new partner, by the way—Detective Taite—and he seems to think the guy was homeless, too. But he didn't even want to admit the poor guy had been hit over the head, even though I saw the blood. Anyway, the man Declan and I found was wearing clothes with dirt on them, but he also had a nice watch and had recently shaved. Except for his hands, he looked bathed and, well, healthy." I made a face. "Other than, you know, being dead."

They all stared at me. I realized that after talking with Quinn, and then Taite, and then Declan as he drove me and Mungo the few blocks to the bakery to pick up my car, I perhaps sounded a little callous. But they didn't know about the nice breakfast now burning a hole in my stomach or the headache slowly building in my temples.

"Did Quinn tell you who the victim was?" Jaida asked.

I shrugged one shoulder. "He said the guy didn't have a wallet. Didn't seem all that excited about giving me information." I sat back and said in a louder voice, "And that's fine. It's none of my business."

"What else?" Mimsey said. The usual twinkle had left her eyes, and she kept her voice so quiet I had to strain to hear her.

I couldn't help but echo her low tone. "What do you mean, what else?"

"There's something you're not telling us."

"Why would you say that?" I frowned.

"Because my shew stone says so. What are you leaving out?"

"Nothing! I mean . . ." But for some reason I didn't want to tell them.

Bianca finally spoke. "If we are being called upon to help the unfortunate man who died, you must play your part, Katie."

Now I was the one staring at her.

"Is there something else, dear?" Lucy asked from

beside me. Her gaze radiated kindness. It worked better than the most forceful questioning could have.

"Well . . . he had a tattoo."

Cookie raised one eyebrow and exchanged looks with Bianca.

Ben turned in his seat to face me. "What did it look like?"

I raised my shoulders, still reluctant. "Like a wreath, kind of. With lines coming out of it."

"Was it black? Or that gray color you see in prison tattoos?" he asked.

"Prison?" I squeaked at the same time Lucy said, "Good heavens!" with her hand at her throat. Heads turned our way again, and I swore under my breath. "How am I supposed to know what a prison tattoo looks like, Ben?" I asked.

"Well, what color was it?"

The image was so clear in my mind, I didn't really have to think at all. "It was green. Dark green against his pale skin. And the lines were dark yellow. Amber."

The bell over the door tinkled again. Two women were leaving. Ben called good-bye and began to turn back to our conversation when one of our regular customers who made the Honeybee his office away from home walked up to the counter.

"I'll be right back," Ben said, and hurried to take the man's refill order.

I slumped back into the cushy sofa and held my palms up. "That's it. There's no more for me to tell you. And I can't imagine what that tattoo could have to do with your shew stone, Mimsey."

She didn't say anything. The other ladies exchanged glances. Jaida said, "Could it be a gang symbol?"

"He seemed a bit old to be in a gang, but you never know," I replied.

Cookie shrugged and stood. "Probably some personal symbol, like mine is."

"You have a tattoo?" Though I wasn't all that surprised.

"Of course. I'd better get back to work. That sourdough sponge won't mix itself." She paused as she walked away, her hand on my shoulder. "Don't be too concerned, Katie. The dead rarely torment those who have not done them harm." Then she continued on to the kitchen.

Jaida laughed at my expression. "Don't mind her. You know how dramatic she likes to be with all that voodoo stuff." She stood. "I'm meeting Greg for a late lunch at the River House, so I'll see you all later. Katie, don't worry. Detective Quinn took your statement, right?"

I nodded.

"That should be the end of it, then. But if you need me for anything, just give a call."

Bianca rose, too. Tall, with long dark hair and translucent skin, she was the witchiest-looking of us all. She tended toward natural fabrics that flowed with her movements, and today she'd chosen a layered silk dress in hues of lavender, violet, and mauve.

"I need to pick Colette up from the babysitter. I'll see you tomorrow afternoon at the book club meeting, okay?" She leaned down. "I am sorry to hear about your morning, Katie. Just remember that death is but a passage onto another plane, and not a tragedy by any means."

Trailing her signature scent of cinnamon, Jaida winked at me as they passed by.

"Thanks, everyone—" I stopped as my eyes met Mimsey's and I saw the deep worry there.

"Do you think you could draw that tattoo, Katie?" she asked.

Beside me, Lucy stilled at the tone of her old friend's voice.

Chapter 3

Mimsey pushed a piece of paper across the low coffee table, followed by a pen from her purse. Nodding, I pulled them toward me and began to draw. Art had never been my strong suit, but my memory of the tattoo was vivid and its design relatively simple. Soon I'd completed a depiction to the best of my ability. I glanced at Lucy, who had watched with great interest from her perch on the cushion beside me, turned the sheet around, and pushed it back across the table to Mimsey.

My aunt's eyes were wide, her gaze glued to my representation of the wreath. It had three sets of two spokes emanating from its center to extend beyond the edges of the stylized leaves. Mimsey stared down at it without moving at all.

"Darlin'! I just have to show you the book I found in here the other day." The voice was deep with Southern flavor.

I looked up to see two women in their mid-thirties with perfect blond-streaked hair and flawless makeup approaching the bookcase.

The speaker continued. "It's exactly what you need to deal with that wolf you work for."

Such interruptions were inevitable when your library was stocked by a coven of witches who had strong and unerring instincts for what volumes would help Honeybee customers. The result was a hodgepodge of strangely useful literature that ran the gamut from classical Jane Austen to Jon Kabat-Zinn's meditation yoga.

Mimsey stood with alacrity, sweeping my drawing off the table and folding it in half. "Katie, may I talk with you in the office?"

My head swiveled toward the newcomers, but they appeared oblivious to the idea that they might have interrupted us or the notion that Mimsey was being rude. She wasn't really, though. I was just used to the inordinate pleasure she usually took in assisting and witnessing how the library helped people.

"Sure," I replied, and stood to follow her.

Lucy popped up, too, and we trouped to the register. I'd been too distracted by drawing the tattoo to notice that several more customers had entered the bakery, and now Ben was trying to ring people up in between making coffee drinks. Seeing his dilemma, Lucy retied her apron and hurried behind the counter to help. When I paused, Mimsey took my elbow and gently steered me toward the kitchen. Ben glanced up as we passed, eyebrows raised.

Cookie was slicing a batch of toffee-studded biscotti to go into the oven. She looked up as we made our way through to the office, curious, but she obviously had her hands full at the moment.

Mungo stood up on the small club chair from which he reigned whenever he was at the Honeybee, tail wagging furiously until he got a good look at Mimsey. He watched as she closed the door and sank into the swivel desk chair. He tipped his head to the side with an expression of expectation very similar to the one he donned when I cooked bacon at home.

I folded my arms, leaned one hip against the filing cabinet, and waved at the paper she held in her hand. "You recognize it, don't you?"

She hesitated, then gave a slow nod.

"Why didn't you tell the others?"

She wouldn't meet my eyes.

I waited.

She unfolded the drawing of the tattoo and held it at arm's length. At first I thought it was so she could focus better, but then I realized I'd never seen Mimsey wear glasses. Her nostrils flared slightly in distaste.

What on earth?

"Mimsey," I urged.

After a long moment she leaned down and put the paper on the floor between us and looked up at me. "Yes. I've seen this sigil before. I wanted to be sure it was what I suspected before I said anything to the others."

Mungo leaned forward on his paws, peering quizzically at the drawing.

"Sigil?"

She pressed her lips together. "The depiction of the wreath was lifted from the heraldic symbol of a wreath of oak leaves."

I frowned. "Those don't look like any kind of oak leaves to me."

"That's because they aren't. Those leaves are from a holly tree. *Ilex x attenuata* is my guess."

"*Ilex* . . . ?"

"Nowadays we call it Savannah holly. Oh, now, don't look so surprised. I've been a florist for decades, but I know about a lot more than tulips and roses, believe you me. And these sun spokes coming from the center? They reflect the ancient wheel of Taranis."

"Okay, what the heck is a Taranis?"

"He's the Celtic god of sun and thunder."

"Both?"

"Think of it as yin and yang. It's the solar cross, used by druids for centuries. The spokes represent the equinoxes and the solstices and two other sabbats—Beltane and Samhain. For the ones who are branded with that tattoo, the cross combines with the wheel to have an additional meaning."

I stared down at my amateurish depiction, slightly smudged now from folding, lying on the floor of the Honeybee office. But I wasn't really seeing it. I was thinking, *Branded*.

"Druids?" I drew the word out.

Mimsey sighed and nodded. Mungo barked low in his throat.

"Hush!" I whispered.

Chastised, he laid his head on his paws. I instantly felt guilty. After all, he was as surprised by Mimsey's words as I was.

My attention returned to the older witch. I happened to know that she was seventy-eight years old, but she usually looked like she was in her early sixties, if that. Now she looked tired and drawn. If she'd used magic to enhance her appearance, the glamour had lifted. But somehow I didn't really think the change in her appearance had anything to do with a spell gone awry.

"Mimsey?" I put all the gentleness I could muster into her name. "Are you all right?"

She took a deep breath and forced a smile. "Of course. I'm sorry, Katie. This is so very upsetting."

"Oh, no." I brought my hand to my mouth with a sense of dread. "I never thought—you didn't know the victim, did you?"

She gave a little shrug. "I don't know. Perhaps. I'm not sure who all of them are."

I pushed away from the filing cabinet, scooped Mungo up, and sat down on his chair. "Who are you talking about?" I managed to keep the frustration out of my voice, though I was boiling with curiosity. "Druids?"

"Yes."

"In Savannah?" My voice came out higher than I intended. I probably shouldn't have been surprised, but, heck.

"Not only *in* Savannah, but *of* it. That sigil has been the symbol of a particular group of druids who have been practicing in this area since well before the British sent their prisoners to be tried in Savannah during the Revolutionary War."

"Good heavens," I breathed. "How old does that make them?"

Mimsey laughed, and the tension she emanated lifted slightly, as did a few years from her face. "The group has been around that long, but not the individuals in it."

I reddened. "Oh."

"But membership is strict, passed on from one member to the next for hundreds of years."

Mungo leaned into me as I smoothed the fur along his back. "Tell me more," I said.

She opened her mouth as if to speak, then closed it. "What?" I asked.

"I really don't know that much about them. Only that if one of the members died, there could be consequences. And if he died a violent death, as you say, well, then, darlin', that's a situation we should all stay far away from. That must be what my shew stone meant. That I should steer you clear of the situation."

A frisson of fear ran through me at her words. Sensing it, Mungo snuggled closer.

"Or maybe you were supposed to tell me about the druids. Mimsey, how many times have you told me knowledge is power?"

She blinked. "I don't think—"

I interrupted. "Wouldn't it be better to fully understand the situation in order to avoid it?"

My words didn't appear to make her happy, but after a few moments of consideration she nodded. "I suppose that's one way to look at it. It's not my decision to make for you. And after all, you were the one who found him. There could very well be some significance in that." Worry creased her forehead.

Significance. But I understood what she hadn't come right out and said. Months earlier, when I'd still been trying to come to terms with the fact that I was a bona fide witch—a legacy from my mother *and* father, it turned out—the spellbook club had suggested that I was what they called a *catalyst.* At first that simply seemed to mean that my participation, my very presence, augmented the coven's spell work. But since then a few things we'd read suggested that being a catalyst might mean a bit more.

It could mean that I provided a spark in the meta-

physical web that caused—or perhaps only allowed—
things to, well, to *happen*.

"Forewarned is forearmed," I said, tapping my arm
above the wrist with a forced grin.

Mimsey rolled her eyes. So did Mungo.

Fine. I dropped my hand. "There must be something
else you can tell me about this group of Savannah druids."

Still she hesitated. Then in a soft voice she said, "I
think if you really want to know more you should ask
another friend of yours."

I frowned. "Who? One of the other spellbook club
members?"

Her eyes bored into mine, and she slowly shook her
head. "No, not them. Steven Dawes."

Chapter 4

The skin tightened across my face. "Really?" I blurted. "Why?"

Mimsey used the arms on the desk chair to push herself upright, as if she didn't have enough strength to stand otherwise. "I'm afraid you'll have to ask him that. And please don't say . . . Oh, never mind." She sighed. "He'll know I told you."

I leaped to my feet and deposited Mungo unceremoniously back on the chair seat. "Mimsey, you're not afraid of Steve, are you?" The thought made me cringe. "Because I don't have to ask him anything."

She waved away my concern. "No, no. Go. Talk to him. Learn what you must." She patted Mungo on the head, then put a hand on my shoulder, snagging my gaze with her own. "I'm glad to see that you're wearing your protective talisman. Have you charged it lately?"

I nodded, fingering the silver O hanging from the chain around my neck. I could feel the embossed dragonflies chasing each other around the metal circle. "At the last full moon."

"Good." She squeezed, hard. "Don't take it off. Not when you sleep, not when you shower, not when you go for a run."

She let go of me, winked at Mungo, opened the door, and made her way through the kitchen and out to the front of the bakery. I stood in the doorway feeling stunned and confused—and oddly, utterly inappropriately, thrilled.

Cookie's eyes narrowed in question, first at Mimsey's retreating back and then at me. I smiled, nodded my approval at the tray of molasses scones she'd just removed from the oven, and went back into the office, closing the door behind me.

"Well, what do you think?" I asked my familiar. "Should I see if Steve is available to grab a bite?"

The little dog panted his approval.

"Maybe at Soho South Cafe? I'll bring you a side order of shrimp-and-andouille-sausage soup."

Now he grinned. He loved to lap up the spicy soup, which would have been downright disgusting if he weren't indeed a dog. Though after Declan's delectable breakfast spread, I didn't know how Mungo could even think about more food. I almost groaned at the thought myself, but it was too early for a drink, and I didn't want to invite Steve over for dinner later because, well, because every time he was in my house I seemed to barely escape the encounter without ending up in, shall we say, a compromising position?

Maybe I needed to set some Steve-specific wards to protect myself from his charms. Jaida was good at protection spells. Perhaps she could help me. Besides, from the way Mimsey had acted, I could use all the help I could get on the protection front.

Steve answered his cell on the second ring. "Hey, you."

Two words. That's all it took to make my scalp sweat. My suggestion of a late lunch was met with quiet enthusiasm. As I hung up, I realized that ever since the powerful night when we'd linked our magic together in order to save a man's life, I'd not once initiated an encounter with Steve. It was always him pushing and cajoling, and sometimes even tricking me into spending time with him. But I really wanted to know more about the tattooed sigil.

I paused inside the entrance to the Soho Cafe. From the outside it looked rather small, but it opened into a large space with a hip warehouse feel. Metal support beams and exposed pipes arched overhead. An enticing selection of cookbooks was on sale near the front register, and a plenitude of savory scents greeted my nose. Even though I was still full from breakfast, the smell of sautéing garlic and onions made my mouth water. The high ceilings and cement floor created a cavernous acoustic while swallowing up individual words so that the contents of conversations were more private than one might expect.

A waitress approached. "One?" She beamed at me with a freckled grin. She was tall, but not as tall as me, and wore a many-layered pastel dress with gossamer cap sleeves. A Celtic knot barrette held the frizzy orange hair piled up on her head.

I imagined a stranger looking at the two of us—me with my short auburn locks, lanky runner's physique, and almost dowdy clothing. No way would that stranger pick my unremarkable self as the witch.

Searching the room, I said, "I'm meeting someone."

Steve's waving hand at the back of the restaurant caught my attention.

I waved back. "There he is."

Always the gentleman, he rose when I approached. He wore khaki shorts and a chocolate-colored T-shirt that seemed to make his intelligent brown eyes even darker. The usual length of braided leather held his smooth blond hair in a ponytail.

"Here you go," the waitress said, now beaming at both of us.

Steve never took his eyes off me. He held out his hand, and without thinking I took it. "Katie. You look wonderful." He led me to the other side of the small table and pulled out the chair for me.

"Thanks," I said. The waitress winked conspiratorially and moved away.

Dang it. People always seemed to be doing that when I was around Steve, apparently sensing something that wasn't even there.

Really. It wasn't. Never mind that tingle in my hand where he'd touched me. Or the buzzing beneath my scalp. I shook my head to clear it and smiled at him. "Thanks for meeting me."

"Wouldn't miss it for the world." He settled in across the table and handed me a menu. "Though I am curious to hear what you want from me this time."

"Hey, that's not—"

"Fair?"

I sighed.

"It's completely fair, and you know it. The only time you've ever called me is if you need my help. I can't imagine that's suddenly changed." He leaned toward me. "Or has it?"

His breath caressed my neck, and I swallowed. Hard.

"Has it?"

My shoulders slumped. "No. I'm sorry."

He straightened and opened his menu. "No need. Just making sure I know where I stand."

"Steve, it's just that, well, that you . . . I don't know."

"I scare you. I know that. But we have a connection, and you know that, so one of these days you're just going to have to get over being a fraidy cat and deal with it."

I glared at him.

He grinned back. "I'm going to have the turkey Reuben. You?"

With reluctance, I turned my attention to the lunch offerings. This was exactly the kind of thing Steve was good at. It would have been a lot more infuriating if it wasn't true.

He ordered his Reuben and I ordered a Greek salad. After the waitress left, we sat back and looked at each other. Steve took a sip of iced tea and raised his eyebrows a fraction. Waiting.

Reaching into the tote bag on the chair beside me, I withdrew the smudged drawing of the wreath tattoo and laid it on the table between us. Eyebrows still raised, he glanced down. "What's this?"

Then he really looked, and his whole body stilled. The blood drained from his face, leaving it pale under his smooth tanned skin. The muscles in his neck worked, and then he looked up at me. "Where did you find this?" He sounded almost angry.

Mimsey had acted frightened when she saw the drawing, and now Steve was angry.

Interesting.

"I drew it."

"But you must have seen it someplace. Where? When?"

Taking a deep breath, I said, "This morning. In Johnson Square. On a man's arm. A . . . a dead man."

He stared at me, his face expressionless. Then he closed his eyes and shook his head. "Oh, Katie-girl. What have you gotten yourself into?"

He hadn't called me Katie-girl for months. Of course, I'd asked him to stop, but he seemed to rarely do what I asked, so it was notable. Now I found I didn't hate it as much as I'd thought. Something about the way he said it.

The waitress brought our food, and I ordered a side of soup to go for Mungo. She topped off our glasses of tea and left, shooting a look over her shoulder at Steve as she sashayed away.

But he wasn't paying attention. He took a bite from the corner of his sandwich, put his other elbow on the table in defiance of Emily Post's dictum, and said, "You'd better tell me everything."

I shrugged. "Not much to tell, really. We happened to see a man lying under a rhododendron bush in Johnson Square this morning. I could tell something was wrong, so I took a closer look. Sure enough, it turned out he was dead. That's when I saw the tattoo. De—the police came then, and Peter Quinn interviewed us. Him and his new partner." I made a moue, remembering Detective Taite.

Steve's eyes narrowed. "We? Us?"

Of course Steve had caught my verbal slip.

I raised my chin in defiance. "Declan."

If I'd thought he looked mad when he saw the tattoo, then the expression on his face now was downright fury.

"I know you dislike him. We were just having a bite."

"In Johnson Square."

"Yes."

"A picnic." Somehow he made the notion of eating outdoors sound sordid. And I could see the hurt under all that anger—long-held anger toward Declan for his part in a tragic accident that had killed Steve's brother. Now it had been augmented by his feelings for me. One of those feelings was lust. It was sometimes hard to tell what else accompanied it.

He forked a bite of side salad into his mouth and chewed slowly. Swallowed. "What else?"

"Besides a picnic?"

"No," he said with great patience. "What else did you notice about the man you found? What did he look like?"

"Oh. He was older. Thick white hair, old clothes with dirt on them, muddy boots, nice watch."

Steve put down his fork and took a gulp of tea, blinking rapidly. Were those tears?

I put my hand over his. "You seem to recognize the description."

"Not at all."

I didn't believe him. I pushed the drawing of the tattoo toward him. "You know what this is, don't you?"

Composed again, he asked, "Now, why would you even think that?"

"A little witch told me." After all, Mimsey had given me permission to tell him.

He sighed. "A little white-haired witch, I bet. With blue eyes and a parrot."

"You know Heckle?"

Steve grimaced.

I pushed harder. "You know about the druids who wear this. I know you do."

"Keep your voice down."

"I'm practically whispering. No one can hear us. And I bet you know the identity of the man who had this on his arm."

After not being able to take his eyes off me, now he couldn't look at me at all.

"Tell me," I urged. Without meaning to, I felt a little of my Voice infuse the words. I barely managed not to clap my hand over my mouth.

His eyes flared. "Knock it off! That crap doesn't work on me."

"Sorry. I just thought—"

"You just wanted to get your way."

"Not my way! To know whose body I found today. And . . . why. Mimsey implied it might have something to do with my being a—a, you know."

"What?"

"A catalyst."

"Oh. Right. That."

The tension rode there in the air between us for a long moment before he looked at me again. "I need to talk to someone before I tell you any more."

"But you haven't told me anything," I protested. "At least you could . . ." Something in his expression made my words trail off. "Well, okay. I guess. Not that I have any choice."

"No. You don't." He rose and took a few steps away

from the table. Then he took out his wallet, extracted a bill, and threw it on the table.

"But I asked you to lunch," I said.

"Under false pretenses." He turned and walked away.

I watched him go. A knot of guilt twisted in my stomach. Why was he so upset? Who did he need to talk to?

Katie-girl, what have you gotten yourself into?

Indeed.

The blowsy waitress returned, frowning at all the uneaten food on the table. She held a bag with Mungo's treat. "Is there something wrong with your order?" she asked.

"It's fine. Good. My friend had to leave, though." I felt my face redden.

"Well, I hope everything's all right. Would you like boxes to take home?"

"Yes, please." I couldn't bear to waste such excellent fare. Maybe I'd be hungry later.

At least Mungo would appreciate the leftovers.

Chapter 5

Mimsey had left by the time I got back to the Honeybee to pick up Mungo. Cookie, finished with the day's baking, was also gone. Ben was restocking the toffee biscotti and chatting with Lucy. A woman I didn't recognize sat at one of the bistro tables. She wore a denim jumper and Birkenstocks, and her thick gray hair was braided into a single long plait down her back. I glanced down as I walked by and saw that she was filling out a job application. She looked up, her warm smile accentuating apple cheeks on either side of a slightly hawkish nose. Fine lines radiated from the corners of her eyes.

"Hi, there! I'm Nel."

I smiled back, feeling unexpected gratitude. It had been a very odd day, and a wide smile from a perfect stranger was more than welcome. "Hi, Nel. I'm—"

"Katie? Can I talk to you?" Lucy patted Ben on the shoulder and said something, then hurried through the kitchen and into the office.

"Katie," I stage-whispered to Nel over my shoulder as I followed my aunt.

Mungo jumped into my arms when I walked into the office.

"Good thing you're not very big," I said to him. "Otherwise you'd knock me to the floor with those antics."

"Where have you been?" Lucy said.

I turned. "Having lunch with Steve."

Her eyes widened, and a smile tugged at the corner of her mouth. "Oh, really . . ."

"I had a question to ask him." Mungo's soft tongue lapped once at my neck. I frowned down at him.

"About that tattoo?" Her smile vanished. "Mimsey rushed out of here without saying a word to me, like dogs were snapping at her heels."

Mungo whined low.

"Sorry," Lucy said. "Bad choice of words. But apparently I missed quite an interesting conversation."

I nodded. "She recognizes the tattoo. Said it was the symbol used by a group of druids in town, and that Steve might be able to tell me more."

"Druids," she repeated with a thoughtful expression. "I wonder why that would upset her so much. Druids are typically gentle sorts, with a deep respect for the goddess. A deep connection to nature, too. Was Steve any help?"

"Not really. He said he has to talk to someone."

"Well, heck."

Now I was the one smiling. "Since when are you so interested in obscure tattoos?"

"Since one showed up on a dead man's arm—a dead man my darling niece found, by the way—and since my mentor had such a strong reaction to your drawing."

"Yeah, that tattoo definitely disturbed her. I'll let you both know if Steve decides to come through with any real information. For now, though, I'm going to take the rest of my day off, off." I glanced on the clock on the wall. It was almost three o'clock. "I'm going home to play in my garden."

"Good idea," she said. "How are your spells growing?"

"The witch hazel is doing well, but the jasmine has still been kind of wilty. So this morning I took your advice and brewed a healing tea, then misted the plant with it at dawn. I want to get back and see how it's doing."

"What did you decide to use in the tea?"

"Lavender and nettle," I said.

She smiled gently. "Those are good choices. I knew you'd figure out a suitable combination to heal and encourage growth."

"I hope so." I opened my tote bag. "Say, I saw that woman filling out an application. Do you really think we need another employee?"

Lucy shrugged. "Maybe down the road, but not yet. She came in and asked if we needed any help—apparently she has a lot of experience working in bakeries. I figured it couldn't hurt to have her application on file. Cookie's been here four months already, you know."

I nodded. Cookie switched jobs—and men—every three or four months. "I'd hoped she might stick around," I said. "Having the help is great, and we don't have to be sneaky about our hedgewitchery." The Honeybee's baked goods often came with an extra dose of beneficial magic. A little sage here to encourage wisdom and attract money, a bit of rosemary there to encourage long-lasting love. Cinnamon for prosperity and cloves for healing and courage. It wasn't just the herbs and spices that had magical influences, either. Apples promoted peace and happiness and lemon boosted health. Even the coffee from the espresso counter helped people make decisions and clear deadlocks. Our customers might not know all that, but they sure kept coming back for more.

With Mungo safely ensconced in the bottom of my tote, I followed Lucy out to the front, kissed Ben on the cheek, and headed out to my Volkswagen Beetle. I received a doggy glare when I buckled the bag into the passenger seat with my familiar still in it, but he stayed there, head clearing the top so he could look around.

"I'm sorry, but you know how I feel." I drove down Broughton and took a left on Whitaker. Soon we were buzzing out of Savannah's historic district toward home. "I just don't understand why Steve was so weird today," I said once we were on our way. "He's not usually secretive about magic, at least not with me."

Yip!

"And who did he need to talk to before he could tell me anything? I have a feeling he knows at least some of the druids in that secret society."

The terrier was silent. I looked over at him. His expression echoed my questioning tone.

"Right." It wasn't as if I could read his mind in anything like words; I just knew what he was thinking most of the time. Just like I'd known what my childhood dogs, Sukie and Barnaby, had been thinking when I was growing up. Some dogs are smarter than a lot of humans. Especially dogs who are connected with witches.

"Anyway, Steve does know a lot of people in town, so maybe . . . oh, my goddess—what if *he's* one of them?"

The thought was so distracting that I almost missed the stop sign. I might have if Mungo hadn't barked a warning. I stomped on the brake and the Bug shuddered to a stop as a huge king cab pickup went blaring past, right in front of my bumper. The container of soup flew out of the bag on the floor and spattered all over the passenger-side footwell.

Mungo whined.

"Oh, sweetie, I'm so sorry." Thank heavens I was dutiful about using seat belts.

The smell of shrimp and spicy sausage filled the interior of the warm car. Nauseated, I rolled all the windows down for the remainder of my shaky drive home.

Silly me. Steve wasn't a druid—at least not one of the group Mimsey had told me about. He didn't have the tattoo on his arm.

But maybe they didn't all have them on their arms. Maybe he had a tattoo someplace else on his body. Someplace I hadn't seen. Yet.

That thought was even more distracting than the first one, but I managed to get us both home intact.

Mungo and I lived in a tiny house that had once been a carriage house for a larger home. That estate was now gone, and middle-class homes and pleasant lanes lined with dogwood, crape myrtle, and live oak trees surrounded my little abode. There was a green space behind the houses on my side of the street, so my neighbors and I had room to breathe and a little more privacy. There was even a natural stream that ran across one corner of the yard. When I'd purchased the carriage house I hadn't known I'd be doing spell work outside, but somehow I'd happened upon the perfect place for it.

Well, almost perfect. There had been a few issues.

Inside, I went through the tiny living room to the kitchen. I put some of Steve's sandwich in Mungo's dish, and he tucked in. The memory of the near accident hung about me like a fog. Pouring a half glass of wine, I wandered out to the backyard for some quick garden therapy before tackling the smelly mess in my car.

It was a day off from my Witchy 101 lessons as well as baking. The spellbook club had taken me under their collective wing. Jaida taught me about tarot magic. Bianca focused on Wiccan teachings and moon magic. Cookie was four years younger than my twenty-eight, so she didn't mentor me as much. Still, I'd learned a few things about voodoo and the darker side of magic from Ms. Rios. Mimsey usually instructed me in how to use colors and flowers in spell work, as well as trying to hone my divination abilities. She was trying to teach me how to scry using a crystal ball. I was pretty bad at it, frankly, but she insisted on encouraging me.

Lucy, of course, focused on lessons about our family heritage of hedgewitchery. Mostly that meant working outside and with herbs and other plants. It included using them in cooking, too—at the bakery and at home. So I was learning kitchen and garden magic as well as brewing and herbal craft.

Those were the lessons I looked forward to the most.

I stepped from the small covered patio onto the lawn. When I'd first moved in, the whole backyard had been grass, but I'd carved out an herb garden along much of the back fence, and now all manner of culinary, medicinal, and magical herbs flourished within its curving border. To the right of the herb bed a small stone path led to the section of the stream that ran through my property, and along the right side of the yard a kitchen potager boasted vegetables planted with an eye to aesthetics as well as function. A profusion of heirloom roses climbed up one side of the house, and potted annuals on the patio augmented what I thought of as a kind of personal magical farm.

A recent addition was the small gazebo in the middle of the yard. It was round, and the man who had constructed it urged me to paint it. But the exposed grain of the cedar had a natural energy that calmed me. That was important, because the gazebo also served as my sacred garden circle. No one suspected that the candles sometimes flickering within the quaint structure were anything but festive decoration. As long as I didn't get too rambunctious, the gazebo allowed me to cast in the open whenever I wanted to, in all but the worst weather.

I checked on the vegetables, noting that a few tomatoes were plump and ready to eat. I grabbed my harvest basket and filled it with the heirloom fruits once called love apples, red peppers, onions, carrots, and a head of romaine lettuce. Finally, I added a few late strawberries that I spied peeking out from under their leaves.

The witch hazel I'd planted near the stream glowed with vigor. I'd encouraged its health by burying a moss agate at each of the compass points around its base on the night of a new moon. Despite my rather lackadaisical attitude toward magical paraphernalia, I intended to make an honest-to-goddess traditional wand from one of its branches. As I watched, dozens of multicolored dragonflies drifted in to perch there. It was my good luck that dragonflies—mosquito hawks—were drawn to me. They kept the ubiquitous mosquitoes in Savannah at bay.

The jasmine I'd planted at one end of the herb garden was a little different, however. It was itself a spell. I'd planted it with the intention of increasing—and clarifying—my dreams at night. When it seemed to struggle after the initial transplanting, I'd felt discouraged and asked Lucy's advice. I was happy to see that the nettle and lavender tea had worked so quickly. The jasmine's glossy leaves had perked to attention and tiny flower buds were beginning to form on the vine.

Belly full, Mungo trotted out and joined me. In an abbreviated gesture, I moved my hand in a kind of blessing, from the east to the south, west, north, and again to the east, murmuring, "May the elements of air, fire, water, and earth bring strength and grace to this jasmine and what it represents."

"Katie Lightfoot, don't tell me you're talking to yourself again!"

Startled, I turned to find Margie Coopersmith approaching the four-foot fence that divided my backyard from hers.

Did I mention there had been issues?

Not that I didn't love Margie to death. Honest, I did. However, she not only kept a protective eye on her single neighbor, she also had the uncanny ability to sneak up on me. I didn't know how she managed it, given the baby on her hip and the four-year-old twins who constantly trailed on her heels.

I waved away her words with a smile. "Just talking to Mungo here. He's a good listener."

He dutifully grinned up at our neighbor.

"Can he come over and play?" Jonathan asked.

"Yeah, can Mungo come over and play?" his sister, Julia, joined in.

I looked down at my familiar. "What do you think? You want to go play with the JJs for a while?"

Yip!

"That's what I thought." Familiar or no, Mungo had a puppy's heart, and he liked playing with the tow-headed twins. I lifted him over the fence, and the three of them ran off.

"Haven't seen you around for few days," Margie said, brushing the hair back from baby Bart's forehead. It was blond like hers, and he had her brown eyes and round cheeks, too. "Redding's leaving tonight on a big loop up north, and I wondered if you might want to have dinner next week." Her husband was a long-haul truck driver who often had to leave his family for a week or more at a time.

"Sure," I said, "I'd love to." Margie's culinary talents began at take-out pizza and ended at hot dogs and macaroni and cheese out of a box, but she was such a nice, normal person to be around that I couldn't have cared less.

She blinked, consulting an internal calendar. "How about day after tomorrow?"

I nodded. "What can I bring?"

She gestured at the basket at my feet. "How 'bout something from your spread here? I swear, girl, I don't know how you manage to grow so many good things. Pretty, too. I can't even keep our grass green."

It was true: Margie's gardening ability was on par with her cooking. Her strength lay in being a terrific mother, a feat she managed to make look effortless despite her husband's being gone so much.

"A salad, then?" I'd bring a few extra veggies for them to eat later. As much as she felt protective of me, I always felt compelled to feed her. "Are you guys planning to come to the Honeybee Halloween party?"

"Wouldn't miss it for the world! Wait until you see what these darlin's will be wearing!"

"What?" I asked, amused.

She wagged her finger and looked smug. "You'll just have to wait and see. Those two"—she indicated the JJs, still running around the yard with Mungo and giggling—"are so excited about the party. 'Course, I don't know how much they remember about trick-or-treating last year, but it was pretty miserable. Rained like the dickens. Ugh!" She hitched Bart up on her hip and raised her hand. "This one needs changing. I'll see you later, okay?"

"You bet. Monday if not before."

She moved toward their back door.

"Mungo," I called, stooping to pick up the harvest basket. "C'mon." The JJs waved and turned to clamber up the bright plastic play structure in the middle of their yard.

Mungo ran to the fence and followed me along the other side as I made my way toward the front of the house. I let him out of Margie's yard and together we approached the Bug. The smell of spicy pork and seafood reached us before we got to the car. Bracing, I opened the passenger door.

"Yuck."

Yip!

Sighing, I went in the front door, put the veggies on

the counter, and gathered rags and paper towels. I laced a bucket of warm water with a dose of white vinegar and dish soap and grabbed a couple of plastic bags. Back outside, Mungo grinned at me from a prone position in the grass as I scooped bits of shrimp and sausage into the take-out container.

"A lot of help you are," I grumbled.

Out came the floor mat, which I dosed liberally with the vinegar-and-soap solution and then sprayed off with the hose in the driveway. Then I set to soaking and scrubbing and wiping down the hard surfaces. By the time I was done, I was pretty sure I never needed to eat any kind of sausage again, but at least the smell was largely gone from the car. A few sprigs of parsley in the Bug's built-in vase might look funny, but they would act as a deodorizer overnight.

I, however, desperately needed a shower. Bundling the used cleaning materials into a plastic bag, I grabbed my empty bucket as a car pulled up to the curb in front of the carriage house.

Not just any car. A Lincoln Town Car. As I watched, a man got out from behind the wheel and moved to the rear door. He opened it, and a tall man unfolded himself from the backseat and stood on the sidewalk in front of my house. His driver closed the door behind him and returned to sit behind the wheel.

His driver.

Why the heck was someone with a driver standing in front of my house?

Chapter 6

The man spotted me gawking at him and began walking my way. His precision-cut hair was the color of caramel but heavily streaked with gray. That coincided with the fine lines radiating from the corners of his eyes and mouth. He stopped in front of me, and I looked into those eyes. They were gray, so light as to be almost colorless, with a charcoal-colored ring around the irises. They were eerie, indeed, but the feature that really threw me was the newcomer's mouth.

It was very familiar. Lord knew, I'd spent more time than I should have thinking about Steve Dawes' mouth. About the way the upper lip curved, about how smooth the lower lip was. About how it felt on mine.

The gentleman's lips parted to reveal perfect white teeth and then quirked up in a wry smile. That was all I needed to know for sure. This man had to be Steve's father.

What in blazes? Steve drove a nice car, sure, but this guy was *rich*. He wore a suit the same dark gray as the ring around his irises. I'm no expert on sartorial elegance, but it looked plenty expensive.

"Ms. Lightfoot, it's about time we met. I'm Heinrich Dawes."

I put the empty bucket down on the ground. "Um, nice to meet you." It sounded almost like a question.

He held out his hand. I glanced down and saw that the cuff of his crisp blue shirt was fastened with actual silver cuff links. Who wore cuff links anymore? And not silver. Of course not. They'd be platinum.

Half stunned, I transferred the bundle of plastic-wrapped cleaning rags to my left hand and began to reach out to shake his hand with my right. A soggy hunk of sausage meat dropped onto my foot and bounced wetly to the pavement of the driveway. I jerked my hand back, realizing it was still sticky with a combination of soap and soup, and heard Mungo slurping up the sausage next to my flip-flop. The faint scent of shrimp drifted into my nose.

If I could have crawled inside that bucket, I would have.

"Sorry. Just cleaning up a little accident. Would you like to come inside?" I heard the coolness in my tone regardless of my flushed face, and it made me feel a little better.

He dropped his hand, emanating ease. "That would probably be best."

Best for what?

He followed me up the walk and into the house. As soon as we entered the enclosed space I could feel his power. It was like a live thing accompanying him. Some of it was the simple secular power that came from the kind of wealth Heinrich Dawes obviously enjoyed, but there was something else. Something more. Something from another plane. I was disconcerted to realize it felt familiar, as if it shared a signature, a scent even.

The scent of leather and cloves that I associated with his son.

Heinrich's gaze flicked around the living room, up to the loft above, down the hallway to my bedroom, and beyond the French doors to the yard and gardens.

Examining and assessing.

Judging.

"Excuse me while I dispose of this. Please make yourself comfortable." I nodded toward the purple fainting couch and went toward the kitchen. "May I get you something to drink, Mr. Dawes?"

"Heinrich, please. No, thank you, Katie. If I may call you that?"

"Sure," I called over the sound of water running as I scrubbed my hands clean. A movement in my peripheral vision reminded me that Mungo had followed us in. Now he sat in the corner, eyes boring into me. I raised my eyebrows in question, and his little doggy forehead wrinkled.

When I returned to the other room he followed me as far as the doorway. He seemed to be as intrigued by our visitor as I was—but also leery.

Heinrich had settled into one of my two leather wingback chairs, so I sat on the couch, with the Civil War–era trunk that served as a coffee table between us. After a few seconds of hesitation, Mungo trotted over and joined me. I smiled at Steve's dad and waited.

What do you want?

As if he read my mind, he said, "Naturally you're wondering why I've so rudely dropped by unannounced."

I kept smiling. "It's nice to finally meet you, whatever the circumstances." Did that sound rude?

Nah.

Yeah, maybe. But he had indeed shown up without the slightest warning.

He sat back. "My son thinks a great deal of you."

Surely this wasn't some kind of matchmaking mission? I cocked my head to one side, choosing my words carefully. "I'm quite fond of Steve as well."

"He's told me quite a bit about you."

Like what? Steve had hardly even mentioned to me that he had a father.

But . . . mental palm slap to forehead. He'd said he had to talk to someone before telling me more about the tattooed wreath sigil. Was this the someone? Why else would Heinrich Dawes suddenly feel the need to meet me?

My stomach tightened.

Heinrich's sweeping gesture encompassed the whole dwelling. "I see you are discreet about your practices, even in private."

The fist in my solar plexus clenched harder. "Practices?"

"Please. The five-pointed rosemary topiary by the front door would be enough of a giveaway, even if I didn't already know you're a witch." He settled his elbows on the arms of the chair and steepled his fingers. "And yes, my son is indeed correct. You have tangible power."

Takes one to know one, I thought in silence. I wanted to hear what else he would say before I offered him anything.

"For a woman, of course."

"Excuse me?"

He waved his hand in the air as if my words were nothing more than a tendril of smoke. "The fact that you don't put yourself on display with odd clothing choices or some silly altar in plain view confirms what Steve told me about your ability to keep things to yourself."

I carefully did not look up to where my altar was hidden in the closed secretary desk in the loft above. "I see," I grated out. Steve's dad or not, in only a few sentences this man had cast aspersions on me personally and my gender as a whole.

He smiled, revealing those straight white Dawes teeth again. But now I saw the naked arrogance come through, which made his smile more feral than friendly.

"Steve tells me you happened upon an unfortunate this morning."

I inclined my head a fraction. "That's one way of putting it." Now we were getting to the meat of why this man was in my living room.

"That must have been quite alarming."

"It was . . . unpleasant," I agreed, downplaying my reaction.

"I understand. But you handled yourself with aplomb, and I expect you to do the same regarding the tattoo on the man's arm which has so aroused your curiosity."

Arrogant and a chauvinist. Fine. I could work with that. Allowing my lips to curve up in a demure smile, I looked down at the floor and waited for him to say more.

Instead, he stood up. "So glad we got that straightened out. And of course it's gratifying to get to know Steve's new lady."

I came to my feet, too, dumping Mungo on the couch cushion with a thump. "Hang on."

His eyebrows raised an infinitesimal amount.

"First off, I'm no one's 'lady' and certainly not your son's. Secondly, what do you mean we have this straightened out? Because by 'this' I assume you mean the tattoo, and the, uh, group it implies membership in. Since you haven't told me anything about it, I don't really see a need for any of that *discretion* and *aplomb* you seem to assume I possess."

Heinrich looked down his nose at me. With an effort, I stood my ground and willed cool confidence into my own expression.

His eyes narrowed a fraction. "I see I may have been misled."

Only by your own prejudices.

"All right," he said. "Steve told me that Carmichael woman filled your head with a bunch of ridiculous nonsense. You need to put her fairy tales out of your mind. The tattoo you saw indicates membership in a very exclusive Savannah men's club." He licked his lips. "The Dragoh Society. If you must think of it at all, think of the club as a kind of Sons of the American Revolution."

I considered him. "Really. So this Dragoh Society does the same kinds of things that the SAR does? You're all about education and patriotism and the preservation of history, then? Pretty dull men's club."

His lips turned up, but you couldn't really call it a smile. He inclined his head.

"You're obviously a member," I said.

A slight hesitation before he said, "I am."

"So who did I find in Johnson Square this morning?"

"Ms. Lightfoot, I assure you I don't have the slightest idea. There are many members, and we don't all know each other."

So much for Heinrich and me being on a first-name basis. I didn't believe him, either. He knew who the dead man was.

I said, "Now that you're aware the dead man had the club tattoo, you'll naturally pass the information about this Dragoh Society on to the police."

He frowned. "Why would—"

"To help them identify the body, of course."

"Of course." He turned toward the door. "I'll make that my next stop."

"Detective Peter Quinn," I said.

He stopped in midstride and half turned back. "Who?"

"Peter Quinn. One of the detectives on the case. He's a friend of mine."

Now facing me, Heinrich slowly raised one finger. "Do not threaten me, Katie."

"I wasn't."

The finger waggled slowly back and forth. "Not ever. You are now aware of the existence of a well-established men's club that has been around for a very long time. That's more than most women—people— know. Be happy with that, because you would be well advised to keep out of the society's business."

I heard the Command in the last sentence. It rolled off me like rain on polished glass, but I nodded as if it had worked as Heinrich Dawes intended. He'd told me all he was going to, and suddenly it felt imperative to get him out of my home.

"Okay," I said, injecting a little sweetness into my tone. "Thank you. Say hello to Steve for me. It was lovely to finally meet you." I smiled big and bright.

He seemed to buy it. "Likewise."

I closed the door behind him and watched through the slats of the wooden shutter as his driver opened the door of the Town Car and Heinrich Dawes climbed inside. Mungo joined me. I picked him up and together we watched Steve's dad being driven away.

The dog licked my chin.

"I know. There's something off about that guy. I don't know that it's anything evil. An unfortunate combination of arrogance and power, perhaps." I put Mungo down and thought about what my aunt did whenever she wanted to rid a space of negative influences. "Whatever it is, let's dig out the white sage. You know Lucy would tell us to smudge this place from top to bottom."

Yip!

At least Heinrich had gone back to calling me Katie before he left. I tried to think of that as a good thing.

Chapter 7

Smudging, while effective, can be stinky. Mungo and I used stalks of white sage, the stems tied together with twine. But Heinrich Dawes had unsettled me, and I felt compelled to double-smudge, if you will. So after walking the perimeter of each room with the smoking bundle of sage, I did the same with juniper berry incense. The combination of scents was acrid and heady—and quite frankly a little hard to take. All for the good, though. At least the carriage house was small.

After opening the French doors wide, I went to throw open the windows facing the street to encourage more airflow. It would be just my luck for Margie to pop over unannounced. She did that with remarkable frequency, always when I was up to something witchy. Luckily, most of the time my workings looked like cooking or gardening to my neighbor, and since she avoided doing both she rarely paid attention. Also, for magical rituals that looked odd—or smelled odd—I usually worked late at night, either inside with my windows thoroughly covered or outside where I could draw on the power of the moon. Even so, Margie had interrupted me a few times when she'd sneaked out to her backyard to eat Twinkies and Ding Dongs like a smoker steals an illicit puff.

As I pushed the front windows open, a familiar black Land Rover pulled up right where Heinrich Dawes' driver had parked by the curb. Steve got out and hurried up to the door, not noticing that I was looking out the window. The sound of his fist pounding on the wood made me jump.

"Katie! Let me in! Katie—" His face showed brief surprise when I yanked the door open.

"Stop yelling and get in here," I hissed and stepped back so he could enter. "Do you want the whole neighborhood to hear?"

Sure enough, over his shoulder I saw Margie out by her mailbox. I smiled and waved. After a few seconds Margie waved back, but she still looked concerned.

Steve sniffed the air as I shut the door behind him. I flapped my hands, a futile gesture that did nothing to dissipate the smell of smoke. Before I could say anything, he held up his palms.

"I'm sorry. I'm really, really sorry. I had no idea Father would come over here like that. Did he frighten you?"

More than his apology, the way he said the word "Father" gave me pause, made me wonder what their relationship might be like. After all, Steve hadn't told me anything about his father; in fact, he'd dodged my questions about his family the few times I'd asked. I'd assumed it was because of the tragic death of his younger brother and backed off.

"He didn't frighten me as much as make me angry."

He sniffed the air again. "Yeah, Father elicits that

reaction, too. You seem to have removed any lingering effects, though."

I looked down at Mungo. "We did our best."

Steve leaned down and offered the back of his hand for the dog to sniff. Mungo did, then walked over to the French doors and lay across the threshold. Over a period of several months he'd come to accept Steve, but if enthusiastic greetings counted as votes, then Declan had already won the election.

"Come on," I said. "Let's go out back and let the air clear in here." I thought about offering him something to eat, but decided against it. If he wanted to walk out of the restaurant before finishing his lunch, that was his problem. Instead, I poured two glasses of plain iced tea and topped them with sprigs of spearmint. No more wine for me. I had a feeling I'd need to be on my toes for the conversation Steve and I were about to have.

He followed me out to the gazebo, Mungo right behind him. It was my sacred garden circle, but it was also a great place to sit and chat. At least Steve was a witch. Or something like a witch. I was about to get some serious clarification on a few things. I set the sweating glasses on the table and we settled into mismatched wooden chairs I'd chosen more for comfort than style. Steve pointed at the floor.

"Subtle."

I looked down at the star I'd painted in the center. It was purple, outlined in white, and about ten inches in diameter. Shrugging, I said, "It's not an obvious pentagram." Noticing white granules on the floor, I hopped up, grabbed the straw broom leaning against the wall, and swept the salt left behind from the last circle I'd cast in the gazebo out of the structure. "Guess I could be a bit tidier about cleaning up after I work in here, though."

The scents of roses and mint mingled in the air. I flipped a switch on the wall and the ceiling fan began to stir the warm mugginess. A phalanx of dragonflies drifted in to take up station around the gazebo. The sound of a lawn mower droned from a few doors down.

Steve took a long swallow of tea as I returned to my seat. "I never intended to put you in Father's sights when I spoke with him," he said. "But I couldn't tell you anything about that tattoo until I'd checked with him. It's simply not my secret to tell. Do you understand?" He sounded almost like he was pleading.

I'd never seen him so discombobulated. "Of course."

"So . . . what did he say to you?"

Now I took a drink of tea, thinking. "Oh, you know. All that stuff about the Dragoh Society."

Steve's jaw dropped.

"How long they've been around, what they're all about." I kept my tone light.

"You're kidding."

"Nope. 'Course the word *druid* never came up directly, but there was enough wink, wink, nudge, nudge in our conversation for Heinrich's meaning to be crystal clear." I pasted a knowing smile on my face.

His eyes narrowed. "That doesn't sound like Father."

"Really? Because we got along famously. After all, you'd already told him I'm a witch."

"Um . . ."

"So there was no reason for secrets. He certainly is powerful, isn't he?"

Steve's eyes narrowed even more as he picked up on my sarcasm.

"I mean, I could feel it," I went on. "And it went both ways. Your dear father even complimented me on my 'tangible' power."

"Really." His tone was flat.

The smile dropped from my face. "For a *woman*, of course."

He winced.

I relented. He couldn't help it if his dad was a jerk. "So you're a hereditary, too, then."

He nodded.

"But not a witch, as I believed," I said.

"Magic is magic. But yes, technically, I'm a druid."

"Why do I think your father might disagree? That he might be insulted if he knew I'd thought you were a witch?"

Steve took a deep breath. "The Dragoh Society is a bit different from the druids of old."

"How so?"

"Well, for one thing, they're a bit misogynistic."

"I'll say."

He held up his hand. "It's a problem. Not all of them are as bad as Father, but they do tend to hold rather outdated chauvinistic views. It's one of the many reasons I'm less than enthusiastic about my magical inheritance."

"I don't understand."

He looked into the distance for a moment, then met my eyes. "Membership in the Dragoh Society is quite exclusive. All six members have inherited their position through the decades—centuries, really. Most have passed on from father to son, though if necessary, membership can pass to a grandson, or even a nephew may inherit. But the six bloodlines have remained the same since they first banded together during the Revolutionary War."

I took a careful sip of tea as these new bits of information ping-ponged through my brain. Six members. Yet Heinrich had said he didn't know all the members. Liar, liar, pants on fire.

Steve, apparently taking my silence for disapproval, spoke defensively. "I know I should be honored, but I've always had my qualms about the Dragohs. I believe they're outdated, out of touch, and after all this time continue to cling to a wartime mentality." He paused as if deciding how much to say. "The lack of feminine energy in their magic creates imbalance. It has allowed them to occasionally justify . . . questionable . . . practices."

Well, *that* didn't sound good. "Does your father know you feel this way?"

He sighed. "Yes. Having met him, however briefly, you can imagine how he reacted when I expressed my reservations. Considered it an abdication, as if I were refusing some kind of royal mantle that he was passing on. Which, in a way, I guess he was. It caused a deep rift between us. He didn't speak to me for several years." He paused. Licking his lips, he gave a little nod, as if to himself, and met my eyes again. His gaze seemed to go straight to my toes, and after a few beats I realized I'd stopped breathing.

"Luckily, my brother was willing to join the society in my place," he said. "Despite how much Father disapproved of his becoming a firefighter, once Arnold agreed to inherit the membership, he became the preferred son. In some ways, the only son. Father didn't formally disown me, mind you. Mother, who knows nothing of the society, wouldn't allow that. But he might as well have."

The sadness in his voice twisted around my heart.

"Then Arnie died." He held up his hand. "I know you've heard the story before, at least from Declan's point of view. But there are two sides to every story, at *least* two, and we'll never hear Arnie's side. All I know is, as his partner and his best friend, Declan McCarthy should have saved him."

"But the rules—"

"Rules be damned."

Poor Steve. From what Uncle Ben had told me, if Declan had broken the rules that governed firefighting the only result would have been two dead men instead of just one. But this man sitting next to me couldn't hear that right now. For the first time I felt like I understood why he despised Declan so much for being involved in the accident that had taken away Arnie—his younger brother, but also his chance to avoid becoming a member of his father's archaic magical club.

I put my hand on his arm. He turned, sliding away from my touch. "Old news. But it also means I'll have to try to change the Dragohs from the inside, whether I like it or not. At least the relationship with my father is mending."

Because you're doing what he wants, not what you want. What kind of a father is that? Then I thought of my relationship with my own parents since I'd learned that they'd hidden my magical heritage from me. Perhaps it would be better not to judge.

I was seeing Steve in a new light. I'd always thought of him as arrogant and pushy . . . and hot. But now he'd revealed a new facet of himself. What else didn't I know about this guy?

"Perhaps a whole new generation of Dragohs will help you make the changes you envision," I said.

He looked worried. "Unless the group falls apart completely. There have been other membership issues, and now with Eastmore dead there's going to be another one."

My ears perked up, but I kept my voice calm. "Eastmore?"

"Lawrence—" Steve's eyes widened. "Father didn't tell you?"

"He said he would tell Peter Quinn about the tattoo to help identify the man I found. He also said he didn't know all the members of the society. Made it sound like there was a huge roster."

Steve looked disgusted. "You said he told you all about the Dragohs."

"Yeah, well, I was being a tad facetious."

"Now you definitely know more than you should. That's not good."

I ignored that. "Your dad's not going to the police, is he?"

"Nope."

"I guess I'll just have to, then."

"You can't!"

Mungo barked. I looked up to see Margie looking over at us from her back porch. The JJs continued to play, oblivious.

"Will you keep your voice down?" I said. "Of course I can."

He leaned forward and spoke intensely. "No. You can't. What would you say? How could you know what you know about the tattoo? Besides, if Lawrence's death is related to the Dragohs, bringing the police into the loop would be useless. No one will talk to the authorities. You really think you can convince Detective Quinn that the Dragohs even exist? And wouldn't you rather he didn't find out about your little spellbook club?"

I glared at him. Little spellbook club indeed.

He caught my meaning, and looked down. "I'm sorry. I shouldn't have said that. But you see my point, don't you?"

"What if magic had nothing to do with that poor man's death?"

"Then Quinn will find the killer without any help from us."

"But—"

"No. *Please*, Katie. You can't."

We sat for a long moment, eyes locked. "I don't like it," I said.

"I understand. I don't like it, either. But I need to talk to Father again. Perhaps he knows something else by now." He stood abruptly and stalked out of the gazebo. Turning his back to the house—and to Margie—he stood for a long moment with his hands on his hips, breathing hard.

Slowly, I got up and walked to his side.

He gestured at the gardens. "You're doing a great job here."

"Thanks."

The sound of running water from the stream mingled with the scent of someone starting up their charcoal grill.

"Do you know how much I care about you?" he asked in a quiet voice.

I tried a nod, suddenly terrified of where he might be going.

He let out a short laugh, and I looked at his face. "Relax, Katie-girl. I know you're still getting your bearings in Savannah. In magic. I've never met anyone like you. We're connected. I know you feel it, too. We have a destiny. But in the meantime, you need to know I'm trying to keep you safe when I warn you away from the Dragoh Society."

I nodded again, curiously unable to speak.

"I have to go now," he said.

"Okay," I managed to croak.

Together we walked around to the front of the house.

Stopping by the Land Rover, I put my hand on his arm again, gratified that he didn't pull away like he had in the gazebo. "Steve? Who are the other Dragohs?"

He closed his eyes and sighed

I leaned in and kissed him on the cheek. His eyes flew open and he looked at me with surprise. "I'm still not going to tell you," he said.

"Okay," I said. I turned and went up my front walk. Behind me the Land Rover's engine started. On the porch I paused and looked back, sketched a quick wave.

As he returned it I could see the skepticism on his face.

Good. I liked that I could keep that one guessing.

Or so I told myself.

Chapter 8

After Steve left, I went into the kitchen and eyed the two rounds of yellow cake I'd made that morning before leaving to meet Declan. Since I'd been living in the South I'd learned about several regional specialties, and one had recently snagged my interest—caramel cake. The caramel actually had nothing to do with the cake itself; it was about the frosting. I'd decided to experiment with it at home to see if I could get it right.

I stirred butter and brown sugar together in a saucepan over medium heat until tiny bubbles formed and the smell of caramel drifted up to my nose. I whisked in heavy cream, heated the mixture a little longer, then transferred it all to my trusty standing mixer, where I added confectioners' sugar and vanilla. I let it run on medium for a couple of minutes, whipping air into the frosting, then added a little more soft butter at the end.

Working quickly, before the luscious goo hardened, as caramel tends to, I slathered frosting on one of the rounds, placed the other on top, and covered the two layers with pale brown sugary goodness.

"There." I sank into a kitchen chair and surveyed my

handiwork, still holding the spatula. It looked pretty much plain-Jane, but I was sure it would taste heavenly. I looked at Mungo. "At the bakery I'll just make a sheet cake, and the frosting hardening too fast won't be a problem. We'll sell it in precut squares."

He ignored me, staring a hole in the spatula.

"What? You want some?"

Yip!

I grinned and put a little dollop of frosting in his empty bowl. I could swear that dog ate more than I did and didn't even weigh fifteen pounds. Maybe I'd grab a snack later, but it had been a crazy day. I needed to clear my head and stretch my body. I needed endorphins swishing through my system.

That meant a nice hour-long run.

The clock read five thirty, which left me enough time to work up a good sweat before sunset. Of course, now that I'm a Southern gal I don't sweat; I glow. I changed into running shorts, a sports bra, and a T-shirt, and laced up my trusty trail runners. No trails today, though. The placid streets of Midtown Savannah would suit me just fine. I began to unclasp my dragonfly necklace so it wouldn't bounce in my face as I ran. Then I remembered Mimsey's insistence that I wear it and tucked it inside my shirt instead.

Better safe than sorry.

"Sorry, buddy," I said to Mungo when he looked up from his bowl. "I plan to run hard, and you're too little to keep up."

He gave me a baleful look. If a dog could shrug, he did before turning back to his bowl. Deep down, I suspected he didn't enjoy running as much as I did. Mungo could be a bit prissy at times. And lazy.

"You have frosting on your nose," I tossed over my shoulder on my way out.

Margie's voice drifted through the evening air as I stretched my hamstrings on the front porch. "Come on inside and get your mac 'n' weenies, kids." I shuddered at the thought, then reminded myself to stop being such a snob. And I knew for a fact that her mother-in-law cooked all sorts of good things for those kids—and for Margie and Redding, too.

My footfalls pounding on the cement in time with my heartbeat, I took off slowly to warm up my muscles. As I built up steam and increased my pace, my mind left my body to its activity and began gnawing on all the things that had happened since I'd met Declan for our picnic in Johnson Square that morning. Finding the dead body had been bad enough, but then there had been the unpleasant Detective Taite and Detective Quinn's veiled reference to having done something to make his superior unhappy. I couldn't help but wonder what it could have been. Peter Quinn had always struck me as a real stand-up guy.

I smiled at a bearded man walking a golden retriever and moved toward the curb to let him pass. He smiled back.

Then there was the tattoo, which led to the Dragoh Society. Mimsey's frightened expression, so at odds with her usual twinkly self, loomed large on my mental movie screen. Heinrich Dawes' glowering frown soon replaced it as I remembered his condescension and threats. It *had* been interesting to meet Steve's father, though, even if he turned out to be kind of scary. And what about Steve's revelation that he was a druid and in line for membership in a very exclusive magical club?

Unbidden, his words came back to me: *I've never met anyone like you. We're connected. I know you feel it, too. We have a destiny.*

I ran harder. Faster.

But there was no escaping what he'd said. I could only push it aside with thoughts of the dead man. Lawrence Eastmore. His death was none of my business. Everyone kept telling me that, and I wanted to believe it. But Mimsey's reference to my being a catalyst, the way the wreath sigil on Eastmore's arm had sent shivers down my spine, and the fact that I was already involved—well, sort of involved—with someone who would someday be in the same druid . . . clan? . . . as Eastmore all felt too coincidental. Not to mention that Declan and I had discovered the body in the first place.

My breath rasped in and out of my lungs, ragged and harsh. I wiped moisture off my forehead with the back of my wrist. The scent of sautéing onions drifted from one of the apartments stacked on both sides of the street.

I couldn't help being curious. Getting hit over the head in one of the historic squares of Savannah seemed more secular than magical. How could I tell Quinn who Eastmore was so he could find the killer? Yes, I was thinking in terms of a murder, but Quinn was right—it could have been an accident. It was hard to believe that, but I'd only seen the guy lying under the rhododendron. So it was possible. Either way, the police couldn't investigate properly unless they knew the dead man's identity.

That was silly, though. Quinn was a perfectly capable detective, and he'd said Detective Taite was smart. They'd have people canvassing the neighborhoods around

Johnson Square, taking fingerprints, looking at video footage, and whatever else they did to solve their cases. They probably already knew who he was. They didn't require any help from me.

I needed to get over myself. Katie Lightfoot simply wasn't that important to the equation.

Katie! Go left! Now!

Instantly, I veered left between two cars, into the street and oncoming traffic. A minivan screeched to a halt, and I flung up my hand, as if that would make it stop faster. The horn blared. A woman screamed.

A sickeningly wet crash behind me made my heart buck in my chest. I sprinted five more steps as more dull, moist thuds sounded. I stopped and spun around. An amber projectile streaked down from above, and I instinctively ducked. It exploded on the pavement where I'd been running, followed immediately by another.

My heartbeat pounded in my ears, my chin jerked up, and I frantically searched the sky. It was blue and cloudless.

The barrage seemed to have stopped.

The minivan driver got out and joined me. "Wow. They barely missed hitting you." Her voice shook.

Hand at my throat, I nodded and gulped air into my lungs. "Yeah," I managed at last.

Vivid, flame-colored remnants of several pumpkins lay in shreds and chunks on the sidewalk. Their slimy guts spattered the brick wall of the apartment building, the ground, and the sides of several cars. Over the years I'd seen the result of kids' "tossing" jack-o'-lanterns on Halloween, but this was different. Some of the pieces of pumpkin were recognizable shards, but many had liquefied when they'd hit the pavement. The seeds and pumpkin goo looked disturbingly like the insides of something that had once been alive. What might normally have struck me as mild vandalism instead felt violent and threatening. I shook myself, carefully avoiding the reason why: Any one of those orange missiles could have killed me with a direct hit.

"Oh, my God! I'm so *sorry*!" The voice came faintly from above, and I craned my neck to look up. A dark-haired woman in a purple bathrobe waved her hands from the eighth-story terrace. "Stay there! I'm coming right down." She disappeared into the apartment behind her.

"Are you okay?" The woman who had honked at me only moments before asked with obvious concern. She was a few years older than me.

I blinked back at her. "I guess so." Took a deep, shuddering breath. "Yes. Of course. I'm fine." She could have run right over me. I shuddered again.

But this nice woman hadn't been the one who warned me. I looked around. A few residents had ventured out of nearby doorways to inspect the mess. As soon as they realized no one was hurt and there would be no flashing lights to gawk at, most turned right around and went back inside.

Katie! Go left! Now! I'd heard the words loud and clear and had responded to the directive without a split second of thought. Or question.

Which had probably saved my life. That telltale shiver ran down my spine, and then made the return trip back up to the base of my skull. No one had been anywhere close to me, but someone—something?—had warned me to get out of the way. It had been a familiar voice, too. But not one I'd heard since my grandmother had died when I was nine years old.

"Oh, my Lord, I cannot believe that happened." The woman from the balcony came boiling out of the front door of the apartment house. Her hair, not as dark as I'd thought, dripped with water. Tall and thin to the point of being gaunt, she tightened the belt of her bathrobe and shuffled her feet. I looked down and saw that she was wearing a pair of unlaced yellow tennis shoes.

"I was just turning one of those dang punkins around to see which side my little boy might want to paint, and it tipped right over the balustrade," she continued in a harried, breathy voice. "Right out of my hands. I'm so, so sorry. I tried real careful to keep those dang things away from the edge there. So's nobody'd get hurt, you know?"

Her expression pled with me. I nodded my understanding. In the minivan a child began to cry, and the woman who'd managed to not run me down said, "I'm sorry, but I've got to go. You really are okay?"

"Uh-huh. Just a little shaken up, but no harm done."

Both women breathed sighs of relief, and the first one got into her van and drove away. I heard her soothing murmurs through the open window as the van passed.

"How many pumpkins were up there?" I asked the robed woman in front of me.

"Eight. They were for my little boy's Scout troop. We're having a punkin-painting party tomorrow. Or we were. I'll have to get some more, I guess. Keep them in the car this time." She put her hands on her hips and surveyed the damage. "Guess I have a bit of cleanup to do here, too. Who knew a few little squashes could make such a mess?" Shaking her head, she brought her gaze up to meet mine.

"How many of them fell?" I asked.

She paused and looked away. "All of them."

The amount of orange muck sprayed for yards around us confirmed her statement. It still didn't make sense, though. I chose my words carefully. "I can see how one might tip off the balustrade like that, but all of them?"

She licked her lips and met my eyes again. "You won't believe me if I tell you."

Goose bumps played along my vertebrae. "Try me."

"The first one? The one I was holding? I swear, it felt like something grabbed it right out of my hands. And the ones after that, well, they went down like dominoes, one after another. But, honey? They weren't even *touching* each other. That edge is eighteen inches wide, too. I just can't figure it."

We blinked at each other for a long moment.

"Were you the one who screamed?"

She nodded. " 'Bout scared the life right out of me, seeing you down here. You got some quick reflexes, girl."

I tried a smile, but the adrenaline whipping through my veins made my lips quiver, so I stopped.

She tugged on the purple belt again, peering at me. "You're not gonna sue me, are you?"

I shook my head. The thought hadn't even occurred to me. I was pretty sure that whatever had happened hadn't been this woman's fault. "Listen, I have to go now," I said, surveying the mess in a mild state of shock.

"Okay, honey." She patted me awkwardly on the shoulder. "Seriously, I'm real sorry. And I'm awful glad you're okay."

"Me, too," I muttered.

As I ran home my dragonfly amulet bounced under my T-shirt, near my racing heart.

Chapter 9

I rounded the corner to find a baby blue 1964 Thunderbird convertible parked in the driveway behind my Volkswagen. The top was down, and Lucy and Mimsey got out as soon as they saw me approach.

"Where have you been?" Lucy demanded.

"On a run. Why?"

"You didn't take your phone."

"I never take my phone when I run."

Mimsey pursed her lips. "We tried to call you several times, to see if you'd learned anything more from your . . . from Steve. When you didn't answer, we became worried."

"So we came over to make sure you were all right," my aunt said.

"You said you'd call," the older woman said, then paused, inhaled, and seemed to force a lightness into her words. "I mean, my stars and garters, Katie, darlin', this is a good time to be extra careful."

I thought of the pumpkins crashing down right where I would have been if I hadn't been warned by the mysterious voice. A voice I'd recognized. On the way home I'd thought of nothing else—except for the near miss with the monster truck when I'd almost run the stop sign on my way home from the Honeybee.

"Let's go inside, okay? This isn't something we need to discuss out on the front lawn," I said.

The two other women exchanged looks, and turned in sync toward the porch.

Once the front door was closed and Mungo had greeted both of them, I asked, "Have you eaten? Can I get you something?"

"I've had my supper, but I wouldn't mind something sweet if you've got it," Mimsey said.

I smiled and gestured them into the kitchen. They settled into chairs at the small table, and Lucy moved the potted basil plant to one side. I pointed to the cake on the counter and asked, "How about a piece of this?"

"Is that caramel . . . ? Oh my, yes." Mimsey's eyes twinkled. "No, a larger piece, if you don't mind. And a nice big glass of milk?"

I put an enormous slab of cake on a plate and poured the milk she requested. Mimsey was what she described as "comfortably round." Who was I to argue with her comfort? I watched as she took the first bite and closed her eyes in apparent bliss.

"Did I get it right?" I asked.

"My heavens, yes, right down to the crispy crust on the outside of the frosting."

"Ben's waiting on supper for me," Lucy said. "But he's probably getting impatient. I didn't tell him why we were coming over here. I was afraid he'd worry."

That sounded ominous. "You're obviously worried, though." At one time I would have pooh-poohed my aunt's concern, but I'd learned she was right more often than not. I joined them at the table.

"Those druids can be dangerous." Mimsey dabbed at the corner of her mouth with the corner of a napkin. Half of her cake was already gone.

I crossed my arms over my chest. "And how do you know that, Ms. Carmichael?"

She hesitated, then seemed to make a decision. "We had an incident of sorts. A friend of our family, of my husband's, really, crossed Heinrich Dawes in some kind of financial deal. I don't know the details—Heinrich calls himself a venture capitalist, but I really have no idea what that means. Anyway, suddenly all sorts of bad things started happening to this man. Accidents, a tax audit out of the blue, traffic tickets, even an ugly skin rash. It seemed obvious foul play, of the magical variety. So I did a little divination to find out exactly what this poor man was dealing with."

"And?" I prompted when she seemed to have trouble finding the next words. I couldn't help thinking about what Steve had said about the Dragohs' justifying some questionable practices to themselves. What were they capable of?

"I discovered there was a group behind the, well, the curses, really. That's what they effectively were. Never found out how many were in the group, or much else about them, but I went to Hein—to Steve's father—" She took a sip of milk.

"All alone," Lucy interrupted. "It was stupidly dangerous, Mimsey. You should have told the rest of us. I don't know if I'll ever forgive you."

Mimsey waved her hand in the air as if dispelling a

foul odor. "Lucille, you've already forgiven me, and you know it. After all, it all ended well."

"What did you do?" I asked.

She tossed her white pageboy. The indigo bow stuck to the side of it didn't budge. "I talked to him, of course."

"That's it?"

"At the time that was enough. They'd kept their group secret. Not even their wives were aware, from what I understood. And I told Heinrich I'd keep quiet if he stopped cursing my husband's friend. But he'll find out I told you. I don't know how those druids could react if they felt cornered or threatened."

"So did you find out anything more about them from Steve?" Lucy asked.

Nodding slowly, I leaned back in my chair. "From Steve and from his father. Heinrich himself dropped by."

Mimsey leaned forward. "Oh, my."

"He actually told me the name of the group, though he said it was a men's club." I told them what I'd learned about the Dragoh Society. I ended by telling them who the dead man was. I felt a twinge of guilt, since Steve had let the information slip because he thought I already knew, but it didn't seem like something I should keep to myself. I was surprised by Lucy's reaction.

"Lawrence Eastmore?" she gasped, her eyes widening as she bit her lip. My aunt was as tenderhearted as they came, but this was something more.

"Did you know him?" I asked, shifting in my chair to lean my elbows on the table.

She took a deep breath. "Dr. Eastmore, actually. Mimsey had shared with me that there was a powerful group of druids here in Savannah, but we didn't know he was one of them. Though it doesn't really surprise me to learn that. He was a professor, you see, but he was also an expert in rare books. Specifically, rare occult books." She glanced at her friend, then back at me. "Last year I arranged to borrow a copy of the *Heptama-ron* for the spellbook club to review."

My forehead wrinkled. *"Heptamaron?"*

"It's an ancient Latin spellbook. He had an English translation. It was terribly interesting, wasn't it, Mims? And we were all so grateful for his generosity in lending it to us."

"So you didn't know he was a druid, but he knew about the spellbook club."

"Well, he knew we have a book club, and he certainly struck me as quite intelligent. I'm sure he was able to add two and two and get four."

I pressed my lips together.

"That our spellbook club is really a coven isn't much of a secret," Mimsey said. "In certain circles only, of course. I doubt my husband's golfing friends would think much of his wife's magical affiliations." She winked at me.

"Anyway, I decided it's silly to think I need to help Peter Quinn identify Eastmore," I said. "I bet he did that hours ago and has already developed a list of suspects." I just hoped they were more likely to have committed a crime than Uncle Ben had been when Quinn had considered him a murder suspect.

Lucy and Mimsey exchanged skeptical looks.

"What?" I asked.

"I'm not so sure Detective Quinn will have made much progress," my aunt said.

"You don't think he's good at his job?"

Mimsey shook her head. "That's not it at all. But if these Dragoh druids are as powerful as we think they are, they might be able to keep him from being good at it. If you know what I mean."

"Magically." It wasn't a question.

They both nodded.

Well. That added a sticky element to an already messy situation.

Mimsey said, "And now you've crossed Heinrich Dawes. That's not good. I should never have told you to talk to Steve. I just thought since he lo—cares about you he wouldn't put you in danger like that."

I thought about the pumpkin guts splattered all over the pavement and swallowed.

My face must have reflected my thoughts, because Lucy put her hand on my arm. "Katie?"

I patted her hand. "Please don't worry. I'm a pretty powerful witch my own self, you know."

"You're still so inexperienced," she protested.

I couldn't deny that. "I have this." I pulled the dragonfly amulet from where it nestled inside my T-shirt. Lucy was the one who'd given it to me. "And besides, someone's watching out for me in a big way."

Mimsey tipped her head to one side. "What do you mean?"

"I've had two narrow escapes today."

Now they both looked alarmed. I held up my hand. "I'm fine. And they were both accidents. Sort of. The first one was my fault. I got distracted thinking about . . . things . . . and almost ran a stop sign."

Yip!

I looked down at Mungo. "That's right. This little

guy warned me in time, and I stopped before that big truck—" I saw the looks on their faces and stopped. "That was before I even talked to Heinrich Dawes, so I don't see how it could have anything to do with the Dragohs."

"What else happened?" Mimsey's voice held flat accusation. Lucy blinked worried eyes at me.

"Some pumpkins fell off a balustrade at the top of an apartment building as I was running underneath."

"You mean right before you got here?" the older woman demanded.

I nodded. "Shortly before, yes. It could have been an accident, too."

"But you don't think it was," Lucy said. "I can tell."

Shrugging, I said, "No, I don't. From what I was told, they seemed to move of their own accord."

Lucy's hand flew to her chest.

"Now, stop that. I'm fine. And they were just pumpkins. Lordy, did they make a mess!" I forced a laugh.

No one joined me.

"You said someone is watching out for you," Mimsey said.

I hesitated. Would they think I was crazy? Only one way to find out. "I heard a voice. It told me to move left. No, it *demanded*."

They stared at me. Finally, Lucy turned to Mimsey and said, "Do you think she's clairaudient?"

"Hello? I'm sitting right here. And I've never heard voices before."

A few beats passed; then Lucy patted me on the shoulder. "Well, let's just be glad you did this time, then."

I nodded, silent. Should I tell her the rest? In for a dime and all that. "Lucy? One other thing. The voice

that warned me? It sounded exactly like Nonna Sheffield." Lucy's mother and my grandmother.

I don't know what reaction I'd expected, but Lucy
simply inclined her chin thoughtfully and said, "It
wouldn't surprise me, Katie. Of course she would want
to protect you." She glanced at Mimsey and said, "As
do we." She stood up and strode into the living room.

Mimsey rose and followed her. Raising my eyebrows, I trailed behind.

My aunt went to the coffee table and picked up her
purse. From it she extracted a bottle made of antique
milk glass and handed it to me.

"What's this?"

"It's a house protection spell. If you were building a
home we'd put it right into the foundation, but it will
work fine if you put it out someplace in this main
room."

I shook it and heard a soft rattle. "Can I open it?"

"It would be better if you didn't. I sealed it with
beeswax after setting the spell."

"What's in it?" I asked, curious as anything. We
hadn't talked about bottle spells before.

"Salt, garlic, bay, and basil. Dill, sage, anise, and
pepper."

I quirked an eyebrow. "Salt and herbs. Very hedge-
witchy."

Lucy smiled. "It's what I do, dear."

Standing, I went to the built-in bookshelf and placed
the bottle in the center. It looked like an antique knick-
knack, but I could feel gentle power wafting from it.

Turning, I said, "Thanks."

Mimsey said, "You should mark your property with
the rune of protection. Algiz."

There were so many possible ways to practice magic, and I'd barely dipped my toe into ancient runes. "Which one is that again?"

"Basically a Y, with a middle prong in the middle of the vee. Looks kind of like a pitchfork."

"Right," I said, remembering.

They turned and nodded to each other. "We'd better be going," Lucy said.

"Be careful," Mimsey said.

"I'll be fine," I said.

I grabbed a purple Sharpie and walked them out to the Thunderbird. Lucy backed out of the driveway, and they both waved as she accelerated around the corner. I opened my mailbox. Mostly junk mail, as usual. The setting sun had painted the sky with dramatic ribbons of orange and fuchsia, which lingered in the gloaming. Looking up, I dropped a pizza coupon on the ground in case Margie or another neighbor was watching out the window. I bent to pick it up and quickly pushed aside the nasturtium twining up the mailbox post. With a few strokes of the Sharpie, I drew the rune mark that Mimsey had suggested on the wooden post. The nasturtiums fell into place, effectively hiding it.

I was protected on many fronts now, but there was something else I could do.

Chapter 10

I went around the carriage house checking to make sure all the locks on the windows and doors were firmly in place and secured. No harm in being practical on this plane as well as others.

As I moved from the living room into my bedroom, I realized this was the first time since I'd lived in Savannah that I'd felt any fear in my own home. The tiny clicks of Mungo's toenails on the wooden floorboards as he followed me were a comfort, though, and I scooped him up, grateful for his company and for his canine super senses.

I showered off the run, letting the hot water wash away some of my tension as well. After rubbing my short hair partially dry with a towel, I dressed in comfy sweats and went into the kitchen. I washed up Mimsey's plate and glass, as well as Mungo's bowl. Still not hungry, I poured myself yet another tall glass of iced tea and grabbed my phone off the counter where it had been charging.

Mimsey and/or Lucy had left eight messages on my voice mail, each one more frantic than the previous one. I shook my head and hit DELETE until I got to the last one. It was from Declan. He'd called minutes before I'd returned from my run.

"Hey, Katie. Just checking to see how you're holding up after our adventure this morning. Pretty crazy stuff, huh? Well, I'm sure you're fine, probably out running or something, so, you know, hi. Um, and I really had a good time today. You know—before the dead guy and everything. So maybe you'd want to do it again? I like cooking for you. A lot. Um, yeah. So okay, let me know. Bye."

Sweet. The guy was downright adorably sweet. He had every confidence in my ability to bounce back from finding a body under a bush. Of course, he had no knowledge of druids or magic or secret societies.

Steve did, though. I carried the phone into my bedroom. Settling in amongst the pillows piled up against the iron filigree headboard, I scrolled through the contact list on my phone until I found Steve's number.

Never mind that I already knew it by heart.

"Tell daddy dearest to call off his dogs," I said when he answered.

A pause, and then, "Katie?" As if he didn't have caller ID. "What are you talking about?"

I looked down at the alarm clock on the nightstand. It was almost eight thirty. "Please tell your father and his Dragoh friends to leave me alone."

"What happened?"

I had to give him credit: He didn't waste time defending them. Once again I related the tale of not one but eight pumpkins mysteriously falling from a wide balustrade just as I was running underneath it. As I spoke I became painfully aware of how incredibly silly it sounded. I could just imagine what Declan would have to say if I were to try and explain it to him. By the time I was done I was on my feet beside the bed, feeling like an idiot. "I know it sounds ridiculous, but it happened."

"Oh, I believe you, Katie. Settle down and let me think about this for a minute."

Pacing barefoot on the wooden floorboards, I managed to hold my tongue.

"I don't know what's going on," he said after a few moments. "Let me talk to someone."

"Great. That's what got me in trouble in the first place."

"Not my father. Someone else."

"Who?"

"Will you please just trust me?"

"Because that's worked out so well for me so far." But as I said the words, I knew Steve would never have intentionally put me into harm's way.

"Then why did you call?" His words were flat.

"I thought you could help. I thought maybe you *would* help. If it weren't for you, that group of druids wouldn't be after me." Well, heck. That sounded silly, too.

"Okay, listen," Steve said. "For one thing, I don't know that they are 'after you.'"

"Who else could it be? Your father obviously saw me as defying him."

"Maybe. Or maybe the group as a whole created a magical barrier against anyone who found out about them. In case you haven't realized, they are *very* secretive, and always have been. There are long-standing wards to repel anyone who gets too close. You could have run into that. Or they may have cast another spell specifically for anything—or anyone—who was curious about Lawrence Eastmore, since he was discovered this morning." He hesitated. "Or . . ."

"Or what?"

"It could be something else altogether."

I snorted. "Pretty coincidental if that's the case."

"Not if it's something about why Eastmore was killed in the first place."

I stopped short, and Mungo looked up from where he lay dozing on the bedspread. "You know why he was killed?"

"No." There was real regret in his voice. "But I know someone who might have an idea. I'll talk to him, see if I can find anything out. In the meantime, keep your head down."

"Right."

"Um, Katie?"

"Yeah?"

"How did you know to get out of the way?"

"Instinct, I guess." I wasn't ready to tell him my dead grandmother might have warned me from beyond the grave.

He was silent for a long time, and I wondered what he was thinking. Then he said, "Promise me you'll call if anything else happens."

"Okay."

"Anything at all. Even if you're just feeling nervous. Day or night." The concern in his tone made me kind of nervous. But it also made me feel kind of warm and fuzzy.

"I mean it about keeping your head down. I don't want anything to happen to you, Katie-girl."

"Me, either."

I hung up. As irritated as I was with him, it was surprising how much better I felt after hearing his voice.

I brushed my teeth and settled back into bed to read while my hair finished drying. The waning gibbous moon rose outside my window, bright with encouragement. I sent an intention out to the universe that as the light faded so too would any danger to me or to the spellbook club.

As long as I stayed out of the Dragohs' business, that shouldn't be a problem, I thought as I finally drifted off to sleep.

No problem at all.

An hour later I awoke with a start.

For most of my life I'd suffered from a sleeping disorder. Some people might call it simple insomnia. In fact, some people had—doctors and sleep experts and the like. But it didn't feel like regular insomnia. For one thing, even though I slept only one hour a night, and sometimes not even that, I wasn't very often tired. The reason I'd taken up running in the first place was to burn off energy. Energy I shouldn't have had in the first place.

Once I'd begun practicing magic, the manic need for running had evaporated and my sleep disorder had become a thing of the past. Well, mostly. I still had the occasional sleepless night, and I still averaged only about five hours of sleep each twenty-four hours. As a baker, that left me with plenty of time to have a real life on top of crazy early hours at work and long days. Plus, since magic had taken the edge off, I felt calm and peaceful instead of anxious and jittery.

Looking down at Mungo, I said, "Maybe I can get back to sleep in a little while. Right?"

Yip.

It wasn't to be, though. I spent the rest of the night on the Internet researching druids. At four a.m. I dressed in my usual work uniform of skirt, T-shirt, and sensible shoes, and headed out to the backyard to snip a few stems of fragrant basil and parsley. Back inside, I loaded Mungo into my bag, grabbed my to-go cup of coffee, and locked the front door behind me. The basil was for focus as I drove as well as general protection, and the parsley was for protection and a little practical deodorization after the previous day's mishap. The herbs went into the Bug's vase, Mungo went into the passenger seat, and the coffee went into me as I drove downtown to the Honeybee.

Mungo was a good listener, so along the way I related what I'd managed to dig up during the night hours. Given all the hush-hush that seemed to surround the Dragoh Society, it wasn't surprising that I didn't find any information—or even reference—to it. Not in Savannah or anywhere else. I did find out a little more about Dr. Lawrence Eastmore. Sure enough, he was a professor of art history and aesthetics at the Savannah College of Art and Design, and the few comments from students were quite positive. Apart from his teaching position, he was also a member of the Antiquarian Booksellers Association of America and the Georgia Antiquarian Booksellers Association. There was no reference to spellbooks or to his having a particular interest in the occult.

After digging for a while I'd discovered an obituary from eleven years before for a man named Samson

Eastmore. He was survived by his son, Lawrence, who was about the right age to be the man I'd found, and a grandson named Greer Eastmore. No mention of Lawrence's wife, though he apparently had a sister, Penelope, and a mother named Esther. A bit later I found Esther's obituary, too. She'd died within a year of her husband. Unlike his son, it sounded like Samson Eastmore had died of natural causes.

"I know Quinn wants me to stay out of things," I said to my familiar as I steered around Oglethorpe Square. "But now it's getting personal."

He made a sound in the back of his throat.

"Let's hope he knows all this plus a whole lot more. Right?"

The dog curled into the bottom of the tote and went to sleep. I couldn't blame him. He'd stayed up with me most of the night and was probably exhausted.

I was uncharacteristically tired as well, but did my best to shake it off. Even though the Honeybee was open only until one o'clock on Sundays, as soon as we closed the bakery the spellbook club was meeting at Lucy and Ben's town house. Today Cookie and I would hold the fort at the bakery, while Lucy prepped for our meeting and Ben indulged in his weekly round at the Crosswinds Golf Club, where he had a standing eight a.m. tee time.

Inside the bakery I left Mungo sleeping on his chair in the office and got to work. First the sourdough loaves that had been rising all night went into hot ovens. We sold a lot of sourdough bread for family Sunday suppers, so I usually made extra. The brioche dough was also no-knead, rich with eggs and butter and honey, so that went into molds for a quick rise before following the sourdough into the ovens.

Then I mixed up a batch of cinnamon raisin biscotti, which customers had taken to dipping into the warm apple cider we offered in the fall. As I sprinkled in the cinnamon, I added a short incantation encouraging good luck, prosperity, and general healing. I had just finished when Cookie came in the door from the alley. The morning paper was tucked under one arm.

She was usually a little fuzzy that early in the morning and only mumbled a quick greeting before heading out to the espresso counter. Seconds later she was back, a steaming mug of drip coffee in hand.

"You rock, Katie. Thank you for making coffee before I got here."

"I know it's a challenge to work this early." For most people, at least. "Hungry?"

"Actually, I am. I skipped supper last night."

"So did I." Plus stayed up all night, not to mention my evening run, complete with the adrenaline rush of dodging flying pumpkins. "I have the perfect solution."

After popping the loaf of spicy biscotti into the oven for its first baking, I got to work on my version of *pain perdu*. I liked to think of it as the love child of savory French toast and bruschetta. First I soaked slices of brioche left over from the day before in a mixture of eggs and milk with a tiny bit of Mo Hotta Mo Betta hot sauce mixed in. Then I fried the slices in butter until browned and finished them in the oven as I sliced tomatoes and grated Parmesan. Finally, I topped the *pain perdu* with paper-thin Parma ham, the sliced tomatoes, fresh basil, and the cheese. A quick run under the broiler and breakfast was served.

"Mmmph . . . good." Cookie registered her appreciation around a mouthful. Even though she more resembled a colt—long legs, thin build, delicate bones—she ate like a bull. I had to admit, it was better than having someone merely pick at food I'd served. I remembered her mentioning once in an offhand manner that there had been some very lean times during her childhood in Haiti, and I was glad to see her enjoy the *pain* so much.

Mungo nibbled at his plate with more subdued approval.

I took another bite and reached for the *Savannah Morning News* that Cookie had picked up on her way to work. There was nothing about the dead man on the front page, but when I flipped it open I found something on page four: a brief story in which Declan and I were described as "a local man and woman" who discovered "an as yet to be identified man" deceased in Johnson Square.

Darn it. I was half surprised that Quinn hadn't figured out who the dead guy was yet—but only half, since Lucy and Mimsey had planted the seeds of doubt the day before. Maybe the Dragohs really were throwing some magical monkey wrenches into my detective friend's investigation. The other thing that confirmed the possibility was the image accompanying the news article. It was a line drawing, not a photo—thank goodness—but it wasn't a very good likeness. Could this be more of the Dragohs' "magical barrier" that Steve had referred to last night? Because if I'd known Lawrence Eastmore as a living, breathing human being I might not have recognized him from the picture. I wondered if any of his friends or coworkers would.

Wait a minute . . .

"Cookie, do you recognize this man?" I turned the paper around so she could look at the picture right side up.

She cocked her head to the side. "This is who you found?"

"That's him. Sort of, at least. Does he look like anyone you knew when you worked at SCAD?" When I'd first met Cookie she'd worked at the Savannah College of Art and Design, then moved on to manage an apartment building before stepping in to help us at the Honeybee.

She squinted. Pressed her lips together. "Maybe."

"A professor, perhaps?"

"Hmm."

"Art history? Aesthetics?"

Her face cleared. "Of course. That's Dr. Eastmore."

Chapter 11

Bingo.

I smiled. "I could kiss you."

Her eyes widened in surprise. "I don't—"

"Now I can let Quinn know who the dead man is, and Steve can't accuse me of betraying him." I took a triumphant bite and let the salty ham play over my tongue.

"I'm confused."

"I'll explain later. Right now I need to make a phone call."

Shoving my plate aside, I hurried into the office and retrieved my cell phone. Peter Quinn's direct line at the police precinct was still in my contact list. I dialed it, expecting to get his voice mail at six a.m. However, the man himself picked up on the third ring.

"Hello, Quinn. How are you this fine morning?" Being able to get this information off my chest had lightened my mood considerably. "In kind of early, aren't you?"

"My caller ID says this is Katie Lightfoot. Could that possibly be true? Because why would my friendly neighborhood baker be calling me on my official line only one day after I see her in the vicinity of a homicide case?"

"Funny man. Do you or do you not want to know who we found yesterday?"

"Are you telling me you know?"

I abandoned the question game. "Yes! His name is Lawrence Eastmore." I practically crowed.

"I know."

"But—"

"How do *you* know?"

There was no reason to be disappointed, yet I was a little. "Cookie recognized the drawing in the paper."

"Cookie who works there?"

"Of course. But she used to work in the registration office at SCAD. She met Dr. Eastmore then."

"Ah. That makes sense." There was a little too much relief in his tone. "It turns out she's not the only one who recognized the picture. The main desk got an anonymous call to the same effect about an hour ago."

"Just one other call?"

"Yes. Most people are still asleep." His tone was wry.

"We're up." I sounded smug.

"Bakers and policemen don't exactly keep normal hours. I have a murder to solve."

"At least you know whose now. And, Quinn? This is me saying, 'I told you so.'"

"Yeah, yeah."

Something muffled his voice, and he seemed to be talking to someone else. His words became less garbled. "I'll be right there." He spoke into the phone again. "Katie? I need to go now. But I do appreciate the call. Really. We'll take it from here."

"Okeydokey." If he'd hurry up and solve the murder maybe the Dragohs would leave me alone. "Stop by if you're in the neighborhood. The special today is cranberry coconut cookies." They were Quinn's favorite.

"Sounds great." He was obviously distracted. "But I doubt I'll have time for a Honeybee run today."

"I just love those little cat faces! Where on earth did you find them?" Mrs. Standish, one of our regulars, put her fists on her ample hips and peered at the decorations surrounding the front entrance.

"Lucy and Bianca made them," I said as I filled a box with a dozen assorted muffins. The kitties were cute, based on jack-o'-lantern carving patterns and fastened to the doorframe. The ladies had used yellow felt painted with orange and white stripes so they looked like tabby cats. Actually, they looked like Lucy's familiar, Honeybee, who had inspired the name for our bakery. I loved Honeybee, but she made me sneeze and sniffle like crazy. Thankfully, unlike Mungo, she preferred to stay home.

"We're going for a little scarier," Croft Barrow said from where he sat at a table near the display case. Croft owned the bookstore next door. He and Annette Lander, who had the knitting shop on the other side of the bakery, were planning Halloween parties, too. "You know, spooky music, gross stuff in jars. We even have a cauldron to fill with dry ice on Halloween night."

I smiled. "Us, too." I didn't mention that it was a real working cauldron that had seen its share of brewing.

Behind me, Cookie snorted.

"You girls make Halloween too cute," Croft went on. "Annette's decorations are all made of wool, for heaven's sake. Halloween is supposed to scare the pants off you."

"Well, let's hope that doesn't happen," Mrs. Standish said in a dry tone and handed me a bill. I grinned and counted out her change.

"We won't set any records for scariness," I said. "But it'll be a fun and safe place for kids to come and hang out on Halloween."

I'd always loved Halloween, and was glad to be among so many other people who felt the same way. My parents weren't much for the holiday. They let me dress up and go around to a few houses, but always seemed nervous. Now I suspected it was because on Halloween—or Samhain—the veil between the worlds of the living and the dead was supposed to be thinnest. Given Mama's tendency to overprotect me, she'd probably been afraid of something dire happening.

They never let me wear that witch costume I'd always wanted, either. This year I'd been determined to finally dress up as a real badass: black pointy hat, hooked nose with a big wart, broom and all. Until, of course, Lucy had admonished me for being so willing to perpetuate stereotypes that gave our kind a bad name.

Sigh. Sometimes you just couldn't win. Now I had no idea what to wear. Maybe gear up as a ghost, since Mimsey had told me that in the old times villagers would dress as spirits on Samhain in order to guide the dead to the edge of town at the end of the night.

Traditional, but a wee bit boring.

Croft left a little before noon, holding the door open for three uniformed firemen to enter as he exited. Declan came in last, flashing a grin as soon as he saw me.

"Thought I'd bring in some new customers," he said. "Neither of these guys has been in the famous Honeybee Bakery before."

"Famous, huh?" I rolled my eyes and pointed to a table as I slipped out from behind the register. "Have a seat, and we'll see if we can live up to this one's hype." I gestured toward Declan with my chin.

Declan gave me a quick hug and kiss on the cheek.

"I'm Scott," said the older man. His skin was dark and his short hair was threaded lightly with gray. He moved with an easy grace as he took his chair.

The younger guy was stockier, his face chiseled in planes that reminded me of my father, who was part Shawnee. His uniform did little to hide the muscles underneath. As he sat down he smiled at me with his eyes. I couldn't help smiling back. "I'm Randy."

I bet you are, I thought, but said, "Hey, guys."

"You've got to be Katie," Scott said. "No wonder Deck won't shut up about you."

I ducked my head, but not before seeing Declan's face flush.

Ignoring both of them, I asked what they wanted to order. "Today we have some cranberry coconut cookies that aren't on the regular menu. Or you might want a cupcake—carrot with cream cheese frosting, chocolate cherry topped with chocolate ganache, or lemon on lemon, seasoned with black pepper?"

"Black pepper?" Declan asked.

"We mix savory and sweet a lot around here." Not to mention that from a magical perspective black pepper promoted energy, alertness, protection, and courage—right up a fireman's alley, I'd think. And lemon was good for health in general and healing in specific while giving an energy boost. "You should try the lemon cupcakes. They're really delicious," I urged.

They thought for a moment, then shook their heads.

"How about a scone, then? Lime and ginger, maple cardamom, or blueberry cinnamon."

"Yeah, that last one sounds good," Scott said.

"Maple for me," Randy said. "And drip coffees all around."

"Okay. Deck?" I asked. "A couple molasses oatmeal cookies?" His usual.

He nodded. "Perfect."

The cinnamon in the blueberry mix was good for luck and prosperity, but the cardamom in the maple scones was all about love and sex. It figured that Randy would choose that. I brought their food and went back for the coffees. A group of loud tourists came in, and Cookie took over the register. Coffees delivered, I moved toward the kitchen to restock a few things in the display case just as the door opened again. I glanced over my shoulder and saw it was Detective Taite.

"Oh!" I said. "Are you here for coffee or for me?"

Oh, no. Did I really say that out loud?

All three firemen and the pack of tourists turned their heads. Declan saw Taite and shot a puzzled look at me.

The detective quirked up one side of his mouth without a hint of a smile. "I have a couple of questions for you."

"Um, okay. Can I get you something to eat first?"

"I think not." The way he said it made me feel like I'd offered a bribe.

"All right." Why wasn't Quinn with him?

Mungo was in the office, so I didn't want to take him back there. The empty sofas by the bookshelf were at the opposite end of the bakery from where Declan and his friends sat, so I led Taite over to them. I took off my apron and gestured for him to make himself comfortable. He didn't move until I sat down. Then he chose a seat where he could see the rest of the bakery and carefully perched on the edge of one cushion as if the furniture might swallow him alive. Behind me, the tourists filtered back out to the sidewalk, laughing and talking and munching on various baked goods. Cookie lingered behind the register as relative quiet descended.

Taite leaned toward me. His shirt had one too many buttons open and the resulting vee revealed a chest covered with dark hair. I could see where a comb had divided his thinning brown hair into rows across his skull. Still, he looked to be only in his early forties.

"All righty—shoot," I said, trying for nonchalant.

He considered me for a long moment. "Detective Quinn says you called him. That you identified the dead man from the park."

"The square. And I didn't. My friend did, from the picture in the paper." I would call Cookie over to verify if I had to, but she had a deep-seated distrust of the police—of authority in general—so that would be a last resort.

"Convenient coincidence, don't you think?"

My eyes narrowed. "Detective Quinn told me someone else had already called."

He inclined his head. "Someone who managed to remain anonymous. That's hard to do these days."

"Especially when calling a police station," I said.

"But you don't know anything about that first call."

"No . . ."

"You're sure of that?"

I frowned. "Yes, I'm sure. Why would I call twice?"

"I don't know. Maybe to make sure your friend got the information."

"Detective Taite, are you accusing me of something?"

He searched my face. "Again, how was it that you happened to be in Johnson Square yesterday morning?" His gaze shifted over my shoulder.

"Oh, for heaven's sake. We were having a picnic."

"That information is in our statements," Declan said from behind me. He came around the sofa and sat beside me.

Taite frowned at him. "How convenient that you're here. Despite being on duty."

"What's that supposed to mean? This bakery is owned by the former fire chief. All the firefighters stop in when they can. Not to mention the police."

A speculative look crossed the detective's face. He turned his attention back to me. "You recognized the watch."

"I recognized the *type* of watch," I said.

"So you hadn't seen that particular watch before."

"No."

"Detective—," Declan started.

Taite held up his hand. "We can do this here or we can do it at the precinct." He turned his attention back to me. "What about the tattoo?"

"Ta-tattoo?" I stuttered.

Declan looked at me with surprise.

Taite's lips quirked again. "Yes, Ms. Lightfoot. The tattoo. You remember it?"

"I seem to remember something on his arm," I fudged.

"I think you remember more than that."

I didn't respond.

He shifted in his seat. "Where were you two nights ago?"

"At home. In bed. Why?"

"And you?" he said to Declan.

"The same."

"Together?"

Declan grinned. "I wish. But no."

I felt my face grow hot. To cover it, I demanded, "Is that when he died?"

Taite shook his head. "No."

"I . . . I don't understand."

"Are you sure? You know Lawrence Eastmore lived just a few houses down the street from where you found him."

I stared. "How on earth am I supposed to know that? I had *no idea* who he was when we found him."

"Lawrence Eastmore?" Declan asked. "That was his name?"

Without breaking eye contact with Taite, I patted Declan's arm and said, "It seems so. Though apparently he was *not* killed the night before we found him."

"On the contrary," Taite said. "Someone struck him with a heavy clay pot sometime that evening as he worked in his gardening shed. We found the shards. Blood. However, he seems to have recovered and staggered outside and down the street. He made it as far as the location where you reported finding him, and died around two a.m. Since we don't know how long he lived after he was attacked, we can only guess at what time he was actually struck. A neighbor saw him around five p.m. on Friday, so it had to be after that."

"That poor man," I said with a pang. "If only someone had found him earlier, he might still be alive."

"What's going on?"

I turned to find that Jaida had joined the party.

"Is this the new detective you mentioned, Katie?" Her eyes narrowed.

Taite scrambled to his feet. I stood as well. "Detective Franklin Taite, meet Jaida French. My lawyer."

He looked disgusted.

"Is there a problem?" she asked.

"Just following up on Ms. Lightfoot's statement." He gestured toward Declan with his chin. "And had the good luck to find her companion here, too."

"Anything else?" Jaida asked.

"Not at present." His eyes bored into me.

"I'll walk you to the door," I said. "Unless you've changed your mind about a cupcake or a cookie?"

"I haven't."

Leaving Declan and Jaida to stare after us, I accompanied Detective Taite out to the sidewalk.

"Why did you tell us all that stuff about how Eastmore died? Quinn wants me to stay out of it."

He squinted into the sun. "I transferred to Savannah because there is a hotbed of evil activity here, and I'm going to do something about it. Given what we found in Eastmore's home, it seems he was a part of it."

"A . . . hotbed? What on earth are you talking about? What did you find?" A dragonfly winged by. Then another. A funny feeling settled into my stomach.

"You know what I'm talking about. The occult. Witchcraft. Magic. If you're truly unaware of such things, then all's well. But I think you know exactly what I'm referring to. And I think you understand a lot more about the tattoo on Lawrence Eastmore's arm than you're telling me. Even I know it's a druidic sigil, and that was confirmed by the number of books and papers about black magic that he had hidden."

The flutter in my solar plexus blossomed, and my heart rat-a-tatted in my chest. Taite knew about druidic sigils? Who was this guy, really? Should I tell him that Dr. Eastmore was an expert and a collector but not necessarily a practitioner of the dark arts? How would I explain how I knew about his rare books at all? Mention Lucy borrowing the *Heptamaron* for our spellbook club?

Hardly. I didn't know nearly enough about this New York transplant who spoke as if all magic was evil. I kept the puzzled expression on my face and waited in silence.

Taite pointed at me. "I don't know where you stand in all this, but I understand that twice now you've been involved in homicides in ways you shouldn't be. I can only hope you're on the side of good. But if you're not?" He smiled and shrugged. "Then you're not. And I will find out." And with that he turned on his heel and strode away.

I stood in the bright sunshine and watched his receding figure.

Who was this guy? Had he just threatened me?

Yes, he had. And frankly, I was getting pretty darn tired of being threatened.

Chapter 12

Jaida had been downtown already when Cookie called and told her I was being questioned by the police, so she'd buzzed right over. After Detective Taite left, she tried to reassure me. "Don't worry. It sounded like he was just shooting in the dark."

"Yeah, but he's shooting at witches," I whispered, glancing over to where Declan had rejoined his friends.

"What?"

So I hustled my coven mates into the kitchen and told them what Taite had said.

Jaida closed her eyes. "A witch-hunter. Great."

"Really? In this day and age?" I asked.

"In every day and age, unfortunately," Jaida said.

I lifted my palms toward the ceiling in exasperation. "But we haven't done anything wrong."

Cookie said, "He will think that practicing magic itself is wrong."

"We'll talk about it at the meeting," Jaida said. "I have errands to finish." But she looked uneasy as she grabbed her triple latte and left.

The firemen left right behind her. "Deck's right,"

Scott said. "That scone was great! See you soon." The bell on the door rang as they opened it.

Declan paused. "Are you worried about that detective?"

I shrugged.

"Well, try not to be. I'm tempted to call up Peter Quinn and give him a piece of my mind." He gave me a one-armed squeeze and followed the other two out.

I glanced at the clock on the wall. Just after twelve thirty. Two women sat and chatted in the library area, but the other customers were primarily tourists stopping in for coffee and treats to go. In between serving them, Cookie and I began the process of shutting down the Honeybee.

Herbs and flowers crammed the small yard in front of my aunt and uncle's town house. Cookie and I walked up the narrow path between the plants to the front door. Ben opened it before we could knock.

"Come on in, ladies. You're the last to arrive and the wine is open and waiting upstairs."

Cookie gave him a broad grin. "Excellent." She went to the steps that led to the roof garden and proceeded up.

"I'll be there in a second," I called.

Dozens of houseplants reached out of pots on the floor and tables and hung from the vaulted ceiling above. Ivy clung to the brick fireplace. Yet despite the jungle of greenery, their home felt light and airy. Two skylights and tall windows streamed sunshine. White sofas and chairs glowed against cherrywood floors, and boldly patterned rugs defined the seating areas.

"How was golf today?" I asked my uncle as I bent down and deposited Mungo on the floor.

"Shot a ninety. Some pars, couple of birdies, couple of snowmen."

Whatever that meant. But he sounded happy enough. I smiled and nodded.

Honeybee, Lucy's orange tabby, approached on soft paws and stopped at my feet. She did that squinty thing at me, and a ladylike purr emanated from her furry chest.

I sneezed.

Oh, well. At least my aunt's familiar had the good manners not to rub against my legs.

I sneezed again.

Mungo and Honeybee touched noses as a Great Dane walked out from the sunroom. Anubis was Jaida's familiar, and it always cracked me up to see him and Mungo together. It was hard to imagine they'd both descended from wolves.

"Where's Heckle?" I asked.

My answer was a squawk and a flurry of wings. I ducked, and managed not to squeal. After once startling me into a squawk very like his own, Mimsey's familiar now tried to do it all the time. I straightened and glared at the parrot.

"Katie is a scaredy-cat. *Wawk!*"

Ben laughed. I turned away and saw Honeybee glaring at the bird, too. Bad choice of words, Heckle my dear. Oh, well. The familiars could work it out amongst themselves.

"You going to watch the game this afternoon?" I asked over my shoulder as I followed in Cookie's footsteps.

My uncle nodded. "Thinking about heading over to Five House and watching it with the guys."

"Have fun."

"And say hi to Deck?"

I paused. "Sure, but I just saw him in the Honeybee this morning. Brought a couple of his friends in."

Ben stroked his beard and beamed.

It was a little unnerving how badly he wanted Declan and me to be together. He no doubt had visions of white picket fences, a dog, and lots of kids that would be almost like grandkids for him and Lucy. But I'd done the engagement thing, the plan-your-perfect-life thing, when I lived in Akron. It hadn't turned out so well. Now I had the dog and the house, and I didn't feel a need quite yet for a husband and kids. I had time.

And I love my life now, I thought as I stood in the doorway that led out to Lucy's rooftop garden, inhaling the heady scents of lavender and rue. There were at least a hundred pots, from teensy starts in one-inch terra-cotta containers to large wooden structures Ben had built along the edges. Thriving vegetables, herbs, medicinal plants, flowers planted for aroma and beauty—and all for magic, because every growing thing is magic in its own way. Lucy's hedgewitchery manifested in whimsical touches, in the careful arrangement and frequent rearrangement of her container garden, the combinations of plants she chose, and the many additions tucked here and there. A tiny glass fairy gazed up from one pot, the edge of a coin she'd buried from another. In addition to their beauty, practicality, and magical essences, many of these plants were spells themselves, growing into manifestation. I knew many of them had offerings or spell-specific items buried next to their roots.

And there at the wrought-iron table in the middle of the verdant space were my coven members. The spell-book club. How I loved those ladies, each and every one.

"Get on over here." Jaida beckoned. "You are at least one glass behind on the wine." She'd changed into white capris and a deep red shirt that glowed like spice against her dark skin.

"Bit early, isn't it?" I slid into a chair, pulling out our book club selection for the week, *Get Off Your High Broom*.

"Darlin'," she said in an exaggerated drawl, "it's never too early on a Sunday in the South."

I noticed Bianca's glass was still unused. She noticed me noticing. "I have to pick up Colette after the meeting."

"Ah. That hardly seems fair, since you always bring the wine." Bianca owned a wine shop called Moon Grapes, and always insisted on providing the libations for our meetings.

"Such is the life of a single mom." Her face lit up in a smile. "But I wouldn't have it any other way."

"We were just updating the others on what you told us about the Dragoh Society last night," Mimsey said. "And Jaida told us about the visit you had from that nasty detective."

Bianca nodded. "I heard the term *Dragoh* once, at a party. Some vague rumor about secret societies, but nothing else. But I had no idea your Steve's father was a member."

"He's not my Steve," I said for what seemed like the zillionth time.

Bianca, with her talent for getting in on financial bubbles, riding them, and then ducking out before they popped, was among Savannah's nouveaux riches. Nouveau or not, all that money allowed her entrance to some pretty fancy hoedowns. No doubt the rumors she spoke of were whispered among the upper crust of Southern society. I was starting to think the existence of the Dragohs wasn't as secret as they believed.

"So we know Lawrence Eastmore and Heinrich Dawes are members," I said. "Were. Whatever. I wonder who the others are."

"I know of one," Jaida said.

"Who?" we chorused.

"Someone I defended in court once."

"Who?" I asked again.

"I think that might fall under attorney-client privilege."

Hmmph.

"Shall we talk about this week's book?" Lucy asked, obviously changing the subject. "There have been several reviews on Web sites that say they don't like the author's casual approach, but I found it refreshing."

Jaida smiled. "So did I. It's accessible."

"A little too casual, if you ask me. No respect for ritual and tradition," Bianca said.

"I liked how she gives a framework for developing your own spells," I said. "Like a how-to book about method and how things in the world correspond magically, and then she encourages readers to make up our own spells. It reminds me of some of my favorite recipe books."

"I fall in the middle," Cookie said. "Like Bianca, I

like the ritual, but sometimes you need to tailor a spell to very specific needs, and she gives advice on how to do that."

Voices drifted up to the open doorway. Male voices. For a moment I thought Declan had come over to watch the game with Ben, then realized he was still on duty. Besides, my uncle wouldn't have invited him when the spellbook club was meeting upstairs.

"I need to see them, sir. I'm sorry, but no, I won't wait. Are they up here?"

"Now hang on there," Ben said. "Who do you think you are? Wait!"

Footsteps followed, and we all came to our feet as a man burst onto the garden terrace, with Ben right on his heels.

The newcomer was about my height. Skinny. How had he managed to get past Ben? His eyes were magnified by glasses with black plastic frames. I guessed his age at forty-three or forty-four, and if nerdy was the new cool he was about as cool as it got. His head jerked nervously as he looked around at us.

"Please. I need your help."

Jaida stepped forward. "Andersen, what's going on?"

"I need your help," he said again. "Someone killed Larry."

My stomach swooped. We all exchanged looks.

The man noticed. "I see you already know that." Then he focused on me. "You."

I could feel the color drain from my face, but I held my ground. "Me?" I wished the word had come out an octave lower.

"You're the one Heinrich was telling us about."

Us? I looked at Jaida, who nodded slightly. This was

her druid client? "You're a member of the Dragoh Society, then," I said.

"Andersen Lane." He stepped toward me. Out of the corner of my eye I saw Ben take a step, too. "At your service." The smell of bourbon drifted through the air between us. Of course, with the wine we'd been sipping, everyone except Bianca probably had some kind of alcohol on her breath.

Which actually made it more notable that I could smell it coming off Andersen. With reluctance, I shook his outstretched hand. "I think we're okay up here, Ben."

"I'm not going anywhere." My uncle stood with his arms crossed, eyes glinting at Andersen from behind his rimless glasses.

Lucy went over to Ben, took his elbow, and turned him away from the rest of us. I heard her murmur. A pause. Then more murmurs. Finally his shoulders drooped and he turned back.

"Okay, I'll give you your privacy. But I'll be right downstairs." He looked down at his wife, his affection for her obvious even under those circumstances, and said, "And I'll be back to check on you." He gave Andersen a hard look, then spun on his heel and went back inside.

So much for going to the firehouse. Still, it made me feel better to know Ben was nearby. I had no idea what this guy really wanted.

I turned back to Andersen, alarm and curiosity warring under what I hoped came across as a calm demeanor. The air fairly crackled with potential now, but potential for what, I didn't know. Magic? Violence? Both? I looked around the group to see if they noticed it.

But they all seemed focused on our visitor. Lucy looked worried. Mimsey frowned, as unhappy as I'd ever seen her. Bianca nervously fingered her bracelet as if the charms on it were rosary beads. Jaida's unsmiling brown eyes bored into Andersen as if she were trying to read his mind. Not that that was possible, of course. Cookie was the only one who didn't seem upset. She leaned forward with frank, rapt attention.

Andersen looked at Jaida. "Please, Ms. French." Then at me. "If Larry's killer isn't found, an unspeakable evil could be released into the world."

We all looked at each other with alarm. The air vibrated with unasked questions.

Chapter 13

Andersen Lane sank into a chair and eyed the open bottle of wine. No one had offered him any. Finally he drawled, "May I?"

I handed him Bianca's unused glass, which he promptly filled to the brim. He took a long swallow and wiped his lips with the back of his hand. The gesture was at odds with his geeky facade.

Ah. Yes. It was a facade, I realized. Good to know.

"Tell us why you're here," Mimsey said. Her words were abrupt, and not terribly friendly.

"I couldn't think of anyone else to go to," he said. "Ms. French already knows I'm a member of the society. I let it slip once during our . . . professional association."

Which confirmed she'd defended him in court. I was itching to ask what legal line he'd crossed.

"Heinrich told us about you, Katie. How you found Larry yesterday morning and then started asking a bunch of questions. I thought maybe you all could help me ask some more."

I sat back down. Slowly, the others did the same.

He looked around. "I'm afraid I've not made the acquaintance of you other lovely ladies, though." He stopped at Cookie, and something like a leer curved his lips.

Her mouth turned down.

"Andersen," I said, dispensing with the niceties of using his last name. "How did you know where to find us this afternoon?" I was afraid I already knew the answer.

"Your boyfriend told me."

Boyfriend indeed. I was going to throttle Steve. How dare he tell this tipsy druid where to find our coven?

"And why would he do that?" I asked.

"Well, for one thing he wanted me to give all y'all something." Andersen reached in his pocket and pulled out a small pouch made of light blue silk. I sensed rather than saw the aura surrounding it.

I blinked and tore my gaze away. "What's in the bag?"

"Apparently you're in need of a little protection from a protection spell. At least Steve and I think that's what you ran into yesterday. Literally ran into, I understand." He laughed.

My eyes narrowed as I tried to get a read on him. My phone call to Steve last night resulted in this visit? "Do tell," I said.

His smile faded. "We have a sort of a general protection spell, to keep anyone from finding out about us. You were magically attacked last evening, weren't you?"

Jaida, Bianca, and Cookie all turned to look at me. I ignored them.

"If you mean having a bunch of pumpkins almost concuss me—or worse—then yes."

"What?" Jaida leaned toward him. "Andersen, what's the matter with you? Protection spells aren't supposed to hurt anyone, only . . . protect."

"Let's just say the Dragohs are fond of rather, um, *proactive* protection. If you know what I mean." He held his hands out. "Hey, stop looking at me like that, ladies. I brought you these." He fished into the pouch and withdrew six silver circles in varying sizes. Each was thin as a wire, but they glinted madly in the sun, sending off shards of reflected light that made me squint. He stood and handed one to each of us.

"Wear these and you'll be safe. At least from spells like the one you attracted with all your questions, Katie."

"How do you know that's what happened?"

He grinned. "Have you been up to something else to attract the attention of magicians? Negative attention, I mean? Because I can certainly see how you'd attract attention."

Oh, brother.

I sighed. "Well, I guess you'd better have your say."

Mimsey shifted in her chair.

"Right," he said. "Okay, so you all know who the Dragohs are, right?"

Silent nods all around.

"And you know Larry Eastmore was one of us."

More nods.

He paused. Took a sip of wine. The red liquid sloshed as he set the glass back on the table.

"He was also my very good friend. Not all of the others appreciate me, you know. In fact, none of them ever really liked me, except for Larry. When my dad died and I took my rightful position in the society, he took me under his wing." Another sip, and his eyes filled with tears. He blinked them away.

"Anyway, Larry was an expert in occult books and ephemera."

Out of the corner of my eye I saw Lucy nod in agreement.

Andersen had locked onto me, though, as if I were the only one there. I waited, trying not to show my impatience.

He leaned forward. "One of his books is gone."

"A valuable one, I take it?"

"Precious indeed, but not necessarily in a monetary sense. I doubt any auction house would know what to do with it. But I do believe someone killed him for it."

"Why?" breathed Lucy.

He flicked a glance in her direction, but answered as if I had asked the question. "It's a small volume that contains the Spell of Necretius. It's a particularly dangerous spell."

"What does it do?" Bianca asked.

This time he directed the answer at her. "It's a spell for summoning a spirit—a very dark spirit named Zesh."

The spellbook club exchanged blank looks. The name seemed innocuous, even silly—but repugnance slithered through me when he said it.

"This spirit, this entity, is said to have the power to bring great worldly success." He licked his lips, considering the drink on the table beside him. Didn't pick it up. "Problem is, Zesh cannot be contained. In the past, once it has been given entry to this plane it has always turned on its summoner."

"Maybe that served them right," Bianca said. She

could be a bit of a Goody Two-shoes when it came to magic.

"Possibly," Andersen agreed. "But it has always happened with violent results that rippled far beyond the spell caster."

Our stunned silence was broken only by Bianca's sharp intake of breath. A raw gust of cold air whipped the cocktail napkins off the table and tugged at the sweet potato vine twining up its trellis. It seemed to blow straight through my veins, stealing my body heat and leaving me with goose bumps despite the warm air.

Then it was gone.

A feeling of doom had settled across my shoulders at Andersen's words. "What do you think we can do about it?" I asked. The summoning of dark spirits was wa-a-a-y beyond my lessons in Witchcraft 101.

"If you can find Larry's killer, then we might be able to stop him from casting the summoning spell in the first place."

"Prevention," I said slowly, thinking out loud. "Yes, much better than trying to fix the problem after the big spooky is invited to this plane."

"And I happen to know you successfully solved a murder in the not-so-distant past, Katie. With the help of these ladies, no doubt."

"No," Mimsey said. "I'm sorry, but Katie can't help you with this. We can't."

"I agree," Bianca chimed in. "We should stay away from anything to do with such dark magic."

I looked at Lucy, who was looking at Mimsey. She nodded agreement with her mentor. In fact, the older woman was really mentor to us all. What Mimsey said carried a lot of weight.

"I'm sorry, Andersen, but I agree with the others," Jaida said. "This isn't our fight."

"How can you say that?" Cookie jumped up and began pacing. "Katie's right. If we can keep something horrible from happening, we should. Even the Wiccan Rede supports that, Bianca." She looked around the group. "Do you really want to have to deal with the evil once it is here? Because I've seen true evil. And I don't want to ever again." She looked into a distance that wasn't there and hugged herself. I could almost see the emotion rising off of her.

"There's more," Andersen said.

Cookie stopped pacing.

"The spell is most potent on Samhain. The killer would know that and cast it then."

Halloween.

Three days away.

"Why can't you Dragohs handle this yourselves?" Mimsey demanded.

"Because there are only four of us left now," he said. "And because it's likely that one of the other three is the killer."

Chapter 14

Stunned silence fell over the group. I got up and retrieved the wine bottle from the table beside Andersen Lane. Though I'd taken only a few sips, I topped off my glass and set the now empty bottle on the tiled floor by my feet. In my peripheral vision, Mimsey squeezed her eyes shut and rubbed the bridge of her nose.

"Why do you think Eastmore was killed by one of the other Dragohs?" I asked.

He glanced at his empty glass and frowned before his gaze flicked up to meet mine. "Because to the best of my knowledge no one outside of the society knew about the Spell of Necretius."

"No one?"

He shrugged. "As I said, to the best of my knowledge. Surely at some point in the past others knew. But Larry's collection has been in his family for generations. They've been the caretakers of those books for centuries, before the society existed, indeed before Eastmores ever came across the pond from England. Possibly even before England existed."

"But you knew about the Spell of Whatshisname."

Andersen looked impatient. "We all did. The Dragohs have always been allowed access to the Eastmore archive."

I looked around at the curiosity, skepticism, and fear on my friends' faces.

Mimsey nodded slowly. "All right, Mr. Lane. Lawrence Eastmore, you, and Heinrich Dawes," she said. "Who are the other members of the Dragoh Society?"

"Hmm. Yes, I suppose you'll need to know." He grimaced. "All right, then. In for a penny and all. Victor Powers and Brandon Sikes."

"Oh!" Cookie said.

Mimsey shot her a look, and Cookie's lips closed on whatever else she had been about to say.

I'd heard of Powers, of course. Everyone with a television or radio or who read the newspaper had heard of him. He was on a fast track to the U.S. Senate and his campaign ads were all over the place. Sikes' name seemed familiar, but it took a moment for me to realize why: In my Internet travels the night before, I'd seen that he was a frequent guest lecturer at the Savannah College of Art and Design. Apparently he was quite a renowned artist in his own right.

"That makes five," I said. "There were six of you, right? Why only four left after Eastmore's death?"

Andersen nodded. "Lars Sandstrom was the sixth."

Jaida made a noise, and we all looked at her.

"He was a respected Savannah judge for decades," she said.

"That's right," Andersen said. "Of course you would have known him. Well, he died about six months ago of a massive coronary. Unfortunately, he only spawned a daughter." His choice of words earned him glares all around, but he didn't seem to notice. He continued. "Lars' dying without male issue left us in a real jam. The society recently contacted his closest living male relative as a possible replacement candidate."

"That is the most archaic thing I've ever heard," Bianca said.

He shrugged. "That's the way it is. Like Mrs. Sandstrom, the daughter has no knowledge of the society, and likely less interest. She came back to take care of things when the judge died—her mother had already passed—but she'll likely be on her way back to Athens soon. Lars had a nephew, though, lives up in Kentucky. He looks promising."

"How can you, you *druids*, keep something that's such a huge part of your lives secret from your families like that?" I couldn't keep the disapproval out of my voice.

Andersen gave me a look. "Lots of practice."

I thought about what Steve had said regarding the lack of female influence in the druids' magic and how that had affected their judgment. The "proactive" protection spell that had almost killed me was evidence of that. The spellbook club believed that anything we manifested would come back to us threefold. It was a guiding paradigm that shaped our actions whether we were practicing alone or together. The Dragohs didn't seem to buy into the Rule of Three—indeed any rules at all but their own. What the society needed was for a woman to elbow her way in.

"Don't even think about publicizing your newfound knowledge," Andersen said as if reading my thoughts. His voice echoed with warning.

I blinked.

It sure didn't sound like Steve would have any help from Andersen when it came to changing things from the inside. If Steve ever did become a Dragoh, that was. Heinrich looked like he'd be going strong for a long time. Perhaps Steve could still find a way to avoid his supposed destiny.

"What about Lawrence Eastmore? Does he have a son?" I asked, knowing the answer from my research.

Andersen's face slowly cleared, and he nodded. "Greer Eastmore. He's been living in Europe for the last twenty years, with no contact with his father in all that time. It almost broke Larry's heart."

"Why did his son cut him off?" Maternal concern etched Bianca's features.

"Doesn't approve of the society, he said. Doesn't want to take on the responsibilities, his inheritance, now that his father is dead." He made a sound of disgust. "Like he has a choice. It's not like I was thrilled to be included in the group, either, but it hasn't turned out so bad. He'll get used to it just like I did."

My respect for Andersen Lane dropped another notch.

"Can't he out and out refuse?" I asked.

"He can try, sure. But the others can be quite, shall we say, persuasive. And God knows Greer won't be willing to give up his *other* inheritance." He smirked.

"Which is?" I asked.

He rubbed the tips of his fingers and thumb together in response to my question. "Money, honey. Lots of it. That's one thing about being a member of the society—wealth is almost guaranteed."

The spellbook club exchanged glances, and I could see I wasn't the only one who found him distasteful.

Except for Lawrence Eastmore, Andersen didn't seem terribly fond of his fellow druids. If they really didn't care for him, either, as he'd stated earlier, I could understand why.

The guy exuded a combination of childish self-satisfaction and a sense of entitlement that was quite off-putting. Bianca pursed her lips, and I wondered if she was thinking of her gains from playing the stock market.

He glanced at his watch. "I'm afraid I have to go, ladies."

"Oh, no you don't." Mimsey jumped to her feet. "You think you can come dump this problem on us and then just waltz out of here?"

He rose as well. "Madam, I assure you I am willing to do whatever it takes, both to bring justice to my friend's killer and to prevent the evil influence of Zesh in this world. Unfortunately, my hands are tied by my association with the very person—or people—who may be responsible for his death. They already suspect that I suspect them, which is why I came to you. Anything you need that is within my ability to deliver, I will. Just let me know." He handed me a business card. All it had on it was his name and a phone number.

Mimsey scowled at him.

"In the meantime, I will seek access to Larry's collection before his son gets here. Eastmore Junior is coming in from Barcelona tonight, then driving down from Atlanta in the morning. What I need is inside a climate-controlled vault, but I know the combination and I have a key to Larry's house."

A vault. Of course. Well, if it was full of books on

dark magic, I could see why a witch-hunter like Taite might jump to conclusions about Lawrence Eastmore.

"I doubt the police would approve," I said.

"Then it's just as well that I don't plan to ask their permission," Andersen said. "Stop looking at me like that, Ms. French. In the next few days, I'll be looking for a suitable counterspell to prevent the summoning in case you're—we're—unsuccessful in finding the killer in time."

"Hang on," I said. "What about you? We don't know anything at all about you. Why should we even believe you?"

"What would you like to know?"

"Well, for one thing, what was your 'professional association' with Jaida here? She's an ethical attorney, so she's not about to tell us anything about you."

He looked at his watch again. "Ms. French, you hereby have my permission to tell your coven anything they want to know."

"Anything?" she asked with a skeptical look.

"Yes. I'm serious about finding Larry's killer, and revealing my foibles is the least of my worries."

"Andersen," she said in a slow voice, "there's something else you should be aware of."

"And what, my dear, might that be?"

"The police know who Katie found Saturday morning. They know it was Dr. Eastmore."

"That's hardly surprising."

Jaida considered him, then took a deep breath. "One of the detectives is new to Savannah. He's here with a mission, however." She looked over at me, and I nodded. Her attention returned to our visitor, whose eyes had widened at her words. "He's a hunter, Andersen. And from the brief encounter Katie had with him earlier today, we don't know whether he's discerning or not."

Discerning?

"We were talking about that when you arrived," Lucy said to me. "Some witch-hunters understand the difference between black magic and white magic. Others, not so much. Some consider all magic evil."

Andersen asked in a thoughtful tone, "What's his name?"

"Franklin Taite." I didn't feel great about sharing the information with this druid, but if Taite was really dangerous then it was the right thing to do.

Unless the Dragohs were more dangerous. I hated that we were in the dark about so many things. We needed more information about them all.

"Thank you for the warning." Andersen nodded. "Yes, indeed." With deliberate steps he walked to the door leading down from the terrace.

"You're not driving, are you?" Jaida asked.

He turned. "Of course not. Once was enough, thank you." Looking around at each of us, he said, "Thank you, Katie. All of you. Even though you haven't done anything yet, and Ms. Carmichael here may still convince y'all not to help me. But you've listened, at least." He held up a finger. "You do know, of course, that if you use magic when looking into Larry's murder, the other Dragohs will sense it. And believe me, they will react badly."

We watched him pivot and make his way downstairs.

"I can't tell if he's drunk or sad," I said when he was gone.

"Both, I suspect," Jaida said. "I defended him on a drunk-driving case, but he was doing well since that. His friend's death seems to have knocked him off the wagon."

"Great," I said. "What kind of help will he really be?"

They all looked at me.

"Well, we're going to do what we can, aren't we? I don't like it, but it seems that finding Lawrence Eastmore's killer is up to us."

Mimsey's gaze lasered to me, and after a moment she managed a smile. "No doubt that's why Katie was the one who discovered him in the first place."

I held my palms up. "Sorry."

Chapter 15

"Are you familiar with Brandon Sikes' work?" Cookie asked. Ice cubes clinked against the side of her glass as she poured from the pitcher of lemonade Lucy had carried up to the roof garden. So much for a Southern Sunday afternoon of book club and wine.

We'd tabled the spellbook discussion until the next meeting so we could figure out just how to go about investigating Lawrence Eastmore's death. Getting close to the druidic movers and shakers might prove difficult, especially given our deadline. Three days until Samhain.

Deadline, indeed. The very notion of Zesh sent a reptilian quiver through me.

"It's marvelous," Cookie said. "Sikes creates these huge pieces, usually on a background of thin plywood rather than canvas, with paint, fiber, papier-mâché, metal, even clay. Large, but intricate. The longer you look at them, the more they say to you." She was positively enraptured.

"Sounds interesting," Lucy said.

"He's single, too," Cookie said.

Uh-oh. "What are you thinking?" I asked.

"I think I should go to Xana Do! Gallery, where his new show is opening."

"When?" I asked.

She sat back, feline contentment on her face. "To-night. I know I can find out more about him. I met him a few times when I worked at SCAD. He's quite friendly."

Cookie went through boyfriends like she went through jobs, and as luck would have it, she currently happened to be between beaus. The last thing we needed now was for one of the spellbook club to hook up with a druid who was a possible murderer.

Though reluctant, I agreed. "But do not let him know that you know he's a member of the Dragoh Society."

She looked offended. "Of course not. I know to be careful. In fact, why don't you go with me, Katie? So you can keep an eye on me and make sure I don't mess up."

"That's not what I meant," I said. "Though I wouldn't mind seeing his work." And him. I some-times got intuitive hits off of people, so it couldn't hurt to try.

"Of course you have to go," Mimsey said to me, then looked around at the others. "Katie is the common de-nominator. She discovered the body, found out about the Dragohs, drew the magical attack, and was the rea-son Andersen Lane found his way here to us this after-noon."

She didn't use the word *catalyst*, but I, for one, was wondering about it.

"Whatever you do, don't try to use magic on him,"

Bianca warned Cookie. "Like Andersen said, he'd know. I bet all these guys are quite powerful sorcerers. I can certainly see how Victor Powers could be."

"You know him?" Mimsey sounded surprised.

"I've met him."

"At one of those fancy parties you go to?" If that sounded like I was jealous, I wasn't. I wouldn't have minded wearing some of her beautiful gowns, though.

"Indeed. In fact, there's—" She bit her lip.

"There's . . . what?" I prompted gently.

She let out a breath. "A fund-raising breakfast for him at the Westin Hotel. Tomorrow morning." A kind of defeat weighed her features. "I could get tickets, Katie. For you and me."

"I have to work," I said.

"Cookie and I can cover for you," Lucy said. "Mimsey's right. You should go."

"What if they know what Katie looks like?" Jaida said. "Won't the druids get suspicious?"

"Why would they know?" I asked. "You think Heinrich showed them pictures of big, bad Katie Lightfoot so they'd know what to watch out for? Because I guarantee he doesn't think enough of me, or any woman, to feel threatened."

"But the pumpkins—," Lucy said.

"Andersen said the spell was designed for general protection, not specifically directed at me." I stood. "Okay, we have a plan, or at least the beginnings of one. Cookie, do you need a ride home?" She didn't like to drive and usually relied on public transportation.

"If you don't mind."

"And I'll pick you up tonight at eight."

*   *   *

Back home, I let Mungo out to roam the backyard and settled into one of the mismatched chairs in the gazebo. Margie's car was gone, and all was quiet on the Coopersmith front. The stream gurgled over stones by the back fence, the sound blending with the low drone of bees moving drowsily through the garden beds. Iridescent dragonfly wings flashed in the late-afternoon sunlight, and the breeze had turned cool with the promise of rain. I filled my lungs with the electric air.

Things were out of control on so many fronts. My life of early mornings, baking all day, learning magic and gardening had suddenly turned into a dead body, questionable druids, the attack of the killer pumpkins, a witch-hunter, and the looming threat of an evil spirit.

With mixed feelings, I dialed my cell and hoped Daddy would answer the phone in Fillmore, Ohio.

No such luck. Mama picked up on the third ring.

"Katie! How are you, sweetie?" I could hear the strain behind her forced cheerfulness. When Lucy had informed me I was a hereditary witch, a rift had formed between my parents and me. Well, mostly me and my mother, who had been the driving force behind their lying to me most of my life about who—and what—I was.

Over the past few months Daddy and I had talked it out. He'd apologized, and I accepted, since I did understand their motivations, at least in part. How could they have known that their attempt to protect me from myself would boomerang and mess up my life? I firmly believed that things happen for a reason, and maybe the way I found out about my magical heritage was exactly the right way and at the right time.

At least that's what I told myself in the middle of the night.

Mama, however, was not on board with the ideas of serendipity and forgiveness. The relationship between her and her little sister, never that great, had soured even more since Lucy's revelation that I was a witch. Mama was furious, determined not to forgive Lucy and none too happy with me for pursuing magic, either.

"Any news?" she asked now.

"I learned how to plant a prosperity spell." I wasn't proud of myself for baiting her, but I couldn't seem to help it.

There was a long silence. Then she said, "I ran into Andrew the other day. He was house hunting."

Touché.

"In Fillmore?" I forced myself to ask.

"He said he's tired of Akron. He has a new job here, at the school. Vice principal." She sure seemed to have a lot to say about him, given that she'd made no secret of her dislike of Andrew when we'd been engaged.

"Fancy doin's," I said. "In a town with only five hundred and sixty-three people in it." About to be 564, it sounded like.

"His girlfriend was with him."

Okay, make that 565. Maybe. Andrew wasn't great at the commitment game.

I sighed. "Of course she was, Mama. Is Daddy around?"

Another pause, pregnant with regret and frustration and a few other things I couldn't readily identify.

"Hang on. I'll get him."

Mungo bounded up the two steps leading into the gazebo, turned around three times on the purple star, and lay down smack-dab in the middle with a little snort. I didn't know for sure how much he knew from the afternoon doings at Lucy and Ben's, but I figured it was a lot. Maybe I should consider sleeping in the middle of a pentagram, too.

I heard a rustle on the other end of the phone, and then, "I don't know what you just said to your mother, but she's got a very unhappy look on her face." Daddy's voice was low.

"It went both ways, believe me."

He exhaled. "Well, anyway. How are things in Savannah?"

"Strange," I said.

"How so?"

"Well, I found a dead man under a rhododendron bush yesterday morning, and it turns out he was a member of a secret druidic society. Since then another member of the society warned me off with thinly veiled threats. I've been assaulted by flying pumpkins, and the newest detective on the police force is apparently on the prowl for magicians of all sorts."

"Assaulted? Are you all right?" At least he sounded matter-of-fact, despite my reference to airborne squash. Mama would have gone into instant hysterics.

"I'm fine."

"God, Katie. How do you get yourself into these things?"

"It's not like I tried to find a body."

"Well, how about you steer clear of the situation now?"

"I planned on it. I did. But today things changed again."

I heard a door close, and now my dad's voice was a

little louder. I guessed he'd gone into his den. "Tell me," he said.

So I related Andersen Lane's visit and his plea for the spellbook club to help him find Lawrence East-more's murderer. Daddy listened without interrupting.

"If he's telling us the truth, then it's not just a matter of justice. We don't have much time, either."

Daddy finally spoke, his words careful and considered. "Do you have reason to think this Lane fellow is lying to you? Does your intuition tell you not to trust him?"

"Hmm. Not really. He's an odd duck, that's for sure, but he seemed sincere. It's just that I'm naturally suspicious of a request of that magnitude from someone I've never met before, and it seems there might be more to the story than we know."

"That's logic talking, and it's good logic," he said. "But for now if your gut is telling you he's telling the truth, I suppose you have to go with it. I really, really don't like the idea of you going up against something like this Zesh, though. You make sure you keep the rest of the coven around you, and if you do find anything out let those crazy druids take care of it themselves."

"Oh, Daddy—"

"You're still a newbie, Katie, still wet behind the ears. You simply don't know enough to be safe."

"Okay, okay," I said. "I will be careful, I promise. But there's something I haven't told you yet. About Nonna."

The reference to my maternal grandmother was greeted with a long silence, and then Daddy said, "Nonna?"

"When the pumpkins fell? A voice told me to get out of the way. There wasn't anyone around." I paused and licked my lips. Would he think I was crazy? "I could swear it was her, Daddy. Remember that strong Boston accent of hers?"

I heard him suck air in through his teeth. "Oh, my. Well, that doesn't entirely surprise me."

The muscles in my shoulders relaxed. I hadn't realized how steeled I'd been for his disbelief. "It didn't surprise Lucy, either."

"Your grandmother Sheffield was a powerful witch. Stubborn and protective of her loved ones, too. I wouldn't put it past her to watch over you. In fact, the idea makes me feel slightly better about this whole situation."

"How can I get her to talk to me again?" The thought of being able to communicate with my witchy grandmother was strangely exciting.

"I don't think it works that way."

"So," I said, thinking out loud, "I'd have to be in danger again?"

"Katie! Don't even think such a thing."

"Oh, for heaven's sake. I'm not going to do anything stupid. I was just wondering."

"You promised to be careful. Just stick to that," he said. "So you're going to meet one of these druids tonight?"

I fingered the thin silver band Andersen Lane had given me. It only fit on my thumb. "Yes, and I need to go get ready so I don't stand out too much in Savannah's artsy-fartsy crowd."

"What do you hope to learn?"

That gave me pause. What exactly was I hoping to gain from tonight's outing? "I want to meet this Brandon Sikes," I said. "See if I get any kind of intuitive hit.

See if he seems desperate enough to kill a fellow druid in order to summon this Zesh character. Maybe even find out where he was the night of the murder." I sighed. How the heck was I going to do that without arousing his suspicions?

"Katie?" Daddy had heard my sigh.

"Just thinking about what to wear tonight. I suppose I ought to do something with my hair, too."

He laughed. "Once a tomboy, always a tomboy."

"Right. A tomboy who cooks for a living. Somehow I don't think that's in the definition. I'll talk to you soon, okay?"

We hung up. For a long moment I watched a jet paint a snowy contrail against the blue sky, right above the treetops down the street. When talking to Daddy, I'd made pretty light of the prospect of someone summoning Zesh onto this plane, leaving out Andersen's other dire warnings. No reason to worry my dad even more. I'd left specifics about Franklin Taite out of my tale as well. I didn't need any I-told-you-sos from Mama, and who knew how much information Daddy would share with her?

"Come on, Mungo. Help me pick out something to wear."

He stood and stretched into a wide yawn that showed his startling pink tongue.

In my bedroom, I stared at the items hanging in the two matching armoires that served as my closet. Lots of skirts and T-shirts for work, and my nonwork wardrobe was just as casual. But there, in the back. I pulled it out and nodded to myself. A floor-length, silk tiered skirt, tie-dyed brown and orange and gold. Lucy had given it to me because it was too large for her tiny frame. I added a shimmery brown tank top and a nice pair of sandals. I should be set for the Bohemian crowd.

The glint of the thin ring on my thumb caught my eye. No reason to advertise anything given me by a Dragoh. I slipped it off and, unhooking my dragonfly amulet, slid the ring onto the chain. It hung perfectly hidden behind the O of the necklace, slightly cold against my skin.

In the bathroom my reflected eyes gazed back at me, assessing my features for a moment before I shrugged and reached for the hairbrush. I liked my face well enough to leave it out there bare of makeup most of the time, but my short hair needed help tonight. First I tried to slick it down, but hated that, so I loaded it with styling product and ruffled it up all over until I thought it looked, well, artsy.

I checked the time. It would have to do, or else I'd be late picking Cookie up. I slipped into the skirt and tank, grabbed a little sweater, and glanced over my shoulder into the full-length mirror one last time. Lucy had been right: The color combination complemented my auburn hair and set off my eyes.

Even if I did say so myself.

Chapter 16

The gallery opened at seven thirty, and Cookie and I arrived at eight fifteen. It was not fashionably late by any means, but we figured Brandon Sikes would be there for his whole show in order to meet and greet as many potential buyers as possible. The fewer competitors for his attention, the better.

Of course, we were wrong.

Inside, the air-conditioning was going full blast, and I was happy for the small amount of warmth my sweater offered. Black track lights hung from the high ceilings, focused on the oversized artwork on walls and partitions painted the color of roasted red peppers. The spotlights left the areas between in relative shadow. Several knots of people murmured amongst themselves. A group of high school students huddled together uncomfortably in a back corner, and I wondered if Sikes' opening might be an art class assignment. A hint of something savory in the air—bacon?—snagged my notice for a moment before it was overcome by a whiff of expensive perfume.

"Welcome to Xana Do! Gallery."

Cookie and I turned to find a woman in her mid-thirties wearing a sleek black sheath that hugged her every curve until it widened below her knees and fell in a dark chiffon froth to the tops of her very shiny and very pointy shoes. Her hair, streaked too many shades of blond to list, was gathered in a sleek French twist at the back of her head. The updo accentuated the diamonds glittering at her ears and diving down to a respectable cleavage.

I suddenly felt like something Mungo had dug up in the backyard.

"I'm Xana Smythe. So very happy you could come! Are you fans of Brandon's?" Her smile revealed a small gap between her front teeth, and her eager-puppy demeanor was at odds with the crusty British accent. I found myself utterly charmed, and forgave her for being so well put together.

Cookie wore a cobalt blue minidress that barely covered her posterior and heels so high it was hard for me to imagine her taking more than three steps in them. Her dark, eggplant-tinted hair flowed straight down her back, accented with only a single orchid. She was supremely comfortable in her own skin, and frankly, of the two of them, she looked more at ease in the red-tinged light. She marched up to Xana and embraced her like an old friend. "I'm Cookie, and this is Katie."

A startled look crossed the gallery owner's face, but then she relaxed into another smile.

"I adore Brandon's work," Cookie said. "Always have. Katie has not been exposed to his talent before, however." She let go of Xana and searched the room. "I don't see him anywhere . . ."

"Brandon darling will be here soon." Xana's eyes

darted toward the entrance, though, and as they did, stress rolled off her in waves.

Brandon darling was late.

"Please help yourself to some hors d'oeuvres and take a look around. Oh! Mrs. Cisco, welcome!" And she was off to talk to a new arrival.

My companion looked at me with raised eyebrows. "I wonder where he is."

"I wonder where he was when Lawrence Eastmore was killed." I took a step in the direction Xana had indicated. "Are you hungry?"

But Cookie stood riveted in front of one of Brandon Sikes' masterpieces.

Moving to her side, I leaned my head back in order to see the whole thing. "That is one of the ugliest things I've ever seen on a wall. Or a floor, for that matter." Then I saw the price on the placard that stated the title of the work: *Afternoon Destiny.* "Good Lord, Cookie! How could anyone pay that much for this?"

"Shh!" she hissed. "Someone might hear you."

"Why is he so famous, again?" I whispered.

"Can't you see?" She spread her arms out in a wide gesture. "His unique use of media, how he mixes paper and wood and paint in with the images?"

Squinting, I ticked my head to the side. She was certainly right about his mix-and-match method, but the piece left me cold. Though modern art wasn't generally my thing, I had to admit that much of it left an emotional impression, or at least an aesthetic one—for good or bad. But this was devoid of effect. Empty and dull.

Yet, somewhere deep down I had a curious desire to purchase it. *What the* . . . "Oh, Cookie." Looking around to make sure no one was standing nearby, I leaned toward her ear and spoke in a low voice. "This piece is glamoured."

She blinked. Took a step back. After a few moments she turned and looked at me with wide eyes. "I feel so stupid. How could you tell?" She didn't come right out and say anything about my being a newbie to magic, but I knew that's what she was thinking.

I shrugged. "Not sure. But it's a good job, don't you think? Subtle."

"I'll say." She moved to the next piece on display. "This one feels the same way. And even though I can tell it's charmed, I still want it."

"No wonder he's so successful," I said, glancing around at the thickening crowd. Xana was posting a SOLD sign next to a piece near the front door, looking pleased.

"Cookie!" A goth vision approached, dripping black leather and metal buckles and sporting black lipstick and hair spiked straight up. The voice and the five o'clock shadow identified the newcomer as male despite the heavy eyeliner.

"Damien," Cookie responded, hugging him. "It's so good to see you. This is Katie."

I wondered what his real name was as I shook his hand. His grip was firm, and he nodded at me with intelligent eyes. "Cookie has mentioned you. It's nice to finally meet you."

My mouth opened in surprise, and he smiled. "We met when she worked at SCAD and dated for a while after that." If anything, my surprise deepened, though it shouldn't have, given Cookie's diverse interests in men.

"There are a bunch of us here from the college," he said. "Come say hello."

"You go ahead," I urged Cookie. "I want to look around a little more."

"Okay. I'll find you." She moved off with Damien.

I, of course, headed toward the table of food set up against the back wall.

It was a larger spread than I had expected, but unfortunately not very original. Hummus and pita chips, rumaki, pallid shrimp with a standard red cocktail sauce for dipping, bowls of chilled crudités and spinach dip. My thoughts turned to what I might have made for the event—sausage-stuffed mushrooms, tiny balls of fresh mozzarella marinated in sherry vinaigrette, bruschetta slathered with olive tapenade, slow-roasted tomatoes or walnut pesto, a rustic caramelized onion tart cut into thin wedges, and artichoke Parmesan dip loaded with grated horseradish and a dash of Worcestershire sauce.

All items that would travel well, could be eaten at room temperature, and easily done in the Honeybee kitchen. But then, we had catered only one event, and that had ended badly enough that I put the idea of expanding operations firmly out of my head.

I loaded my plate with rumaki and prosciutto-wrapped melon tidbits, grabbed a glass of red wine, and stepped into a nearby corner to people-watch. One man was talking to his four companions with exaggerated seriousness, and I couldn't help but wonder what he was saying. As he gesticulated, his friends' faces took on stricken expressions. After a few moments the group disbanded, each going to another group of people. I watched as faces fell throughout the room in a kind of domino effect. The level of energy in the gallery lowered.

Then I saw the man who had started it all come to the buffet table. Trying to be surreptitious, I stepped over and snagged a cocktail shrimp in time to hear him say to a lanky young man, "Have you heard?"

The other man shook his head. "Heard what?"

"Larry Eastmore was found dead in Johnson Square yesterday morning."

Ah. Of course. As an art historian and professor at the Savannah College of Art and Design, Dr. Eastmore would be well known by many, even most, of the people at Xana Do! tonight. News of his death was only now beginning to circulate.

"Holy cow," was the response. "What happened?"

"No one seems to know for sure, but the police are involved. Two detectives questioned several of us this afternoon at the school."

"Katie."

I turned away from the gossipy guys to find Cookie standing next to a man, her arm twined through his. He wore faded jeans, a red and orange dashiki, and a worn leather messenger bag strapped across his chest. His dark skin stretched over high cheekbones and his hairline dipped in an exaggerated widow's peak centered above a proud nose and bright green eyes. He exuded "hip" and "cool."

"I want to introduce you to Brandon Sikes," Cookie said.

"The genius himself," I said.

A broad smile lit up his face. "If you say so."

I smiled back, not sure what to say to an artist who imbued his work with more magic than creativity. I decided on, "Great turnout this evening."

Scanning the room, he nodded. "I'm quite pleased.

Xana has already sold several pieces." He met my eyes. "Are you a patron of the arts like Cookie here?"

"Well, *patron* might be a bit strong, but I do like to support artists in the community." I shifted my weight to the other foot. "If I can afford to, of course."

He laughed. After a couple of seconds, Cookie joined in. I didn't think it was particularly funny, especially if Sikes' spell work resulted in someone's buying something they couldn't really afford. On the other hand, people did that all the time, with no magic involved beyond good advertising and the human desire to keep up with the Joneses.

"I was afraid I wouldn't get a chance to meet you, Mr. Sikes."

"Brandon, please. Yeah, I was a bit late. Prior engagement and all. Busy life of an artist."

"Do tell," I said. "What the life of an artist entails, I mean."

"Creating art is a full-time job."

I allowed my skepticism to show.

"I donate a lot of my time, too." Now he sounded defensive.

Cookie laughed again, and I shot her a look. She was giddy as a schoolgirl. Had Sikes charmed her, too? Or was she just flirting, Cookie-style? Whatever was going on, she wasn't picking up on the fact that I was trying to find out more about his schedule. Or maybe she was. I couldn't tell.

And worse, I couldn't get any kind of solid hit off Sikes himself. He didn't seem terribly trustworthy, but I was basing that on his creative dishonesty, which I found mildly offensive. But other than that, I couldn't tell what kind of person he was at all. He knew East-

more was dead, I was sure of that. Was his easy demeanor a cover for his grief, or did he really not care
that a friend and colleague had died? Or had they even
been friends? I couldn't imagine being in a coven with
people who weren't my friends, but maybe it was different for men. For druids.

Or for a murderer.

It took only a few seconds for those thoughts to race
through my mind. Conversation flowed around us,
and I saw Cookie lean toward him and point at Xana
Smythe posting another SOLD sign next to one of his
paintings. He nodded as if that was the most normal
thing in the world. Andersen Lane had said whoever
stole the Spell of Necretius wanted to summon Zesh to
bring great success on this plane. How much success
did Brandon Sikes need?

A pointless question, perhaps. Some people were
simply never satisfied, and he was obviously willing to
employ magic to increase both fame and fortune. But to
the point of summoning a dangerous spirit? He didn't
emanate power like Heinrich Dawes had, that was for
sure. Like his artwork, Sikes struck me as more dull
than driven.

A movement over Sikes' shoulder drew my attention, and I glanced up to find Steve Dawes staring at
me from across the room. A stunning young blond
woman spoke to him, head tipped back to gaze into his
face with great earnestness. She wore nearly as much
jewelry as Xana, and her dress looked expensive. As I
watched, her hand rose and she stroked his bare forearm with her fingertips. Unexpected jealousy arrowed
through my solar plexus.

I blinked and looked back at Sikes.

His eyes had narrowed. "What's your name again? Katie?"

Silently willing Cookie to keep her mouth shut, I smiled. "It was wonderful meeting you. Wonderful work you do." I sidled to the left and waved to a non-existent friend. "I just saw someone I need to say hello to. Best of luck with the show, Brandon!" I strode toward the middle of the gallery with a welcoming smile directed at no one in particular.

Darn it! What a waste this whole evening had been. If Brandon Sikes was the murderer, I was no closer to proving it, and now he seemed suspicious of me. Great. At least I'd had the pleasure of seeing Steve out with a beautiful woman.

My attention flickered around the gallery, desperately seeking the restroom. I needed to take a breath, regroup, figure out if there was any way to salvage something from this venture.

"No-o-o!" A tall, rail-thin woman wailed, and I turned back toward the buffet table. "How can you say that? Larry loved *me*!" Even from fifty feet away, I could see that her tears had melted through several layers of mascara and dribbled in black streaks down her face. She pointed at another woman, with short blond hair and a dozen silver studs running up the outside of each ear, also crying near the wine station. "You're lying."

The murmurs of individual conversations quieted as all heads turned their way.

The blonde made a sound deep in the back of her throat, took two steps, picked up a piece of bacon-wrapped chicken liver from a platter, and threw it at the other woman. It bounced off her collarbone, leaving a greasy smear visible even in the low light. A collective intake of breath echoed through the crowd.

We watched slack-jawed as Tall-and-Skinny scooped up a handful of sun-dried tomato hummus and threw it at Silver Studs—who ducked. It hit Brandon Sikes in the messenger bag. Cookie skipped aside with a look of surprise. Sikes' eyes blazed and his mouth opened in protest. But neither woman paid any attention to the artiste. They were busy flinging pita chips and shrimp cocktail at each other between shrieking accusations and swear words. A glob of spinach dip sailed through the air and splattered on a painting. I watched, fascinated, as it oozed between the metal rivets attached randomly to the piece.

Silver Studs shrieked as a sploosh of red wine hit her square in the face. Xana Smythe and two men stepped in as she growled and reached for the full platter of rumaki.

Then Sikes started yammering about suing them, and both women, now restrained, burst into tears again.

"Come on," Steve said in my ear. "Let's get you out of here." His fingers closed on my elbow as I turned to look.

I pulled away. "I'm fine."

He frowned. "I'm not worried about you."

"What?"

"You don't think you had anything to do with that?" he indicated the mess of spilled food and wine.

I stared at him. "I don't even know those people."

Everyone seemed focused on what had just happened. A couple of people made halfhearted attempts to wipe the spinach dip off Sikes' painting. A shame, really. The culinary addition was a definite improvement to the aesthetics of the artwork.

Steve tugged at my arm again, and I let him lead me to the front of the gallery. "Your very presence can exacerbate a situation. You know that."

"Oh, come on," I protested.

"Why are you here, anyway?"

"What did you expect after you sent your buddy Andersen to Lucy's—to her *home*, Steve?"

He looked down at my hand. Grabbed it and lifted it. "Where is it?"

"What?"

"The ring," he hissed.

"Oh. Right here." I turned my dragonfly necklace around so he could see how I'd attached the ring to the chain in back.

Relief flooded his face. "I asked Andersen to come see you all, for your protection."

"Well, I didn't think it would be very smart to let another Dragoh know I had it. Luckily, Cookie's fits on her toe . . ." I trailed off, seeing his expression.

Steve's eyes narrowed. "How did you know Brandon is a member of the society?"

"Oh, for Pete's sake. Andersen told us who all of them are, after he asked for our help."

He looked confused. "Help? Help with what?"

"Ooooh." I lowered my voice even more, and Steve leaned closer. "Are you going to tell me you don't know about the Spell of Necretius?"

I could tell by his expression he had no idea what I was talking about.

"Wow," I said. "Your friend—at least I assume he's your friend if you saw fit to ask him to give us these"—

I gestured toward my neck—"took advantage of your request to drag us even further into Lawrence Eastmore's murder investigation."

Anger flickered behind Steve's eyes. "I should have known better than to trust him. Listen, can we get out of here? I need to hear the rest of this."

I snorted. "What about your date?"

His forehead wrinkled. "What date?"

"Ms. Blond Bombshell with the Italian shoes. I saw her, you know."

His lips parted briefly, and delight played across his features. "Katie Lightfoot, you're jealous!"

"I am not."

"You are." His self-satisfied smile continued to curl up one side of his mouth.

I wanted to swipe it off. Instead I felt my face growing hot.

"I'm covering the opening for my column. Modern art in old Savannah, that kind of thing. Though the food fight does put a twist on things." He grinned. "And I don't bring dates along when I'm working, FYI."

"Oh." I looked down at my feet. Why should I be upset if he was dating that woman? How many times had I told myself I didn't want to get involved with Steve? Still, he'd pursued me so steadfastly . . .

Perhaps I shouldn't take that for granted. I pushed the thought to the back of my mind. Time enough to think about such things later.

"I don't want to leave quite yet," I said. "I'm hoping I can find out more about where Brandon was the night before we . . . I . . . found Eastmore dead."

He ignored my oblique reference to Declan. "Well, I can tell you that."

I felt my eyebrows climb my forehead.

"Brandon was at Father's house."

"What? Why?"

"Some confab about a big piece of installation art Brandon wants to do on the Talmadge Bridge. Father's helping him get permissions from the city. He ended up staying."

"All night?"

"All night."

"How do you know?"

"I stayed in the guesthouse."

"Why didn't you go home?"

He shrugged. "I was tired, and I'd had a couple of drinks. So had Brandon. That's why he stayed overnight."

"But not in the guesthouse."

"No, but I saw him leave the next morning."

"What about your mother?"

"What about her? She was home, but went to bed early. She's not interested in Father's business dealings."

"So your mom doesn't know about the Drag—" I cut myself short as a woman rounded the partition closest to us, saw Steve, and made a beeline our way.

He shook his head, though whether in answer to my question about his mother or as a warning, I didn't know.

"Stevie Dawes, as I live and breathe. You have turned into quite the fine-looking young man." She looked familiar, and then I recognized her as the woman who had filled out the job application at the Honeybee. She'd replaced the denim jumper and Birkenstocks with a flowing red caftan that would have made a gypsy proud. Her gray hair, still braided, was now coiled in a crown on top of her head. Given the fine lines that fanned from her smiling dark blue eyes. I judged her to be in her mid-fifties.

"Stevie?" I couldn't help repeating with a wide grin.

He rolled his eyes. "Katie, this is Nel Sandstrom. How long has it been?"

"Hi, again," Nel said to me, and when Steve looked surprised she explained. "I've been looking for a job, and stopped into the bakery where your friend works."

"She more than works there," Steve said. "Katie and her aunt and uncle own the Honeybee."

"So are you the one I should thank for that burnt toffee biscotti?"

I nodded. "It's my personal recipe."

"Scrumptious," she declared. Then to Steve. "It's been at least fifteen years since I've seen you, darlin'."

"Well, you look just the same, Miss Nel." He could turn on the charm like you switch on the bathroom light in the middle of the night. "And if you're job hunting I assume you're back in town for good?"

"For a while, at least. You know I had to come back to . . ." She glanced at me. "To take care of Daddy's affairs."

He nodded. "Of course. I'm surprised I haven't run into you before now."

"Well, I came for the funeral, of course. You weren't there, I noticed. Then I had to return to settle some things in Athens. Now I'm back for good."

"I am sorry about missing your father's memorial," he said. "I was out of town."

She patted him on the arm. "Oh, that's all right. There was quite the turnout for the judge, though. It was nice to see."

"Father told me."

I'd been listening with a bit of impatience, frankly, wanting to track down Cookie and head home. It was getting late, and I felt like I'd learned all I could about Brandon Sikes for the evening. But then Steve's gaze snagged mine, and something in his eyes gave me pause.

Dead father of a fiftysomething woman who lived in Athens. A judge.

I quirked an eyebrow and asked, "Your father was Judge Sandstrom?" Dragoh number six, who had died without male issue.

Steve winced.

"I'm sorry about your father," I said, ignoring his dramatic shoulder slump. "A friend of mine is a lawyer, and she'd mentioned him as someone she respected a great deal."

"Thank you."

"So, any luck with the job hunt so far?"

"Not yet, but something will turn up soon. It always does." Her words made me think of Cookie's laissez-faire attitude. "I don't really need the money, but I like to keep busy, love to bake, and would like to meet some new people. As you heard me tell your boyfriend here, I've been gone from Savannah for quite some time."

Steve stepped to my side. "Well, I'm sure you'll find the right thing, Nel. You've always been lucky that way."

I cocked my head. What did he mean by that?

"You've seen Brandon?" he asked.

"Oh, yes. After the food fight." Her laugh was

strained. "That man could certainly charm the ladies, couldn't he?"

"Brandon Sikes?" I asked, wondering if he glamoured more than his paintings.

"Oh, no. Though he does just fine. Has a new little filly just tonight."

My heart sank. Cookie had better not do anything stupid.

"No, I meant the man who started that food fight from beyond the grave," Nel said. "Lawrence Eastmore. He always had more ladies flocking around him than seemed justified to me. Quite the player, for an old guy." She winked.

My smile in return felt weak.

Chapter 17

"I'm going to kill Cookie." I shook my head in frustration and leaned one hip against the hood of the Bug.

In the aftermath of the food fight I'd seen her talking animatedly with Nel, and then a few minutes later she'd hustled over to me and said, "Just wanted to let you know Brandon is giving me a ride home, Katie. No worries."

But I *was* worried. When Steve and I had left the party she'd been draped over Brandon Sikes' arm all gooey-eyed. I had to admit he'd looked pretty smitten, too. I just hoped he drove her to her home, not his, and that she kept her head on straight.

Nel had walked out of the gallery with us and driven away in a bright red MINI Cooper. Steve and I had walked on, half a block farther, to where I'd parked, and now he put his elbows on the roof of my car. "Well, you wanted to find out more about Brandon," he said. "If anyone can do that it'll be Cookie."

"I'm not afraid of what she'll find out about him. I'm afraid of what he'll find out about her. I should have known better. She was so excited to meet him." I banged my hand on the metal. "Ow. But I should have known better," I repeated.

Steve laughed. His Land Rover was parked the next block down.

As we strolled to my car, I quickly filled Steve in on what Andersen Lane had told us about the Spell of Necretius.

"I don't know what he was thinking, getting your spellbook club involved with something like that," he said, forehead creased with worry.

"Now who's being sexist?"

"That's not it at all. I know how formidable you ladies can be. But why didn't he tell me?"

I shrugged, unwilling to point out the obvious: Andersen might suspect Heinrich of killing Eastmore in order to get the spell. If so, he would hardly involve Steve.

"What time did Brandon Sikes arrive at your father's house?" I asked. In the gallery, Nel Sandstrom had interrupted our conversation before I'd had the chance to ask whether the double alibi Steve had offered for his father and Sikes covered the entire window of time from five p.m. until two a.m.

"About eight. But we'd been at a function with him since four."

Well, that answered that.

"Get in," I said, pulling my sweater close around my shoulders. The night had turned cool. "I'll give you a ride down to where you're parked."

He opened the passenger door and slid into the seat. I settled behind the wheel. "I'm not being a prude, you know. Cookie has been running her own life for a long time without my help. But Sikes could be dangerous."

I waited for a Prius to pass by, then pulled out of the parking space.

"I know he comes across as kind of a skirt-chaser," Steve said, "but I'm certain she can handle him."

"Let's hope so," I said. "For all our sakes."

"You know, I'm kind of glad you know about the society," he said. "I don't like keeping secrets from you."

My eyes cut toward him, then returned to the street ahead. "Do you have any other secrets you feel like sharing?"

He laughed.

I slowed for a pedestrian. "That's not exactly an answer."

Still smiling, he shook his head. "No. No other secrets. My life is an open book."

"Right."

"Seriously. You can ask me anything. But you know most of my life is totally normal, even boring. Just like yours is. Practicing magic is just part of it."

"I like my life," I said. "And I love learning about magic. But you're right—normal and boring can be awful nice."

I double-parked next to his car. It gleamed black and shiny in the moonlight, reminding me of how much money Steve came from.

He reached for the door handle, then paused. Turning, he leaned close. "Katie-girl." His warm breath against my skin gave me instant quivers. "Things are crazier than I ever thought they'd get. It makes me regret the time we've wasted."

"Oh, Steve. I don't think—"

"You need to stop playing around. You know we're supposed to be together."

I felt my jaw slacken.

"Think about it. Seriously." He got out of the car and shut the door. Leaned down and spoke through the open window. "Please? That's all I ask."

Stunned, I watched him get into his Land Rover. Then I tromped on the accelerator and drove away.

We're supposed to be together? What did that even mean?

Had that been a declaration of love?

Did I want it to be?

Needless to say, I didn't sleep great that night. Still, I dipped into my stash of Lucy's seven-layer bars, the ones she laced with agrimony, and managed to eke out a few hours.

Early the next morning I awoke feeling a bit foggy. Normally I would have shaken it off with a run, but venturing alone into the dark predawn felt dangerous now. I hated that, resented that someone could make me feel that way.

Half an hour of yoga and a nice long shower did wonders for both body and mind, though. As I slipped into my work clothes I eyed the tie-dyed skirt and glittery tank from the night before, now laid over the back of the chair in the bedroom. For this morning's investigative adventure I decided not to pull any punches. Forget casual Bohemian. I had the perfect suit to wear to a late October breakfast with Savannah's political bigwigs.

At least I thought it was perfect. And that was what counted.

"I'm going to be at the fund-raiser with Bianca for most of the morning," I reminded Mungo. "You don't mind staying here today, do you?"

He knew I didn't like to leave him at the bakery when I wasn't there. It was enough that we were breaking all sorts of food police rules by letting him stay in the office so much. But, heck, it wasn't like he was out in the kitchen romping in the cookie dough or anything.

Yip!

"Good. You want me to have Margie bring the JJs over to play?"

He looked disinterested, which I took for, well, disinterest. He loved playing with the kids, but sometimes they could be a bit much for his sensibilities.

"You want the TV on, I suppose?"

Yip!

Looking at the ceiling, I shook my head. "Okay."

I climbed up to the loft that overlooked the living room, and he bounded up the narrow stairs behind me. Once he was settled into the pillows on the small settee, I turned on the TV and flipped to his favorite channel: the Soap Opera Network. "I'll leave your lunch downstairs, okay?"

He ignored me. I'd discovered over the past few months that my familiar *really* liked soap operas. It was like a sickness.

Leaving him to his newfound addiction, I opened the secretary desk Lucy had given me. The folding desk fit in the tight quarters of the carriage house and perfectly hid my makeshift altar. A lace shawl Nonna Sheffield had knitted covered the wooden surface and provided the backdrop for my chalice (a small, swirly glass bowl from the flea market), a worn vintage paring knife that suited this baker's idea of a ritual athame, a collection of stones gathered by rivers and on lakeshores, an Indian arrowhead my dad had given me, and a brilliant blue feather that had drifted into the gazebo only weeks before.

Now I fingered the delicate stitches my witchy grandmother had knitted and wondered again whether she'd imbued the piece with magic of some kind. Though I suspected she had, I'd probably never know for sure. It probably didn't matter, either.

My grimoire sat on a shelf above the objects on the altar, reminding me that I hadn't updated it for a couple of days now. I thought of it as a kind of recipe book for spells. In six months I'd recorded my casting attempts, what worked, what didn't, refining and honing as I went. I promised myself that when this was all over I'd catch up.

Not that there was much to catch up on. Lawrence Eastmore getting himself killed had thrown a real monkey wrench into my lessons with the spellbook club.

After touching each object on the altar, with a mental nod to the four elements they represented, I closed the desk. Mungo didn't budge when I ruffled his ears, so I went down and cut up a portion of Steve's leftover turkey Reuben, complete with sauerkraut and dressing and part of a kosher pickle. It all went into a bowl that then went into a larger bowl of ice to stay fresh for hours until Mungo felt hungry.

Lordy, the things I did for that dog.

Placing the whole shebang on the floor of the kitchen, I called good-bye, then took my change of clothes out to the car. As I locked the front door I wondered what Steve would say about Mungo's soap opera habit. Or the fact that he wouldn't eat dog food but loved pickles and raisins.

Then I wondered why I'd bother to wonder such a thing, firmly pushing his vague request the night before to the back of my mind.

Again.

It was still pitch-black outside when I arrived at the Honeybee, and would be for hours. I tied on a bright orange chef's apron with the white bones of a skeletal torso appliquéd on the front. I'd bought two—the other one was black—to add to my considerable collection of vintage aprons. After preheating the ovens, I put the pans of sourdough that had been rising overnight onto the racks to bake and mixed the batter for brown-butter-and-walnut cupcakes, which would be the special for the day. Or were they muffins? Hard to tell the difference when you mixed savory and sweet like that. I added a hefty dose of powdered ginger to the batter, closing my eyes and invoking its influence to increase energy, love, and courage. By the time Cookie arrived, I'd also mixed three kinds of cookie dough and rebaked a batch of cranberry orange biscotti.

"You're late," I said, instantly regretting my tone.

She blinked at me with bleary eyes. "Sorry. Didn't get much sleep."

Oh, dear. I rubbed my hand over my face, afraid to ask.

Cookie didn't seem to notice. "Brandon and I sat down by the river and talked for hours and hours last night. I barely made it home for a nap and a shower." She twisted up her still-wet hair, pinned it in place, and donned a Honeybee baseball cap. Then she slipped the black skeleton apron over her head and reached behind to fasten it.

"What did you talk about?" My tone was carefully casual as I began stacking biscotti in a large glass jar.

"Oh, gosh. Everything. Absolutely everything. We have so much in common! It's like we've known each other forever." For being so tired she sure was enthusiastic.

I put the lid on the jar and leaned my hip against the counter. "What did you tell him?"

She stilled. "About what?"

"About the fact that you're a witch. About the spellbook club. About what you know about him being a druid, the Dragoh Society, Lawrence Eastmore, and the Spell of Necretius." Frustration blew out on my words. Anger, too, I realized. And fear. Cookie could have jeopardized everything the spellbook club was trying to do to find a killer and keep an evil spirit at bay.

She whirled to face me, hands on her hips. "Just because you're too afraid to commit to either of the men who are obviously in love with you doesn't give you the right to judge me."

"Cookie, I wasn't—"

"Believe me, we had a lot more interesting things to talk about than your murder investigation."

"My—?"

"And yes, Brandon knows I practice magic, but he told me about his practice first. The spellbook club and his society didn't come up. Our childhoods, our lives, our values and beliefs—those were what we talked about. You know what else?" She was practically shouting by now. "He admitted to glamouring his paintings. He doesn't do it with all of them, just enough to keep the money coming in so he has the freedom to pursue his *art*."

Oh, brother. Like that somehow made it better?

"Katie is only worried about you," Lucy said from beside the display case.

We both turned in surprise. "How long have you been standing there?"

"Long enough to hear you two fighting. Now stop it. It makes my stomach hurt to watch you."

I went over and gave her a hug. "Hear that, Cookie? We've made Lucy sick."

After a moment Cookie laughed. "I'm sorry. I get kind of cranky when I don't get enough sleep."

"You're not the only one," Lucy said with a meaningful look at me.

"Moi?" I said.

"Actually, we need to talk about that," Cookie said, her expression serious again.

Uh-oh.

"What's up?" my aunt asked.

Cookie licked her lips. "Well, you know I've been working at the Honeybee for four months, right?"

Lucy and I exchanged glances.

"And I'm not that great at these early mornings . . . Oh, heck. The truth is I really hate getting up this early."

"And besides, four months is about your limit at most jobs, isn't it?" Lucy's voice was kind. "We understand."

Cookie looked over at me, and I nodded. "We've kind of been expecting this. Can you stay for a few more days, while we find someone else?"

She wagged her finger at me. "Ah. You see, I found someone last night."

"Last night?"

"At the gallery. Brandon introduced us. Her name is

Nel. And she's already filled out an application—kismet!"

"Nel Sandstrom?" I asked, thinking hard.

"You met her, too, then." Cookie looked pleased.

"Briefly. And I saw her here when she came in looking for a job. But, Cookie, you know who she is, don't you?"

"Her father is a druid," Lucy breathed.

"Was a druid," I said.

"Does it matter?" Cookie asked. "She's no druid, she's looking for a job, and her background is in baking. She worked at a bakery in Athens for a long time, and—get this, Lucy—she's a cake decorator!"

Lucy's lips turned down in thought. "We could sure use someone else who likes to decorate cakes. It's good business."

"Yeah . . ." I trailed off. I loved experimenting with flavor combinations and trying new baking techniques a lot more than the intricacies of piping and working with fondant. Maybe I just wasn't artistic enough, but cake decorating had been the only pastry course that brought me to tears.

Cookie continued. "When I told her there might be an opening here because I was quitting, she became very excited. She says she's a real early bird, too."

"All right," Lucy said with a decisive nod. "If you think she would be a good fit, the least we can do is interview her."

"I was hoping you'd say that," Cookie said, lifting the jar of biscotti and sashaying out to the front counter with it. "She'll be here this afternoon to talk to you."

"First she went directly against the spellbook club's request not to get involved with Brandon Sikes by spending most of the night baring her soul to him," I whispered to Lucy as Cookie began opening the front blinds.

"Presumably only her soul, though." She smiled.

"And then she had the audacity to arrange for her own replacement by asking a total stranger," I finished.

"I'm sure she felt that she was doing us a favor," my good-natured aunt said in Cookie's defense. "And she does have terrific instincts about jobs, not only for herself but for others."

I harrumphed.

"Everything happens for a reason, Katie. You know that."

"Maybe."

"Definitely. Cookie," she called.

The younger witch turned with a quizzical expression.

"What will you do once you're not working here?"

"I'm not sure yet. Something will turn up."

"It always does," I muttered.

"I heard that," she sang out, her good humor completely restored. "Oh, and Katie? You can cross Brandon off your list of suspects in Dr. Eastmore's murder."

"Why? Do you know where he was?" Wondering if her new beau's story would match Steve's, I followed her to the reading area, where she had started tidying the volumes on the shelf.

"Well, I couldn't very well come right out and ask that, now could I? Not without giving away our interest. But if it's true that whoever killed the professor did it because they wanted that spell to bring them worldly power, well, then, it just couldn't have been Brandon.

See, he's not interested in material success, only in bringing beauty into the world."

Not interested in material success, my patootie. And as for bringing beauty into the world, if that was Sikes' goal he needed to take some more art lessons.

But I just nodded and smiled and went back to the kitchen to pull the sourdough loaves out of the oven.

Chapter 18

At seven forty I took off my apron and went into the office to change clothes. The fund-raiser breakfast didn't begin until nine, but Bianca and I wanted to get there early. Perhaps we'd have a chance to chat with some of Victor Powers' staff, his wife, or at least the sponsor of the breakfast. Anyone who was running for a senatorial seat should have a verifiable schedule—if you had a good reason to know. I considered how I might be able to involve Detective Quinn in the investigation without letting Franklin Taite know what was going on. It didn't seem like much of a possibility, though. Besides, how could I get Quinn to listen to me unless I actually told him the truth?

Not only would that be foolish, but he'd think I was crazy. Not to mention his bad attitude about my poking my nose into murder cases.

In the restroom, I fluffed my hair with my fingers, applied eyeliner, mascara, and lip gloss, and called it good. When I emerged, I discovered Bianca waiting for me at one of the bistro tables, her fingers curled around a to-go cup that no doubt contained her usual mocha.

She wore a formfitting linen sheath the color of ripe plums. The polish on her toenails matched the dress, and a small Coach bag lay casually on the table beside her.

Someone whistled as I walked by, and I frowned until I saw it was Annette Lander from the knitting shop next door, getting her first caffeine fix of the day.

Bianca looked me up and down with approval. "Very nice. Is that Evan Picone?"

I nodded, oddly happy that she'd noticed. "Vintage." I left out that I'd stumbled across it in a thrift store where I was trolling for aprons to add to my collection. I loved the pencil skirt that fell below my knees and the short jacket with a stand-up collar. This was the first opportunity I'd had to wear it.

"That olive green really sets off your eyes."

"Thanks."

"And your hair," Lucy said. "You look positively stunning, dear."

"You should have seen her last night," Cookie chimed in from the register. "Chic Bohemian. Steve Dawes certainly appreciated it."

Lucy raised her eyebrows. "You saw Steve last night?"

I waved my hand dismissively. "For a few minutes. He was working."

"Well, let's get going," Bianca said.

"Let me get my other sandals," I said. As often as I wore heels—or rather didn't wear them—I'd break a leg if I tried to walk on Savannah sidewalks from Broughton Street to the ferry dock down on the river.

"No need. I brought my car. We can park by Moon Grapes and walk from there."

Moon Grapes was on Factors Walk. I nodded, willing to risk the cobblestones and oyster-laden tabby walkways from there to the river. Besides, I rarely passed up a chance to ride in her red Jaguar, even if it was for only a few blocks.

It had turned gray and blustery outside, though, and Bianca kept the top up on the car. We parked in front of Moon Grapes, and she quickly checked in with her assistant before we headed toward the stone stairway leading to the riverfront. The wind held a hint of warning, and during the brief walk the sky began to roil with dark clouds.

Bianca looked upward with concern. "I hope the weather holds off."

"I'll say. We don't want to show up at some fancy fund-raiser looking like bedraggled puppies."

Her glance held amusement. "We wouldn't be the only ones."

I'd been to the Westin Hotel on the other side of the Savannah River only once during the six months I'd lived in Georgia—one day when Lucy and I had met Ben for lunch after he'd played golf on the hotel's championship course. Now the Westin's green and yellow water taxi chugged toward the dock as we approached the ramp.

We joined two nicely dressed couples who I imagined were going to the same function we were. Or maybe not. The Westin had a reputation of attracting moneyed visitors to Savannah, whether they were in town for business or pleasure. Soon two gentlemen carrying golf bags lumbered up to where we stood. Moments later three giggling college-aged girls showing a lot of skin and tossing around flirtatious come-hither looks more from habit than intent tripped down the ramp.

The ferry nudged up to the dock and several passengers disembarked. A few minutes later we all made our way on board, most passengers ducking inside to get out of the wind. Hair streaming back from her face, Bianca looked over at me, and in unspoken agreement we headed for the railing. No harm in a bit of moving air as long as the rain held off. In fact, it felt cool and welcome.

The engine emitted a low growl as folks got settled, then rumbled to life and the ferry began moving back across the river. On the other side, the Westin rose like a pale modern castle. The water below reflected the mercurial sky above, splashing against the hull as we cut across the current. The faint smell of the paper mill made me wrinkle my nose.

I clasped my amulet in my chilly fingers. The thin ring hanging behind it felt insubstantial, and I wondered whether Anderson Lane really had our best interests at heart. Other than Cookie's finding a new boyfriend, last night had been a bust. Well, that wasn't entirely true: Steve had provided alibis for Brandon Sikes and his father. Still, we were no closer to finding the killer. Would this morning change that? Because if it didn't, I didn't know what the next step was.

A political fund-raiser was so not my thing. I didn't care for politicians in general, and while I did do my homework come election time, often it felt as if I was simply voting for the lesser of two evils. It was early in the current election cycle, though, and I'd largely ignored the ads and pontification, so I knew very little about Victor Powers other than the sound-bite rhetoric I'd found when I looked up his Web site after learning he was a Dragoh. Yet here I was, helping him raise money while trying to figure out whether he was a killer who wanted to unleash a great evil in the world simply to further his own agenda.

Raise money. I leaned over to Bianca and spoke loudly to be heard over the wind. "How much do I owe you for the ticket to this event?"

She waved the question away without even looking my way. "Don't worry about it. I know one of the organizers and was able to get us in at the last minute."

"So they were free?" I asked.

"Not exactly," she said. "They were, shall we say, discounted."

"Tell me," I insisted.

She sighed. "Twelve hundred dollars each."

"Oh, Bianca. Why didn't you say something?" It would take some financial scrambling for me to pay her back.

"Because this is a way that I can contribute. I'm not that happy that we're involved in some strange druid's problem, but we are. So I'm committed to helping. You know how I feel about the Rule of Three."

I shook my head. "But—"

"Oh, give it a rest, darlin'. You know I can afford it, so just let it go. Please?"

I hesitated, but I could tell she meant it. "All right. Thank you." I'd been going to point out that she might have just given money to a murderer, and I wasn't sure how the Rule of Three worked in relation to that. It was already done, though, and with the best of intentions.

"Save the thanks for after it's over. I don't know if

we'll find out anything useful at all. Victor Powers may not even be there—he's got some kind of scheduling conflict. But I'm sure we'll be treated to plenty of political posturing."

"Yay," I said with a small sarcastic smile. "I can hardly wait."

She snorted a very unladylike laugh.

On the other side of the river we stepped off the ferry and climbed the concrete ramp to the expansive lawns that surrounded the hotel. No oyster shell–filled tabby mix on this side of the river, just smooth sidewalks, perfectly green grass, and elegant palm trees. The golfers broke off from the group, and the college girls headed for the main lobby. Bianca and I followed the two couples past fragrant flower gardens and a row of lounge chairs. Sure enough, they skirted the teal blue outdoor swimming pool and made their way to the Club Pavilion.

We pushed through the glass doors and paused just inside. Table after table boasted white cloths that echoed the swaths of fabric that swooped in elaborate folds across the ceiling and poised in luscious rolls above the windows. White china place settings reflected the lights from the chandeliers above and the gray daylight coming through the windows. The air swarmed with the welcoming smells of warm food and hot coffee, but I was surprised to see an elaborate buffet table set up at the back of the room. Perhaps white-coated waiters would have disrupted the upcoming speeches.

A woman across the room waved at us and began threading her way through the tables in our direction. Her lipstick was the color of Merlot, matching her dress and shoes. Smooth dark hair swung above her shoul-

ders, and long mascaraed lashes framed her friendly
gray eyes.

"Bianca! I'm so glad you called me last night. We're
delighted to have you join Team Powers, even in this
small way."

My companion smiled widely. "Elizabeth Dwyer, I'd
like you to meet my friend Kathleen."

I shot her a grateful look.

"She wants Victor Powers to represent the great
state of Georgia in the Senate as much as we do. Kathleen, Liz is the driving force behind this lovely breakfast."

We shook hands. "Oh, heck," Elizabeth said. "Just
doing my part for the greater good."

"Good for you," I said. "I'm so pleased to meet you.
I do hope to get a chance to talk with the candidate
himself."

"He has been busy, busy, busy from what I understand. So many people to meet around the state. He's
been out of town for the last four days, shaking hands
and kissing babies. Running for office isn't for wimps!"

"I can only imagine how much work it must be." But
I wasn't imagining that at all. I was thinking Victor
Powers might very well have an alibi for the night
Lawrence Eastmore was struck on the head. "Do you
happen to know where Mr. Powers was on Friday night?"

Elizabeth looked momentarily puzzled, but recovered
quickly. "I'm afraid I don't have his schedule. However,
Carolyn—his wife—will be here soon. It looks like Victor's running late, so she may be speaking in his stead.
She's very charismatic, you know. Perhaps she could tell
you."

"Oh, it's not important," I said. "Will you excuse me for a moment?"

"Of course." She turned to Bianca, and as I moved away I heard her ask, "Are you interested in volunteering for the campaign?"

Bianca was a big girl. She could take care of herself.

The place was beginning to fill, and some people were finding seats at the tables. I snagged a couple of seats near the front, but remained standing. I didn't recognize anyone at first, then saw Mrs. Standish. I had no idea of her political leanings, but that probably didn't matter. Since she was a mover and shaker in Savannah she might have attended the fund-raiser of an up-and-coming senatorial candidate no matter what his views so as to keep her hand in.

She didn't see me, though, and I turned to survey the rest of the growing crowd. They were a well-dressed bunch, though the level of formality varied. Elizabeth Dwyer hurried toward the buffet tables, smiling and nodding at everyone she passed. Bianca found me a few minutes later.

"What time is it?" I asked.

Glancing at her watch, she said, "Eight forty-five."

A male voice announced that the buffet was open, and people began filing in that direction.

"Let's wait for the throng to thin," I said.

Bianca nodded. We sat down at the table for six, and a young couple and two older gentlemen filled the other chairs. We all exchanged pleasantries. The men had already been through the food line, and I surreptitiously eyed their plates. Shrimp and grits, cheddar biscuits and slabs of ham, piled together with peach pancakes and scrambled eggs. The Westin obviously offered a proper buffet. It was a ridiculous display of food, and I wanted some.

"Let's go," I said.

Bianca grinned.

We shuffled down the buffet and returned to the table. My plate had a little dab of everything, while Bianca's held an assortment of melon and a piece of toast. Poor woman was going to starve, eating like that.

Elizabeth Dwyer went up to the podium, adjusted the microphone, and welcomed us all. Next she started in on the same sound bites I'd already heard. Between the food and the people-watching, I largely tuned her out. Then she introduced Carolyn Powers.

Victor Powers was married to a willowy, tan blonde who spoke in a refined drawl. She welcomed all the attendees as well, and then got down to the business of touting her husband's credentials.

"He has worked in the financial sector for most of his life. We talk about the economy, but Victor understands economics. He also understands how things get done, both in business and in the world of politics. With your continued support we can bring the Empire State of the South back to greatness!"

Funny: I thought it was pretty great already.

She went on for twenty achingly long minutes, making vague but enthusiastic promises. Finally, she gave the online link for further donations. "However, we know how busy everyone is, and it's easy to forget. We need your help, and you need Victor Powers in the Senate! So why not break out your checkbooks right now? And if you don't have a check handy? Well, shame on you." She smiled, and a few people laughed. "But you can still donate to the campaign online before you leave the hotel. We have volunteers with electronic tablets who will be moving among you, and we accept credit cards. Or text your donation and the amount will show up on your phone bill." She recited a number. "Thank you so much."

I looked at Bianca in amazement as everyone clapped. She shrugged. The young couple got up and hurried over to a college-aged woman, reaching for the tablet in her hand.

A waiter collected our plates—my eyes had been bigger than my stomach, but I'd made good inroads—and I pushed back from the table.

"Sorry you spent so much to get us in here," I whispered to Bianca. "Let's at least circulate a little more, see if we can find out anything useful." I looked around for Carolyn Powers. She'd know where her husband had been on Friday night. Or at least I assumed so.

I spied her approaching the podium again. She took the microphone in hand, and a short whine screeched through the room. Bianca winced.

"Sorry about that! But I have some very good news!" Carolyn said.

A murmur drifted through the crowd.

"We thought Victor would be unable to attend this morning's soiree, but it turns out he is on his way back from Athens as I stand here. Go, Bulldogs! He's only about fifteen minutes away, and we'd love for you to stay and get to know each other. I know my husband would love to personally meet as many of you as possible."

Of course Powers would want to meet as many of these moneybags as he could.

"Well, now. Maybe things are going to be more interesting than I thought," I said to Bianca and stood up. "Let's at least stretch our legs while we have a chance. Maybe take a look around?"

She nodded, and we started toward the exit.

And there, walking straight toward us, was Heinrich Dawes.

Chapter 19

"Darn it," I said, and veered to the right.

Bianca followed. "What's wrong?"

"That's Steve's dad."

"Oh! Did he see you?"

"Not yet—but if he does he'll know I'm not here because I'm a big fan of future senator Powers."

You would be well advised to keep out of the society's business.

He turned in our direction. I ducked down as far as my long pencil skirt would allow. He strode forward, confident and smiling, toward a cluster of political boosters. Quickly, I slipped into a chair next to a white-haired woman in a navy blue pantsuit. Bianca remained standing, surveying the room as if she were looking for someone in particular.

The grandmotherly woman in the chair next to me looked at me in surprise.

"Sorry," I said. "Not feeling well."

"Oh, dear. Shall I call someone?"

"No, no. I'll be fine in a moment." I pushed a napkin off the table with my elbow. "Oops." I leaned down to retrieve it from under my chair as Heinrich walked by, oblivious. Relief washed through me as I saw his retreating back.

Then he paused by the next table. Stopped. He looked at the faces near him, then turned in a slow circle. It looked for all the world as if he were sniffing the air.

You have tangible power. Heinrich's words came flooding back.

Even though he hadn't actually seen me, he knew I was there. I didn't know how to dampen whatever he was sensing, didn't even know if that was possible.

"Dear, are you all right?"

The nice white-haired lady leaned down to where I remained hunched over in my chair, alarm and concern all over her face.

"Just a little dizzy," I whispered.

Heinrich had stopped turning and was now facing my way, but I was still mostly hidden by the white tablecloth. Movement to his left made him turn his head just before Bianca ran into him.

She'd picked up a half-full glass of freshly squeezed orange juice from one of the tables, and now it dripped down the front of his expensive suit.

"Oh! Heavens, where did you come from?" Bianca turned on her considerable charm full blast, capturing his undivided attention. "I thought I saw Mr. Powers coming up the path outside and became utterly distracted."

I sat up and smiled at my new friend. "I feel much better now. Do you know where the restroom is inside the hotel?"

"Just around the corner from the elevators, dear. You're sure you're okay?"

"Yes. Thanks so much." My words were rushed, and I missed her reply as I stood and sidled quickly toward the exit, watching Heinrich the whole time.

Bianca dabbed at his lapel with a napkin. "Take that off, and I'll get it cleaned up with some nice club soda. Can someone please get me some club soda?"

"Isn't that for wine stains?" he asked in a gruff voice, looking up. I saw his light gray eyes flash.

"Oh, I think it'll work for a little citrus stain. Let's at least try, okay?"

I stepped to the side, putting several people between Heinrich and me.

A cheer went up as the door opened behind me. I turned to find myself facing a large man with a short white fringe of hair running around the perimeter of his otherwise bald head. The tonsure effect belied his powerful shoulders and military bearing. I recognized the face from the television ads.

Victor Powers met my eyes with his own ice-blue ones. Something passed between us, but I didn't know exactly what. Did he recognize me, perhaps from Heinrich's description or even a picture? Or did he sense something the same way Steve's dad seemed to when he walked by?

Whatever it was, it flickered for one long second before he grinned broadly and waved at his supporters. They shifted to allow him passage, and I slid farther behind the crowd until I was finally able to duck outside.

Bianca walked into the women's restroom fifteen minutes later. "I thought I might find you here." She bent down to check under the stall doors. We were alone.

182 Bailey Cates

Leaning against the counter, I said, "Seems the safest place to be right now. Nice job with the orange juice, by the way."

She laughed. "Mr. Dawes is not terribly happy with yours truly. I would have offered to get his suit cleaned, but anyone who can afford that suit in the first place doesn't need my contribution to his household budget."

I grimaced. "No kidding. You're out of pocket enough already. What a fiasco, not to mention a waste of time."

"Oh, I don't know about that."

My chin jerked up. "What do you mean?"

"After her husband arrived, I had a chance to talk to Carolyn Powers. Their grandson turned eleven on Friday, and she made sure Grandpa was in town for the party. In fact, it was at their house, and Heinrich was in attendance. She also mentioned that it was a pleasant—and rare—thing to have her husband home for a full night during this campaign."

"Really. Well, Steve said that Brandon Sikes was with him and his father at a function of some kind, then came home with them and stayed the night at the Dawes' house."

"Why?"

"Something to do with an art exhibit Sikes is planning. It got late, and they'd had a few drinks, so he stayed."

"Ah. Well, I guess that's better than having Jaida defend another DUI."

The door opened then, and a woman came into the restroom holding the hand of a little girl. Bianca and I exchanged glances and I nodded. "Let's go."

Hotel guests, golfers, and political supporters strolled through the Westin's lobby, but there was no sign of Steve's father. Watchful, we went outside and made a beeline for the dock. Halfway there, I spotted him. He stood between us and the river, watching people gather for the water taxi. I tugged on Bianca's arm, pulling her back, but there wasn't really anywhere to hide. We retraced our steps as far as the hotel and tucked ourselves around the corner.

"At this rate we should just get a room and plan on staying until he leaves," I said, frustrated.

Heinrich continued to watch the waiting passengers as the taxi chugged across the water. We could see one of the humongous container ships from China downriver, approaching the Talmadge Bridge.

Suddenly Heinrich spun on his heel, looking across the lawn toward the main entrance of the hotel. He raised his hand to someone and began walking back up. Bianca and I shrank back, but he walked inside without a glance in our direction. Down at the dock the water taxi let off its passengers from the other side of the river.

"Come on!" I said.

Together, we ran across the grass and down the sidewalk, high heels clattering on the cement ramps. We made it onto the taxi just before the attendant closed the gate.

"Whew!" I laughed, trying to catch my breath. "It's a miracle I didn't turn my ankle on that little sprint." The boat pulled away. The wind had blown some of the cloud cover off, and now thin sunlight glinted off the dark water of the river.

But Bianca didn't respond. She was looking back at the hotel. I followed her gaze.

Heinrich Dawes stood above, looking down at us. He'd fooled us by going back into the hotel, I realized. I put my hand on the railing and nodded to him.

His nod in return felt like a promise. Not a good one, either.

Bianca was due back at Moon Grapes. She pulled her Jag up to the curb in front of the Honeybee. I got out and waved as she drove away. Someone had propped the door of the bakery open, and warm, homey smells drifted out to the sidewalk. It was our best way to advertise.

A customer waited at the register while Cookie frothed up a coffee drink behind the espresso bar. I asked if he'd been helped, but it turned out the coffee drink was for him.

"Lucy and Ben are back in the office with my replacement," Cookie said.

I was stunned. "They hired her while I was gone?"

"Of course not. But you will. Hire her, I mean."

Hmm. But I wasn't going to say anything about feeling railroaded in front of a customer, so I pasted a smile on and clicked back to the kitchen on my heels. If I didn't get those things off my feet soon I'd be crippled for life.

Sure enough, my aunt sat in the swivel chair in the little office by the storage closet, and Uncle Ben leaned his forearm on the tall filing cabinet. Nel Sandstrom sat on Mungo's usual chair, gesticulating with both hands.

"Oh, my, yes. I love to create cakes for people's special days. I could whip something up if you'd like to see my decorating skills. I also brought this to show you some of the things I've done before." She handed Lucy a legal-sized leather portfolio.

Lucy began flipping through a series of photos. Her eyes widened. "These are wonderful. Oh! I love this one—the pond with airbrushed lily pads? Just lovely. Heaven knows, I wouldn't mind expanding that part of the Honeybee's business. Katie's too busy with all her fabulous treats, and I simply don't have enough time for elaborate wedding cakes and the like." She looked up. "Speak of the devil, here she is."

Nel jumped to her feet. "Wow. It looks like I'm going to have to up my fashion game if I'm going to work here. That suit is stunning!" She wore a knee-length denim skirt with brown loafers and a white blouse covered with a cardigan. Her hair was in a precise bun instead of a braid today.

Well, no one said you had to look like Cookie to work with us at the Honeybee. Maybe Nel would add a kind of Aunt Bee flavor to the joint. I had plenty of questions for her before it got that far, though.

"Thanks," I said, "but hardly my usual work duds. Lucy, could you reach that duffel for me?"

She extracted it from under the desk and handed it to me as Ben said, "Katie's just been to a political fundraiser."

"Um . . . ," I said.

"Well, good for you." Nel grinned. "I avoid anything to do with politics as much as possible. Keeps my shoes cleaner."

I found myself grinning in return. "Isn't that the truth. Back in a sec."

"Sure! We're having a grand time getting to know each other."

Ben and Lucy both beamed. That was a good sign, at least. They were both good judges of character.

After changing, I grabbed my orange skeleton apron and carried my suit bag into the office. I laid it over the file cabinet so I could shut the door and then managed to tie on my skeleton apron without elbowing anyone. The office was a tight fit for four people. I remained standing, since I didn't have any other choice. My feet still hadn't recovered from wearing high heels.

"Nel has lots of restaurant experience, and some very specific bakery experience, too." Lucy handed me the cake pictures she'd been looking at.

Quickly shuffling through the photos, I had to admit they were pretty impressive.

Nel nodded. "I love to cook, especially baking and developing new recipes. But I'll do anything you tell me to. I'd just like to get back into the atmosphere of a working bakery."

"How do you feel about early mornings?" I asked, thinking of Cookie's bleary arrivals at o'dark-thirty for the last four months.

"I'm up with the chickens. Always have been."

"I'm afraid we get up even before the chickens," I said.

"Oh, that's just an expression. I'm a very early riser."

"Can you tell me a bit more about your baking experience?"

She'd run a small bakery more or less single-handedly in Athens, though she'd never been to pastry school. She had, however, attended a cake-decorating academy. I had to agree with Lucy that it would be nice to be able to offer more of that specialty to our customers, and the truth was I was more interested in flavor than in creating a piece of art, and truly good decorators were fine artists. The more we talked, the more I could see why Lucy and Ben had already taken to her.

"Let us call your references, and we'll get back to you," I said once I'd asked everything I could think of. She seemed perfect, but I still had a few reservations about hiring someone with even a peripheral connection to the Dragoh Society.

"There's one more thing you should know, Katie." Lucy's smile was almost smug.

I raised my eyebrows.

"Nel is Wiccan."

"Really?"

"Yes. So she understands the kind of herbal 'help' we sometimes give our customers, and we don't have to be secretive about our other magical activities."

I looked at Nel, who nodded with a bright smile. "I've always practiced solitarily, but it's nice to be around other people with similar beliefs. I love the idea of working with other witches, in the kitchen if not elsewhere."

Did she know what her father had been? Probably— at least that he was a druid, even if she didn't know he was a member of the Dragoh Society. It would be ideal not having to sneak around. Working with Cookie had been so convenient in that regard, and Nel was far more qualified as a baker.

I opened the door. "I'd better see if Cookie's overrun."

We all trailed out through the kitchen to find her sitting at one of the bistro tables alone. A woman typed on her laptop by the bookshelf, but otherwise the place was devoid of customers.

"Where is everyone?" Nel asked.

Cookie shrugged. "Just a lull. We'll be hopping again in no time. What's the verdict?"

"Well . . . ," I said.

"We love her," Lucy said. "I knew I would when you recommended her, you clever girl."

"But—," I said.

"Good." Cookie stood and took off her apron. "Because I am on to my next big thing."

"And what would that be?" I heard my wry tone.

"I'm going to work for Xana Smythe at the gallery."

"That was fast."

She shrugged. "That's the way it goes, right?"

For her, sure.

"Xana needs an assistant. I can start tonight if I want to. And I do."

Nel took off her cardigan and picked up Cookie's apron. Tying it on, she said, "What would you like me to do first, boss?"

Lucy was grinning so hard I thought she'd hurt herself. "Isn't it marvelous how things work out? How everything happens for a reason?"

Ben raised his eyebrows, watching me.

I'd been about to protest, but Lucy's words gave me pause. My whole move to Savannah, starting the Honeybee, learning I was a witch, my new friends—all of it had come with a big dose of serendipity.

So I smiled back. "Welcome to the Honeybee, Nel."

Ben nodded his approval. "Follow me, my dear. It's time for a lesson in all things espresso."

Chapter 20

Serendipity was wonderful, and Nel's portfolio was impressive, but good business was good business. We ran a small, intimate shop, and checking her references was only practical.

Armed with a double cappuccino with extra-dry foam, I slipped into the office and shut the door. Our new employee was out front learning barista skills, and the sourdough sponge wouldn't need to be mixed for a while. Opening the file cabinet, I extracted the file of job applications. It contained only four completed forms, and one of them was Nel Sandstrom's.

According to the information on her application, she'd worked at the Halcyon Bakery in Athens, Georgia, for almost nine years before returning to Savannah. She'd listed the owner as a professional reference, which was a good sign.

I reached for my cell phone so Nel wouldn't inadvertently pick up while I was talking to her old boss, and propped my feet up on the desk. Ah . . . bliss.

A man answered with a simple "Hello?"

"Is this the Halcyon Bakery?" I asked.

"I own the Halcyon. David Talbot. You've reached my cell phone." His voice was deep, his vowels round and full. A Georgia native.

"Ah." I explained who I was and why I was calling.

"Well, we just loved working with Nel. Everyone was sorry to see her go. I'm glad to hear she's found work again in the field she enjoys so much."

"Would you say she's reliable?" I asked, thinking about Cookie.

"Oh my, yes. Showed up on time—or early—every day. Rarely called in sick. And I already miss her creative approach in the kitchen."

"Sounds like you'd happily hire her back again?"

"In a heartbeat."

I thanked him and hung up, feeling happily satisfied.

The Honeybee phone rang. I grabbed it from the cradle. "Honeybee Bakery."

"Katie?"

There was a click as someone out front picked up, too.

"I've got it," I said, and heard another click as they hung up. "Yes, this is Katie."

"Just the person I was hoping to talk to. This is Andersen Lane."

I sank into the desk chair. "Andersen. Hello."

"Have you had any luck since we spoke yesterday?"

"I wouldn't call it luck. I met Brandon Sikes, saw his horrid artwork, and now he and Cookie Rios appear to be an item. Steve says Brandon was at Heinrich's the night Dr. Eastmore was killed, so unless he's lying—which I'm pretty sure he isn't—or Heinrich and Brandon were in cahoots, that's a bust. Victor Powers was in town Friday, however."

"For his grandson's party. Right."

"How did you know that?"

"I was there. We all were."

"All the Dragohs?"

"Except Larry. And I do wish you'd stop bandying that word about."

"So you didn't see Dr. Eastmore that evening?"

"He said he would be late, but he never showed up at all."

"When did the party start?"

"About three thirty in the afternoon. Everyone got there a little early, so we could surprise the birthday boy. Then it broke up around seven thirty. Why?"

I sighed. "Detective Taite told me Dr. Eastmore was struck at his home sometime after five o'clock in the afternoon, when a neighbor saw him, and two o'clock in the morning, when he died in Johnson Square."

There was a long silence.

Oh, dear. "I'm sorry. You didn't know about that." I took a deep, bracing breath and went on. "Your friend was hit over the head at home, but managed to get to the square before he died."

"I see," he said after a moment. "Well, that complicates things, I suppose." He sounded sad and tired.

"I'm afraid that birthday party ends up being part of everyone's alibi. *You're* part of their alibi."

"Only for a few hours. The others might be lying."

They might be, sure. But why would Carolyn Powers lie about Victor staying home all night? I didn't know her, though. As a woman behind a powerful husband, why wouldn't she lie?

Hard to think the same thing about Steve.

"Andersen? I have to ask."

"What?"

"Where were you after the party?"

"I went home."

"Alone?"

"Yes."

"You didn't stop by your friend Larry's to see why he didn't come to the birthday party?"

"I'm afraid not. You'll just have to take my word."

Though I didn't particularly care for Andersen Lane, it was hard to believe he would drag me into investigating his friend's murder if he was the killer.

I changed the subject. "Any luck with a spell to counter the Necretius summoning?" Unlike *Dragoh*, I didn't like saying *Zesh* out loud.

"Unfortunately, no. I did gain access to the collection last evening, not in a terribly legal way, mind you. But I need one more book to complete the counterspell. This afternoon I spoke with Larry's son, Greer. The police have given their permission for him to stay in his father's home, but he refuses to let me in. He's being quite stubborn about it."

"Well, heck. Now what?"

He hesitated. "I was hoping you might be willing to talk to him. Use your powers of persuasion. Get him to let you see the collection, ask to borrow something. The book I need is called *The 33 Curses* by Anton Maestrada. It may be able to help us."

"I don't know," I said. "Why on earth do you think Eastmore Junior would give me something he won't give you?"

"Because he doesn't like me, and he doesn't know you. I'm not suggesting that you tell him anything—about your coven or your knowledge that his father was a member of the society. Didn't your aunt have some interaction with Larry? He lent her a book, yes?"

"Yes," I said with reluctance.

"Use that. Tell him you want to borrow the *Curses*."

I groaned. "You sure aren't afraid of asking people to do things for you."

"Please, Katie. Will you at least try?"

"Oh, fine. What's the address?"

Andersen recited it. After we hung up, I put my chin in my hands and thought. It made more sense to ask Steve to go with me, but I was feeling uncomfortable about his recent "We need to be together" speech. However, I didn't want to approach Lawrence Eastmore's son by myself. Surely if I was simply trying to borrow a book for our "book club" to read, then it wouldn't hurt anything to invite a brawny firefighter to come along. And he'd be off during the day again after tonight. Afterward I'd make him something special at the Honeybee to pay him back for the excellent picnic grub on Saturday.

I dialed from the office phone again. "Declan? What are you doing tomorrow morning?"

Mungo trotted beside me as I carried the bowl of salad next door that evening. It was almost six thirty, and the remnants of the earlier clouds created another spectacular sunset. Fireflies danced around my familiar's head like an electric halo. His affinity for them matched mine for dragonflies. Though there were fewer fireflies around in late October, they still seemed to find him in the gloaming.

"Hello?" I called through the front screen. The cheery yellow porch light shone down on us.

"Come on in!" Margie's voice beckoned from inside.

I managed to wrestle the door open without dropping the salad—or the lemon vinaigrette—and followed the surprisingly good odors issuing from the kitchen.

"Do I smell warm chocolate?" I asked as we entered. Sure enough, Margie stood over a bowl on the counter, mixing up a dark batter. A can of cola sat next to the bowl, and as I watched, she dribbled a bit out of the can into the batter.

"What on earth are you doing?" I asked.

"Hey, Katie! And you brought Mungo—great!"

"I thought the JJs might want to play." I looked around. Bart was wedged into his high chair, gnawing sloppily on Cheerios, but there was no sign of the twins. "Where are they?"

She put her hands on her hips. "I farmed them out to my sister for the night. The *whole* night. It's just you and me. And baby Bart, and Mungo, of course, but we are free of bath time and whining about teeth getting brushed and the truly spectacular inventiveness employed by a pair of four-year-olds who don't want to go to bed."

I laughed.

"And, darlin', I've got wine." She raised a glass from the counter and took a sip of pink liquid. "Sweet and good. Getcha some?"

"Sure." I set the salad on the counter and peered at the cake batter.

Wine glugged into a goblet from a jug in the refrigerator. She handed it to me and said, "As for what I'm doing, I'm making Coca-Cola cupcakes for dessert."

"Coca . . . you're kidding."

She looked genuinely surprised. "You've never heard of Coca-Cola cake? Good Lord. And you a professional baker."

"Yes, well . . ." It looked like I'd stumbled across another Southern specialty.

Now she began to dollop the batter into paper-lined muffin tins. "They're one of the only things I like to cook, or that I'm any good at, at least. The kids love 'em, so I thought I'd make up a batch to surprise them with when they get home tomorrow. And tonight we can have them all warm and yummy for dessert. They're real good." She winked. "Way better than Twinkies."

"Wow. I know how you love a Twinkie now and again."

Margie whirled around and opened the oven, removed a pie, and set it on the counter, then popped the cupcakes in to bake.

I leaned on the counter and peered at the gravy oozing out of the crust. Inhaled deeply. "Chicken potpie? My goodness. You've gone all out tonight."

She waved her hand. "Oh, honey, those cupcakes are my limit. My mother-in-law brought over three of the potpies last week, all nicely frozen so I can just pop them in the oven. She does make a nice potpie. You'll like it."

"Of course I will."

"Listen, the inside of that thing is like molten lava," Margie said. "Let's take our wine outside for a few minutes and let it set up."

She extracted Bart from his high chair, swiped his face and hands clean, and carted him out to the playpen on the back patio. Mungo trailed behind me and took up station under my chair as I sat down. My feet still hurt from sprinting in high heels that morning and then spending the afternoon showing Nel the ropes at the Honeybee.

"We hired a new employee down at the bakery today," I said.

"Another one? Y'all are going great guns down there." She settled into a lounge chair and took an appreciative sip of wine.

"Not exactly. Our other employee moved on. She found her own replacement, though, and she's very qualified."

"Is she old?"

"Margie!"

"I'm just asking because that other one was so young, and someone with a little more, shall we say, maturity, might stick around longer."

"True," I admitted. I hoped so. Never mind that Cookie was only four years younger than me.

"So what are you going to be this Halloween?"

I frowned and shrugged. "No idea. I thought about going as a witch, but changed my mind." Or had it changed for me.

She took another sip. "Nah. That's boring. You should go as something exciting. Sexy. Wonder Woman or the Green Hornet or something."

Laughing, I said, "Right. What are you dressing up as?"

"Oh, I'm too old for that."

"You're only three years older than me! And you're still coming to the Honeybee party, aren't you?"

"Of course. But I'll leave the Coopersmith costumes to Bart and the JJs."

"I can hardly wait to see them."

"Seriously, you should dress up as something fun. You could always be a zombie secretary. Or a zombie baker! Just wear what you normally wear but with zombie makeup and dirt in your hair!"

I started to protest, then paused. "You know, Margie. You've given me a great idea."

She leaned back in her chair, looking pleased.

Beside his mother, Bart dragged himself to his feet and clung to the edge of the playpen, staring at Mungo, who blinked placidly back at him. Then the baby let go, wobbled, and sat down with a *thump* on the padded surface. His mouth formed an O of surprise, and then he laughed, which set us off, too.

"Who are you taking to the party?" Margie asked, trying to sound casual.

"No one. Why?"

"Not your firefighter? Or your reporter?"

"It's a party, but I'll be working."

"They don't really like each other, do they?"

"Not so much."

"A regular soap opera triangle."

"It's complicated, Margie, and it has nothing to do with me."

She blew a raspberry, which made Bart laugh. She grinned down at him, then up at me. "Sister, you are so full of it. And I think you're on the edge of making a decision between those two."

"Why do you say that?"

"Because the yummy firefighter hasn't been over

lately, but the other one has. You look pretty intense around him, too."

"Who needs a neighborhood watch with you around?" I said.

She took it with good grace. "Heck, I have to watch something besides these kids. Let's go dive into that potpie."

The four of us went inside. I dressed the salad while Margie cut the pie into wedges. She even knew to put some on a plate for Mungo, who wiggled his behind in enthusiastic thanks when she set it on the floor in front of him. Sitting there at her kitchen table, Bart mashing pie onto his face between happy baby squeals, chatting with possibly the most normal woman in the world, I felt a slight shift in perspective. Spell work was fine, and seeing the world through the eyes of magic was wonderful, but sometimes I needed to remind myself that normal, everyday life had a magic of its own.

It was after ten by the time Mungo and I left. Margie had put Bart down to sleep and poured herself another glass of sweet pink wine, and we'd spent the next couple of hours gossiping and laughing like schoolgirls.

Before leaving I'd snagged a copy of her recipe for Coca-Cola cake—those cupcakes had turned out to be fantastically moist and yummy, not to mention that she'd frosted them with Coca-Cola frosting. Who knew?

The fireflies zeroed in on Mungo again on the return walk, circling him in a sparkling nimbus. The clouds had returned to seethe in the sky above. The temperature had dropped, too. I shivered and hastened toward the carriage house door.

Mungo yelped, and suddenly the phalanx of fireflies

seemed to explode, flying outward from where they'd gathered around my familiar's head. Several dropped to the ground.

I twisted around, searching the shadows. The air felt electric, a storm brewing on the horizon. Shaking my head at myself, I scooped up the little dog and hurried inside.

As soon as we got in the house, I checked his paws. "Did you step on something in the yard?"

He whined, but I didn't see anything wrong. When I put him down, he hightailed it into the bedroom. I followed after locking the front door behind me. It took several seconds before I discovered Mungo huddled in the corner behind the armoire. I knelt in front of him.

"Sweetie, what's wrong?"

His pink tongue snaked out and licked his black nose. His dark eyes blinked at me in the dim light of the bedside lamp.

Frowning, I stood up. Why was he acting so strangely?

I got undressed and put on my version of pajamas: a pair of soft gray yoga shorts and a white spaghetti-strap tank. As I tossed my clothes into the hamper, an arrow of pain shot behind my eyes, then vanished.

I pinched the bridge of my nose, hoping it wasn't the beginning of a migraine. I'd gone through a spate of nasty headaches right after Andrew ended our engagement. But when the pain didn't return, I went into the bathroom and washed my face. I flossed and brushed my teeth and reached for my brush to give my hair a few quick swipes.

Great. I'd brought in my Evan Picone suit from the

car, but left the duffel in which I'd packed my work clothes out in the Bug. I ran my fingers through my hair, consulted briefly with myself in the mirror, and decided it could wait.

The shooting pain hit again as I was climbing up to the loft, but disappeared just as quickly. Still, I found myself gripping the railing with white knuckles. I needed to put Dr. Eastmore's murder on the shelf and get a good night's sleep.

Upstairs, I opened the built-in cupboard and lifted a white box off the floor. Closing the cupboard, I turned off the light and took it back down to my room. Placing the box on the bed, I whipped off the top in one motion. A pile of frothy white lace spilled out over the top.

Speaking of Andrew ending our engagement . . .

"Now *that's* a costume," I said to Mungo, laying my never-worn wedding dress on the bed. "How fitting to be a zombie bride for Halloween, eh?"

But my familiar continued to hunker in the corner.

"Come on out." I reached toward him. "I need a Mungo snuggle."

He backed away, as far into the corner as he could get.

Then I realized he was shaking. "Oh, gosh. Honey, are you sick?"

He made a noise in the back of his throat that sounded like a negative. A badly frightened negative. Now I was getting scared. Glancing at the alarm clock, I saw it was late, at least for phone calls. Lucy and Ben would both be asleep by now. But I didn't know who else to call, and I needed help.

Mungo needed help.

Looking into his eyes again, I tried once more to figure out what was going on. A sense of foreboding dropped across my shoulders like a lead weight.

"I'm going to call Aunt Lucy, see if she can help. You stay here."

He made another little noise, but at least it sounded like agreement. He lay down and put his nose on his front paws, blinking up at me.

Okay, that seemed a little more normal. Quickly standing, I hurried into the living room, where my cell phone sat on the coffee table.

I reached out my hand, but the phone was so far away. My movements slowed. Everything slowed. The walls began to rotate around me. Dizziness unlike anything I'd ever experienced made me stumble. I fell to one knee, hard, on the wooden floor. Pain shot up my leg. The walls whirled. The ceiling turned. Yet I knew they weren't actually moving.

Fear stabbed through me. This was way worse than any migraine I'd had before.

"Help," I croaked. Maybe Margie was still up. Maybe she was outside and could hear me. But my windows and doors were closed and locked tightly against intruders.

But someone was here. Inside the carriage house.

No. *Inside my head.*

This was no migraine.

I shook my head, trying to clear it, but that only made things worse. My stomach twisted, and I retched. The phone was still on the coffee table. On hands and knees I inched across the floor.

Nine, one, one. That's all I needed to be able to do. Dial nine, then one, then one again.

A yellow-green mist seemed to rise around me,

punctuated with streaks of maroon. Pain arrowed behind my eyes again, and this time it didn't subside. I squeezed them shut and felt myself fall, heard my body strike wood.

There would be no help from emergency services.

Fight back, Katie. Fight back now.

It was the voice that had saved me from the falling pumpkins.

"Nonna?" I felt my mouth forming the word, but no sound came out.

Find the trigger. Push the trigger. I'll help you.

Trigger? What the . . . ?

I smelled gardenia. It was my grandmother's favorite flower, and she always wore gardenia perfume. Then I felt the mental nudge, and knew it was her. I opened to it, grasping it and holding on to its intention. I opened my eyes, concentrating around the pain so I could follow where it led.

A dog was barking somewhere.

A great darkness rose in my vision, boiling like the clouds in the night sky. I forced myself to crawl toward it. My approach, halting as it was, seemed to make the dark pause. The gardenia scent grew stronger. Something feral and lupine flashed through my consciousness, the impression of cool white eyes and fangs. It was so familiar. With a shock, something deep inside me realized it was *my* familiar, that Mungo had joined the fray.

I struggled forward, breath rasping in my throat, accompanied by gardenia and wolf. The dark grew infinitesimally smaller.

Shrinking. And emanating surprise.

Closer and closer I crawled, inch by aching inch.

With a determined gasp, I reached out and touched it. For a moment the texture of the black ran across my fingers, jagged and brittle like flakes of rusting metal.

I *pushed*.

A flash ripped across my vision.

A scream lashed the air.

And I fell to the floor again.

The scent of gardenia enveloped me. The soft touch of a warm pink tongue was the last thing I felt before I lost consciousness.

Chapter 21

I awoke to the acrid smell of burning hair and Mungo frantically licking my face. I looked up at the high ceiling of the carriage house. Turning my head to the side, I saw the peach walls and the built-in bookcase. On the floor in front of it, jagged shards of Lucy's milk glass spell bottle lay among a scattering of dried herbs.

But the room was steady as a rock.

"I'm okay, buddy. I'm okay. How about you?" Gingerly, I sat up and gathered the little dog into my arms. He radiated relief. I ran my hands all over him, looked into his eyes. He appeared completely unharmed.

Sniffing the air again, I winced at the horrible smell. With trepidation, I reached up to feel my own short locks.

Everything seemed fine.

I held on to the fainting couch, as wobbly as baby Bart had been in his playpen earlier. Except for the broken spell bottle, the room looked exactly as it had when I'd walked in from Margie's. My cell phone still sat on the Civil War trunk, right in front of me.

I clutched at my dragonfly amulet. It was still there, but something had changed. I held it away from my neck to see it better. My breath hitched in my throat.

The Dragohs' ring had fused to the back, as if it had originated from the same piece of metal. I ran my thumbnail over the ridge it formed. But the other change was what made it hard to breathe. No more did tiny etched dragonflies follow each other around the circle in perpetual chase. All the embossing was gone. Only smooth, slightly warped metal remained.

I ripped off the necklace.

After all my precautions—the amulet, the ring, the double smudging and protection spells, the rune on the mailbox post, rosemary by the front door, nasturtiums in the front yard, and potted basil in the kitchen—I had been attacked in my own home.

And not in a small way.

Hedgewitchery was a gentle magic, Lucy always said. She was right. No doubt there were layers and layers of the Craft for me to learn, and at some point in the future perhaps I could have fought off the attack by myself.

You did it yourself, something whispered. *I only guided you.*

Nonna? I called mentally.

But there was no answer.

"Nonna!" This time out loud. Mungo watched me with wise eyes.

Again no response.

"Okay, I get it," I called. "But I want to say thank you. So, you know: Thank you."

I'd have felt silly if I didn't think she could really hear me.

I eyed the phone. I could still call Lucy. In fact, *should* still call Lucy, if only to tell her what happened.

I picked up the phone and dialed Steve's number.

It was just after midnight. The witching hour. I sat on the velveteen fainting couch with my legs tucked under me, Mungo on my lap. He still seemed okay, though I kept running my hands over him, looking for missing fur, bruises, anything that hurt. He did the canine equivalent, sniffing me all over. We were both utterly unscathed, at least physically. I couldn't speak for Mungo, but I was still pretty shaky inside. And scared nearly out of my wits.

"You were very brave," I said to him. "Thank you."

He blinked and nosed my hand, then licked it. *It's what I do*, he seemed to be saying. I ruffled the fur along his back and tried to think.

Someone had breached all my protections and entered my mind. My *mind*. It was a terrifying realization. Under the tutelage of the spellbook club I'd come to think of magic as primarily beneficial, and at worst benign. It was, indeed, both of those things. It just turned out that it could be a whole lot more, too.

Maybe Mama had been right to be frightened for me, I finally admitted.

Mungo sighed, at last relaxing enough to lean against my chest.

Tires screeched on the street outside. I got up and peeked through the slats in the window shutter. The black Land Rover sat at an awkward angle in the driveway behind my Bug. For a moment I wished Steve could have been a little more subtle about his arrival, but truthfully I couldn't have cared less. As long as he'd come. He doused the headlights, jumped out, and ran toward the house.

I had the door open by the time he reached it.

His honeyed hair hung loose against the shoulders of a black T-shirt. His dark eyes, wide with worry, searched mine.

"Katie." He wrapped his arms around me, holding me tight while he kicked the door shut behind him.

I clung to him, burying my face in his shoulder. The tears I'd been holding back stung my eyelids.

"It's okay, it's okay, you're okay." He held me away from him, looking me over, stopping at my eyes and holding my gaze. "Aren't you?"

My lip trembled.

He pulled me back against him. "Oh, Katie-girl."

Swallowing convulsively, I fought back the tears still. I hadn't called Steve in order to cry on his shoulder. Despite our sometimes confusing relationship, I trusted him. And he knew the Dragohs. I was sure Lawrence Eastmore's murderer had been my attacker. There was simply no other explanation—no other motive. I needed Steve to help me figure out what had happened, and how to fight back.

Standing straighter, I dropped my hands from his shoulders and stepped away. "Thanks."

But he stepped with me, his lips seeking mine. His palms pressed into my back and the room went dark as I closed my eyes into the kiss. This was not the light, teasing way we'd flirted before, but intense and urgent. I felt the tears threaten again as my resolve—to resist, to be strong, to fight the evil that had found me—wavered. His lips moved to my earlobe, then descended in tiny kisses down my neck. He slipped his finger under the strap of my tank and tugged it aside to access my bare shoulder.

I didn't have a logical thought in my head by then, only the desire to know I was still alive, and to be alive with this man. I plunged my fingers into his long, smooth hair, savoring the crackle of energy between us.

Without warning, Steve pushed me away. A gasp escaped my throat as I stumbled. I turned and our eyes locked. "No," he croaked. "Not like this."

Confusion and desire rooted me in place for a long moment. Then I buried my face in my hands, struggling to tame the myriad emotions crowding my tired mind.

His fingers touched my arm. "I'm sorry. But you're so vulnerable right now. You don't need me pawing you."

Yes, I do!

I took a deep breath and dropped my hands. "You're right."

"You do need something to eat. So does Mungo, I expect. Come on." He tugged at my arm.

Silent, I followed him into the kitchen and sat at the table while he rattled open the refrigerator door.

"Bah," he said, dumping the limp leftover Greek salad from the Soho in the garbage. He assembled eggs and cheese, green pepper and onion on the counter, followed by bread and butter.

"Where can I find a skillet?"

I gestured wearily toward a lower cabinet. He got out a pan, set it on the burner, and plopped a pat of butter in it. As it began to melt, he left the kitchen and returned moments later with my robe. Only when he placed it around my shoulders did I realize my skin was ice cold.

"Thanks," I said.

"Why is there a wedding dress on your bed?"

I rubbed my eyes. "I was thinking of wearing it for Halloween." It seemed like I'd opened that box on my bed eons ago.

He smiled. "Eggs'll be done in a minute."

"I had a big dinner," I protested, slipping my arms into the warm sleeves.

"Just trust me."

Turning back to the stove, he browned peppers and onions, then poured in beaten eggs and covered the whole shebang with grated cheese. It wasn't complicated, but I had to admit it smelled like heaven. Soon the aroma of toasting bread drifted to my nose as well, and I found myself absolutely ravenous.

"Do you like peppers and onions?"

"Of course," I answered before realizing he was talking to Mungo.

My familiar raised his head from where it rested on my bare foot.

Yip.

He was obviously as tired as I was.

"Mungo likes peppers and onions just fine," I said. "He was a big help tonight, you know."

Steve considered the dog, then gave him a slow nod of approval. "I'm glad to hear it." He took the skillet off the burner and set it under the broiler to melt the cheese and finish cooking the frittata. Looking over his shoulder, he said, "You didn't say much on the phone—I could only tell how frightened you were. That's not something I've witnessed before, so it must have been pretty bad."

My shoulders hunched as I remembered. "It was . . . I don't know how to describe it. It was something, in here—the house, I mean—and in *here*." I pointed to my head.

His eyes flared in alarm. "What did it feel like?"

I described it, or tried to: the inky blackness, the feel of decaying metal. "It's hard to define, but it wanted to hurt me."

Steve took the pan out of the oven. He sliced a hefty wedge of the frittata and put it on a plate. I saw his hand shaking as he set it in front of me. A smaller wedge went into a bowl for my little wolf.

I dug in and seconds later so did Mungo.

Sliding into the seat across from me, Steve asked, "Who did this to you?"

A shrug. "I don't have the vaguest idea."

"Well, they'd need something of yours—or you—in order to cast this kind of spell."

"Like what?" I asked around a mouthful of frittata. "Can I have some juice?"

He got up and went to the fridge. "Like hair or fingernails."

I stopped chewing and stared at him. Swallowed. "Really?"

"I can't think of any other way they could get directly to you like this. But we need to know who it was."

Okay, that was kind of gross, and furthermore I couldn't think of anyone who had access to my personal . . . pieces.

"Maybe that explains that horrible smell," I sniffed the air.

Yip!

"What smell?" Steve asked.

My lips parted in surprise. "You can't smell it? It's like burning hair. In fact, I was so sure it was burning hair I thought either Mungo or I must be half bald."

"Damn. That's not good. And no, I can't smell it. But that's probably what he used. We need to bind the caster, so they can't touch you like that again."

"I'd prefer they didn't touch me at all again, thank you very much."

"Me, too, Katie-girl. But we can't bind someone unless we know who it is."

"It's whoever killed Lawrence Eastmore."

"You're sure?"

"Who else would it be? Or do you think your Dragohs were just *protecting* themselves from being exposed?"

"They aren't my Dragohs."

"Yes, they are."

He sighed.

"Though the killer might still be one of them—alibis or no alibis. In fact, I can't think who else it could be. Unless . . ."

"Unless what?"

"Well, Andersen Lane doesn't have an alibi for the hours after the party broke up. There's also Lawrence Eastmore's son. Greer. I was planning to talk to him tomorrow."

Steve grimaced. "Yeah, I heard he came back to town. You know, he had even less interest in taking on the Dragoh mantle than I do."

"Is there an inheritance involved that's perhaps a bit more secular?" I asked. "A bit more financial?"

"Well, sure. None of the Dragohs are exactly desti-tute, though Andersen is certainly the worst about managing his gains. But Greer would have inherited the money regardless."

I remembered what Andersen had said about how persuasive the druids could be when it came to forcing the next in line to join their group. "Are you sure?" I took another bite.

One shoulder rose and fell. "Not positive. I could find out, though."

"From Heinrich?" I used his first name because in my mind he was still as much of a suspect as any of the other Dragohs, and I hated thinking that he was also this man's father. "Steve, when did you get home last Friday night?"

"Pretty early. Eightish."

"After Victor Powers' grandson's party," I said, thinking out loud.

Declan had always told me Steve was a player, a heart-slayer. And now he was going to kiddie parties and then staying home on a Friday night?

He pursed his lips. "Father mentioned he saw you at the fund-raiser this morning. He wasn't very happy about it."

My chin jerked up. "Do you think he's the one who came after me tonight?"

He shook his head vigorously. "My father may be a lot of things, and some of them I don't like, but he would never attack anyone like that. Never."

"Okay." I didn't have it in me to argue.

"Do you want more frittata?"

"No thanks." Forming words seemed to take all the energy I had.

"Come on, then." He put one arm around my shoulder and another under my elbow, helping me to my feet.

"What are you doing?"

"Putting you to bed."

Fear shot through me, and I shook him off. "No! I can't go to sleep. What if it happens again?"

Chapter 22

Steve's voice was calm. "Whoever did this is recovering, too. Working such magic takes great energy, and I can't imagine they'll be up to the same shenanigans for a while."

It usually exhausted me to work magic, too, but in a really good way, like a long run through the woods blew the cobwebs out of my mind. It was a lovely feeling, but the defense I'd put up earlier had been something else. I felt utterly sapped.

"You know, I had protections all over this place," I said. "Plus my amulet."

"You're not wearing it now."

"It changed."

"Changed?"

"Um. Yeah."

Curious, he asked, "Where is it?"

"Someplace on the living room floor. I tore it off and threw it away from me when I saw what had happened to it."

His eyebrows rose when he heard that.

Even breathing seemed to take effort. I reached

down and picked up Mungo. "Poor little guy looks about ready to drop."

"Here. I'll take him."

Mungo didn't seem to mind riding in Steve's arms, and I was tired enough to allow him to carry my familiar into the bedroom and put him on the bed. I started to collapse beside him, but Steve stopped me, took off my robe, and then pulled back the covers. I snuggled underneath, and he tucked me in.

"Thanks," I mumbled, oddly grateful to be taken care of even though it made me feel like a weakling at the same time.

"Go to sleep."

The last thing I remembered was Mungo burrowing in next to me and beginning to snore softly.

I awoke to daylight streaming in through my bedroom window and the sound of male voices in my living room. It was so strange for me to wake up after dawn that for a long moment I simply stared at the sunshine splashing across the quilt. Then I looked over at the bedside clock. It was after nine o'clock.

I sat straight up and rubbed my eyes.

The events of the night before came flooding back. In the light of day I could hardly believe it had happened at all. I searched for Mungo, but he wasn't in the bedroom.

Holy cow, was I ever late for work. Lucy must be frantic with worry.

"This isn't about you," I heard Steve say from the living room. "This is about Katie."

"Like you know what's good for her. Like you *care* what's good for her."

I recognized Declan's voice, and my stomach sank.

Throwing off the covers, I leaped out of bed and ran into the living room. Mungo sat on the purple velvet couch watching the two men face off. Steve stood with his hand on one of the wingback chairs. His hair, so wild the night before, was smoothed into its usual sleek ponytail, but he wore the same clothes. Declan stood next to the other wingback, five feet away. His blue T-shirt read, FIRST IN, LAST OUT, and his jeans were faded and worn. His jaw slackened when he saw me.

"Katie? Are you okay?"

I nodded. "I'm fine."

His mouth clamped shut and his eyes turned hard. "I went to the Honeybee to pick you up, and Lucy told me you were *sick*. So I came by to see if there was anything I could do." His hand struck the back of the chair, and I flinched. "Obviously you don't need my help— not with that little favor you asked me for, and not with anything else, either." He turned to glare at Steve. "You've been here all night." It wasn't a question. His attention transferred to me, and his eyes swept me up and down. "And obviously you're feeling anything but under the weather."

I became aware of what I was wearing and looked down at my tank and knit shorts. Great. Crossing my arms over my chest, I said, "Deck—"

He held up his hand. "I don't want to hear it. You've made your choice."

"No, wait. You don't understand. And I do need your help."

Incredulity infused his features. "You've got to be kidding me."

"What favor?" Steve asked me, his gaze running over my body.

"I wanted him to go with me to see Greer Eastmore."

"You don't need him for that," Steve said. "I'll go with you."

"It's none of your business, Dawes," Declan said.

"It's more my business than yours," Steve countered.

"Katie and I found that man in the square, not you."

"There's more going on than you know, McCarthy, more than you're equipped to deal with."

The muscles along Declan's jawline flexed dangerously.

"Will you two stop it?" I said.

Declan turned to face me. "Yes. I will. You're on your own. Good luck with this guy, Katie. I'm done playing your game." And he strode out the door. It slammed behind him. I heard his pickup start up out front and the squeal of tires as he accelerated away.

A low whine issued from the back of Mungo's throat.

Margie would be asking all sorts of questions about the screeching comings and goings in the last twelve hours. With a sigh, I pushed the thought out of my mind. Enough time to think about that later.

"You stayed here all night?" I asked Steve.

"Did you really think I'd leave you alone?"

"I was too tired to think anything," I said with a grimace. "But thank you."

"Sure got you in trouble with your firefighter."

"He's not—" I started to protest, then saw him grinning. "Stop it."

Steve shrugged and changed the subject. "I called

Lucy around five this morning—luckily she was up and heading out the door to the bakery already—and told her you weren't feeling well. She said she'd call your new employee in to cover for you."

My shoulders relaxed a fraction, then tensed again. "You didn't tell her about last night?"

"No. I thought that should be your decision."

"And she knew you were here."

"Yes." Amused.

Great. More explanations. Though knowing Lucy, she would applaud any forward momentum in my love life.

"Katie, go shower and put on some clothes, will you? You're driving me crazy in that getup. I'll throw together something to eat, and we can discuss Greer Eastmore."

Despite the after-midnight nosh, Mungo and I both wolfed down the breakfast Steve had set out on the back patio: bowls of my homemade granola topped with yogurt and fresh strawberries from the garden. A couple cups of strong, steaming coffee didn't hurt, either. As we ate, Steve played with my amulet, running it over and through his fingers like a Las Vegas showman.

"I've never seen anything like this."

"I don't want it anymore," I said.

He paused in his machinations, considering, then nodded. He reached back and unwrapped the leather braid from his ponytail. His hair swung forward, obscuring his face as he worked something out of the plait. It flashed in a wayward ray of sunlight that had found its way under the patio roof. When he held it up, I saw a thin silver wire circle.

It was one of the Dragoh rings.

"Steve, no."

"Hush." He removed the ruined amulet Lucy had given me, and slipped the thin ring onto the chain instead. Then he stood and fastened it around my neck. His fingers ran lightly across my jawline, just once, and he sat down again.

The thin metal felt cool against my warm skin. I watched him tie his hair back once more.

"This is your protection, isn't it? But aren't these to repel Dragoh magic?"

"It's supposed to fend off all potentially harmful magic, actually. Father gave one to me and one to Arnie when we were children."

"You can't give this to me," I protested again.

"I just did. Besides, I don't know how much good these really do, you know? The one Andersen gave you didn't help much last night."

"We don't know that," I said. "It might have been part of what saved me."

"Well, Arnie's sure didn't do him much good."

I knew by now it wouldn't do any good to point out that his brother had perished as a result of bad judgment, not magic. So all I said was, "Thank you."

Half an hour later my big, powerful wolf from the night before was sitting in my tote bag as Steve drove us to the Honeybee. I'd insisted that we stop by and put Lucy's and Ben's worries to rest. Besides, Nel was still brand-new, and it seemed like a lot to ask her to cover for me on her very first full day as an employee. Even though Steve suggested I check in via telephone, I knew I wouldn't feel right until I'd stopped by and made sure everything was okay. Besides, it was only blocks from the Eastmore home.

After breakfast, I'd showered, and now I wore sedate khaki capris, a short-sleeved camp shirt, and flip-flops—unsexy and mundane. Still, I kept catching Steve's eyes cutting to where I sat in the passenger seat, looking at me in a way that reminded me of how Mungo looked at steak sizzling on the hibachi.

I remembered the break in my resolve the night before, how I'd clung to him. The feel of his hands on my back, his lips on my neck . . .

"Whatcha thinking about?" he asked.

I realized I'd been staring straight at him without speaking for over a minute. A deep blush crept up my neck and flared in my cheeks. "Nothing. So what do you know about Greer Eastmore?"

He shrugged. "Not much since I was a boy. He's in his late forties, and he left to live in Europe when I was about fourteen. So he would have been in his twenties still. I remember him as a pretty cool guy, actually. He'd toss a ball around with me—something my father never had the time or inclination to do. Greer took me hiking right before he left, on the Tupelo Trail in the wildlife refuge. We made a fire and cooked our lunch over it. Fried baloney on a stick." His laugh held bitterness. "Can you believe that? But wow, did I feel like a real Boy Scout."

I thought of fourteen-year-old Steve, poor little rich boy, thrilled with the experience of eating baloney toasted over a fire in the woods.

"Then he went away," he continued. "And he ended all contact with his father for decades. I missed him, but it broke Lawrence's heart."

"That's what Andersen said." The fear I'd been successfully keeping at bay suddenly swooped through me. "Do you think Greer attacked me?"

"I don't know." He sounded almost angry.

"Does he practice magic at all? Or did he turn his back on it altogether when he broke off contact with his father?"

He lifted one shoulder and let it drop.

"We really don't know anything about him. Maybe he needed money." I was thinking out loud. "He obviously wasn't close to his father. What if the murder didn't have anything to do with the Dragohs or the Spell of Necretius? Maybe he killed his father out of old-fashioned family greed."

"Then why is the spell for summoning Zesh gone?" Steve asked.

My throat tightened at the name. "Right. I don't know. Maybe someone else took it? What does Greer do, anyway? Is he obsessed with worldly success?"

"Not unless he's changed a lot. He used to be kind of a Bohemian, actually. The family money was part of the problem between him and his father."

"Heck." I thought for a moment. "Who knows? Perhaps Eastmore Junior will turn out to be another ally in this investigation. At least be able to shed some light on what happened. Seems like we could use all the help we can get, you know. Tomorrow is Samhain."

"Just be careful when you're talking to him."

I put up a hand. "I'm not going to spill the beans. Andersen suggested I ask to borrow another book from Dr. Eastmore's collection for our book club."

Steve rolled his eyes. "Right."

"No, really. He wants me to get a copy of *The 33*

Curses for the counterspell he's working on in case the killer tries to summon this Zesh character." But something had been bothering me ever since I'd talked to Andersen the day before. I waited, allowing the thought to gel. "Steve, do you think . . . Could Andersen have asked me to help him in order to divert attention from himself? He's the only druid who doesn't have an alibi. He told me he got into Dr. Eastmore's collection and took a couple of books to help with the counterspell, but what if he didn't? What if he wants me to get this other book because he can't get in? I mean, something called *The 33 Curses* doesn't exactly sound like it's full of nice fluffy magic."

Steve's expression was grim as he pulled to the curb a few doors down from the Honeybee.

"But we have to do *something*," I said. "If whoever came after me last night has the additional power of this Zesh character behind them, things are going to get really bad really fast."

Chapter 23

I slowed as we approached the entrance. "You might not want to mention going to see Greer in front of our new employee," I said.

Steve looked at me in surprise. "Okay."

"Not that you would anyway, but I rather suspect she knows him. She sure knew you, 'Stevie.'"

He stopped. "You're kidding. Nel?"

I nodded. "Cookie roped her in after we left the gallery the other night. As her replacement. She'd already filled out an application, and it turns out the early-morning hours of a bakery are a bit much for Ms. Rios."

He snorted. "That doesn't surprise me."

"It also turns out your old friend has plenty of experience working in a bakery, a portfolio of cake decorating, and her arrival dovetailed perfectly with Cookie's plans. Andersen said she didn't know anything about her father's druidic activities, but she told Lucy that she's a practicing Wiccan. Lucy was so relieved that the spellbook club wouldn't have to sneak around and that we could continue to practice our hedgewitchery at the bakery."

He shook his finger slowly in my face. "I knew you hexed your baked goods." His voice was triumphant.

"We don't hex! We . . . help."

"Whatever. Still, I'm glad it worked out with Nel. Like Greer, she's quite a bit older than us, but she was awfully nice to Arnie and me and the other kids."

"So you all socialized?" I said, opening the door. The bell tinkled over our heads.

"All our families have been friends for a long time. Oh. My. God."

As I followed him inside I saw what he meant. Our adorable, homemade, kitschy Halloween decorations still festooned the bakery, but there were a few additions.

"Katie! You're okay! Thank goodness!" Nel bustled toward us. Her skirt was cotton today, bright orange and covered with black cats. She wore a tall black witch hat with the top bent over, and a pair of false buckteeth jutted over her lower lip. Boots with long, curled toes adorned her feet, and she wore striped stockings like something out of *The Wizard of Oz*.

So much for perpetuating the witchy stereotype. Still, she looked both dorky and adorable, and it was hard not to laugh. She looked tired, though, and I felt bad for making her come in early after she'd worked until closing time the evening before.

Ben waved at me from the register. "Glad you're feeling better, Katie! How do you like what we've done? Nel had all sorts of suggestions."

"And supplies," she said in a low tone. "I must say, Halloween is my favorite holiday—you can guess why, of course—and my dear father had lots of decorations stowed away in a back closet. I'm so glad to have a chance to bring them out and dust them off."

A booming *hwa-ha ha* right by my ear made me jump. I turned to find a full-sized skeleton leering down at me, its eyes flashing green. Apparently it had some kind of movement sensor that prompted it to sound off.

"Sorry! Let's just turn this guy off until the party tomorrow night, okay? The kids will love him."

I nodded. "That's a bit too realistic, though!" I pointed to the big hairy spider, a foot in diameter, which now hugged the wall by the bookshelf. A wide smile split Ben's face. Maybe Croft had been right: Men like Halloween to be a little spookier.

A scarecrow in prison stripes crowded next to my uncle behind the register, but he didn't seem to mind. A withered hand lay across the jars of biscotti on top of the display case.

"It certainly does look . . . festive," I said.

Lucy came out of the kitchen then. Her forehead cleared when she saw me. "I thought I heard your voice. How are you feeling?"

"Better."

"Really?"

I nodded. "Still have that little errand I mentioned to you yesterday. Steve's going with me. Then I'll come back."

If I'd expected her to so much as give me a suggestive look at the mention of Steve, I'd been wrong. My aunt obviously wasn't worried about my love life right now. But she was still worried about me.

Nel hovered nearby.

"I'll tell you about everything later, okay?"

Lucy inclined her head. "I'll look forward to that. See you in a few hours, then?"

"If not before."

Outside, I asked Steve, "You sure you didn't tell her anything about the attack?"

"Nope. But she's an intuitive lady, and she loves you very much. She knows something went on. And I don't mean between us."

I let that drop, still unwilling to talk about what had happened between us.

Or almost happened.

Lawrence Eastmore's house was relatively small, but obviously old. Gray bricks made more than a century earlier from the unique mud on the Hermitage Plantation accented the windows. Those bricks were associated very specifically with the area but had become quite rare and expensive. Iron filigree swooped through the railing that enclosed the small second-story balcony overlooking the street. The top of the railing boasted wickedly sharp spikes. Elaborate gargoyles with large ears and leering expressions peered down from the corner downspouts, and the front door had been painted deep red.

It was the kind of architecture you'd find all over Savannah—and elsewhere in the South, save for the unique gray brick—but I could see how it might strike Detective Franklin Taite, self-appointed hunter of witches and their ilk, as sinister.

In fact, standing in front of the place and knowing that its owner had been murdered made *me* think it looked a little sinister. Too bad, though, because if Greer Eastmore had been the one who'd invaded my head the night before, I had a bone to pick with him.

"Stay in the car?" I asked Mungo, rolling the window down all the way.

He blinked his acquiescence.

With Steve on my heels, I marched up and whacked the big lion paw knocker against the brass plate. I shifted my weight from one foot to the other as we waited. After about a minute, Steve reached around me and tried the knocker again, this time with a little testosterone behind it.

Nothing.

Scanning the area revealed no doorbell. It was the knocker or nothing.

"He's not here," Steve said. "Let's go."

But now that we were here, on Lawrence Eastmore's actual property, I didn't want to go. Not just yet. A cool breeze brushed my cheek, caressing it with elemental fingers. It made me think of the spirit who had recently inhabited the physical shell Declan and I had found Saturday morning.

Only one day until Samhain. The day when the veil between the dead and the living was the thinnest. I wondered how far away Lawrence Eastmore's spirit really was at that moment. I managed to stop myself before actually looking around to see if it was nearby.

Because that was just silly. Right?

"Let's go around to the back, see if maybe Greer is there." I pulled at Steve's arm.

He pulled back. "I don't think that's a good idea."

"Why? He wouldn't be able to hear the knocker from back there."

"Didn't you tell me that Larry was struck in back of his house?"

"In the potting shed, Taite said."

"You're curious, aren't you? You want to see where. Katie, that's pretty macabre."

"No, that's not it at all. You really think I want to look at a murder scene? That's so icky." I tipped my head to one side. "It'll be cleaned up by now, don't you think? Come on."

"I hope so, for your sake," Steve muttered as he followed me around the corner of the house.

Dr. Eastmore's backyard was anything but spacious. The eight-by-eight potting shed took up most of the far left corner of the garden. A tin roof covered the structure, which had slatted walls open to the rest of the yard. Wisteria had twined muscular branches through the slats, creating a charming organic enclosure. The yellow police tape draped around it looked almost festive.

A tall, spiky hedge accented the back fence and created even more of a barrier between the yard and the alleyway that ran behind. One of the trees teetered in a five-gallon pot near the gap in the hedge where it was obviously meant to go. I went over and found a large hole in the ground.

Lawrence Eastmore had been wearing old gardening clothes, and my bet was that the dirt Declan and I had seen on them was from digging this very hole.

I took another look at the plant. Shiny, waxy leaves ended in spiked scallops. It wasn't the typical Christmas holly, but it was holly nonetheless.

I felt rather than heard Steve at my side. "Savannah holly," I said, without looking at him. Like Lawrence Eastmore's tattoo. "Do you have one?"

"A holly tree?"

"No. A holly tattoo."

He was silent. Then, "No. Not yet."

Good.

"There are six of these trees," I said, looking around. "Is that significant?"

"Probably."

The rest of the yard was nicely landscaped, but not in any particularly creative way. There were few flowers, only a few of the herbs used in all sorts of spell work—lavender, sage, rosemary, rue—and no vegetables at all. Eastmore had not been a hedgewitch; he'd been a druid. There was no real reason for him to have a potting shed if he wasn't much of a gardener.

But the birdbath was also a sundial—and, upon further inspection, a moondial. The space we stood in had a magical feel to it. I approached the potting shed, and the feeling grew stronger.

My footsteps quickened.

"Wait." Steve strode ahead of me and stopped, blocking the entrance. "There's nothing here," he said. "Nothing to see."

"Then there's no harm in my looking."

"Katie."

Gently, I elbowed him aside.

"Fine," he said. "Don't believe me." He stalked back toward the house.

I put his crankiness down to nerves. Heck, I felt pretty jittery, too. But Samhain was only a day away, and the idea that someone might summon that awful spirit or entity or whatever it was gave me the creeps more than ever. Before, Lawrence Eastmore's death had been disturbingly real, and I'd felt a compelling need to see his killer brought to justice after finding his body in Johnson Square. It had been the psychic attack, how-

ever, that made me truly realize the magical consequences should we fail to find Dr. Eastmore's murderer.

A feeling like tiny mouse claws ran across my neck.

The police barrier banned actual entrance, but it
looked like Steve was right about the innocuous potting
shed. Inside, a waist-high bench ran along the back wall.
An assortment of garden tools was tucked into a vivid
green pot, and larger tools hung on the wall. Then I noticed that not all of the tools were those a typical gardener would possess. The wicked blades of two scythes
curved next to a hoe. A bundle of peacock feathers sprouted
from another pot in a festive bouquet. Pot, or cauldron?
A long staff, taller than a typical walking stick, was
propped in a shadowy corner. Pressing slightly against
the yellow tape, I leaned in to take a closer look. The
gnarled surface was carved with runes and symbols I
didn't recognize at all. A long strip of leather studded
with glass beads wound around the top.

This was more than a potting shed. It was Lawrence
Eastmore's equivalent of my gazebo: a sacred circle for
spell casting, ritual, and ceremony, outside, like the
druids of old would have done.

No doubt this shed would have put a hunter of
magic like Detective Taite on high alert. He'd said Dr.
Eastmore had been struck with a large pot. Not a scythe?
Maybe the killer hadn't seen them. Or maybe the pot
came easier to hand. Not very well thought out, then. I
looked at the ground, but there was no trace of the murder weapon. The police would have taken it away, of
course. But before I turned away I spied a semicircle of
smooth stones embedded in the walls. My bet was that
there had been more that formed a full circle. The police
must have taken some of those, too.

The air inside the potting shed felt tainted, dark shreds of violence hanging invisible in the atmosphere. The place needed some serious cleansing, and I didn't mean the soap-and-water kind.

Tentatively, I reached out with my mind, as if dipping my toe into unknown waters, to see if I could recognize the flavor of the evil that remained within the wisteria-covered walls. I got a brief impression of cold, something beyond mere ice. I flinched away, then steeled myself to try again.

"Greer? Hello?"

I looked over my shoulder to see Steve leaning inside the back door of the house. "What are you doing?" I hissed.

He turned his face toward me, but his eyes were still trained inside the house. "Tried the door. It's unlocked. Don't you think he'd lock it if he went out?"

"How would I know?" I looked back into the potting shed. It would make sense to lock the door if his father's collection remained inside the house—unless Greer was really home. Had he ignored our knocking? Did he know who I was? My resolve shattered, and I whirled around. "We should go."

But Steve was gone.

The door gaped open. From my vantage I could see the corner of some white wainscoting, a rug inside the entry, and a pair of rubber boots. With reluctant steps, I walked across the grass until I reached the small cement step.

"Steve?"

Another step took me close enough to touch the doorframe.

"Greer?"

The smell of burning hair curled through the air, making my eyes water.

"Steve!" I yelled.

Pushing the door open all the way, I ran inside, hands out in front of me as my pupils struggled to adjust to the dark interior. Frantic, I passed through the small mudroom and ran down a hallway. My pounding footsteps echoed against the wooden planks. On the right, a cheerful modern kitchen beckoned, but when I paused and stuck my head in, no one was there. A dark wooden door on the left opened when I twisted the knob, revealing a richly furnished den.

Also empty.

Continuing down the hallway brought me to a bathroom appointed in brass and marble. A part of my brain noticed, of all things, a bidet. Opposite, a stairway rose to the second floor. It was narrower than most. Old. Beyond, a large living room sprawled, facing the street outside. I got the impression of thick Oriental rugs, gilded frames, and the aged patina of bulky antique furniture, but when it was obvious that no one was in the room, I turned back.

The acrid smell increased at the bottom of the stairs.

Muttering to the archangels under my breath, and throwing in a plea to my Nonna as well, I started up to the next level.

Chapter 24

"Stay down there," Steve called when I was halfway up the stairs. He appeared at the top.

"You're okay?" The words squeaked out of my tight throat.

"I'm fine."

I sank to the step, my usually strong running muscles suddenly turning to jelly. "Thank goodness."

"Yeah, well, I think we'd better call the police."

"Why?" I pulled myself up by the banister, glad to see that my legs could hold my weight after all, and started up the stairs again.

"Just turn around and go back downstairs. I'll be there in a minute."

I stopped, hands on hips, and looked up at him with eyes still burning from that horrible smell.

The creases in his forehead deepened. "Why are you crying?"

"I'm not crying. Can't you smell that?" But I could tell he was oblivious.

"What?"

I sighed. "Burning hair."

Slowly, he shook his head. He hadn't been able to smell it the night before, either. My stomach roiled at the thought that whatever—whoever—had attacked me had been in this house.

Or was still in this house.

Sudden anger swept through me. So Greer Eastmore had killed his father and come after me. The thought made my scalp positively tingle with fury.

I went up a few more steps until I reached the one right below where Steve stood. "Is Greer here now?" I whispered. He might not have answered the door when he saw who it was. Or he could be sleeping off the aftereffects of last night's hostilities.

He reached out and brushed a strand of hair from my face. "I don't think you have to worry about Greer anymore."

My apprehension deepened. I gripped the railing. "Why not?"

"I'm sorry, Katie. He's dead."

I felt my eyes go wide. *"Dead?"* Slowly, I sat down on the top step. After a few moments, Steve sat beside me and put his arm around my shoulders.

"Is it bad?" I asked.

"I didn't see any signs of violence, if that's what you mean. Maybe he had a heart attack or an aneurysm." Steve bent forward to see my face. "But it wasn't a heart attack, was it?"

I bit my lip. "How would I know?" But I was afraid I did. I leaned back so that I could see more of the upstairs hallway. More wooden floor, another intricately woven rug, and a burled-walnut sideboard topped with a tall mirror at one end. Five doors opened off the space. One was a bathroom, one revealed bookcases, and I could see enough of two more to know that they were bedrooms.

He took his cell phone out of his pocket. I put my hand on his arm, and he paused, eyes searching my face. "Katie?"

"You really can't smell that stink?"

"Uh-uh."

I swallowed convulsively, not wanting to say the words but knowing I had to. "Do you . . . do you think I killed him?"

His head jerked back. "What?"

"When he . . . when I, you know, fought back last night?"

"No. No, of course not. No."

He thinks I did it.

"I want to see him before you call the cops."

He rolled his eyes and shook his head.

I stood and stepped onto the upstairs landing. "Where is he?"

"Katie, wait!" By the time Steve got to his feet, I was moving down the hallway.

I glanced in the bathroom, saw nothing unusual, and kept going. I stopped in the doorway of the first bedroom. A huge sleigh bed dominated the room, which reeked of masculine presence in everything from the scent of citrusy cologne to the boldly striped curtains on the window overlooking the backyard to the solid reading chair and clean lines of the lamp beside it. A navy blue bathrobe lay across one corner of the fully made bed.

Citrusy cologne. The burning smell was fading if I could smell that. I inhaled with relief, feeling like I could take a full breath again.

"This was Lawrence's room," I said to Steve, who

now stood watching me. He had an odd expression on his face, something like irritation mixed with admiration. But I didn't have time to pick it apart, or respond to it. I turned my back on Eastmore Senior's digs and marched to the bedroom opposite.

Suddenly Steve was by my side, his hand closing on my arm. I curled my fingers over his. "I have to see," I said, pushing the door open all the way with my toe.

Unlike his father, Greer Eastmore was pale and wore his dark hair cut quite short. His full lips and hooked nose reminded me of the body in the square, though, and I winced. I couldn't tell what color his eyes were, because they were squeezed shut. He lay on top of the wrinkled sheets, wearing green-and-white-striped pajamas. There was no blood, no bruising on his visible skin, and the room was tidy as could be.

"Are you sure he's dead?" I breathed, grabbing the doorframe for support.

Steve put his hand on my shoulder. "I'm sure."

I turned away, then forced myself to look again. "He looks like he was asleep when he died."

"Probably," Steve said.

"He wouldn't have cast a spell from there," I said. "But he might have gone right to bed after casting it." I ran my hand over my face. "Could my backlash really have done this?"

"You can't know that was Greer last night."

"But that smell—"

"Which was all over your carriage house, right?"

I nodded. "Oh. Oh, dear." I rubbed at my face with both palms. "Of course. Whoever came after me could have killed Greer."

Killed. Last night had been an attempt on my *life*.

"Which means just because this poor guy is dead, this business with the Spell of Necretius and finding his father's killer may not be over after all," I said. A wave of weariness washed all my anger and fear away. I just wanted to go home and take a very long nap.

Steve shrugged. "It's possible. So are a lot of other things, most of which involve Greer dying of natural causes. It happens. Katie, you can't blame yourself. Even if he *is* dead because of some kind of magical backlash, that's not your fault."

He didn't use the term *self-defense*, but I could tell he was thinking it.

That sure didn't make me feel any better. I sighed. "Okay. Let's call the police. But there's probably something you should know about Detective Quinn's new partner."

Steve made the call from the hallway. When his back was turned, I tiptoed into Greer's bedroom again. If the younger Eastmore had been the one in my head the night before, then we were home free. But if he was a victim, as I'd been . . . then why?

Keeping my back to the silent form on the bed and muttering, *Sorry, sorry, sorry*, I sidled across the room to the closet. I grabbed a tissue off the dresser and used it to open the door. It looked like he'd already unpacked. Clothes were hung in a neat row, each hanger spaced two inches from the one next to it. I counted two pairs of slacks, two of jeans, two silk T-shirts and three cotton ones, three collared shirts, a sports coat, and a charcoal gray suit. The dress shoes on the floor looked new and matched the suit. With a start, I realized he'd been planning to wear them to his father's funeral.

"Oh," I said out loud, and closed my eyes. I didn't have the heart to go further. Despite my original intentions, someone else would have to go through the pockets.

Sorry.

On the other side of the closet from the dresser, a matching chair and ottoman backed into the corner. A floor lamp like the one in Dr. Eastmore's room loomed above the chair. A biography of the writer Conrad Aiken lay in the center of the ottoman. Between the chair and the bed was a small writing desk—yet another antique. A laptop sat open on the surface.

Turning my back on the bed, I moved sideways to the computer and pressed ENTER with a tissue-covered forefinger. The screen sprang to life. Program icons were scattered across a photo of the Parthenon, but I didn't see any files. Greer Eastmore had been a very tidy guy. Freakishly so.

"What are you *doing*?" Steve asked from the doorway.

"Just a quick look, that's all," I said.

"Come on," he urged.

I retraced my steps toward Steve waiting in the doorway. But I stopped when I saw the cell phone on the dresser top. Ignoring my companion's frantic gestures, I carefully picked it up and scrolled through to the recent calls.

One number caught my eye.

My cell number.

I stared at it, unable to process what it meant.

"Katie. What are you doing?"

"Nothing."

"Put that down! Let's go."

I placed the phone back where I'd found it and

shouldered past him to the hallway, thoroughly shaken. Taking a deep breath, I tried to focus. Before leaving I had to check out the room with the bookcases. It was still possible to get the *The 33 Curses* for Andersen Lane. I could decide later whether to actually give it to him or not. Sure enough, when I pushed the door open I discovered a small library. I noted the lovely musty scent of yellowing paper and old ink—the burning smell was definitely fading. I moved quickly down the shelves, scanning titles.

As I expected, the volumes were primarily related to the occult. However, none looked all that old, and the book Andersen wanted me to borrow from Greer was not in the section that seemed devoted to spellbooks. Then I saw the metal door at the far end of the room, so out of place in that atmosphere of leather, wood, and money. It appeared sturdy enough to withstand a bomb and no doubt housed the climate-controlled atmosphere that Andersen had mentioned—the one that Lawrence Eastmore employed to preserve books like the Spell of Necretius for future generations of Dragohs.

The 33 Curses would be in there.

My thoughts whirled as Steve grabbed my arm and pulled me out into the hallway. With a murmured "Come on, Katie-girl," he hurried me down the stairs to greet the authorities. My stomach felt like someone had run an old-fashioned eggbeater in it. Why was my number in Greer Eastmore's recent-call list? Had it been a dialed call or a received call? I wasn't familiar enough with his model of phone to know, and I berated myself for not looking closer. But either way, I hadn't received any calls from strangers lately, and I sure hadn't called Greer Eastmore.

I should have deleted the number. My gut did another twist. No, that wouldn't have worked. The police would still have Greer's phone records.

Nonetheless, there was still a part of me that wished I'd hit that DELETE button.

Detective Taite boiled out of the passenger side of the unmarked Caprice before it had even stopped moving. He strode to where we stood waiting on the front step while his partner exited the vehicle, closed the door, and paused on the sidewalk across the street to take in the whole scene. An ambulance and two Savannah patrol cars had arrived moments earlier, and we'd told them where to find Greer Eastmore inside.

"Katie Lightfoot. Imagine seeing you here." New York–accented sarcasm oozed from all six words, and he looked at me like he wanted to suck every secret out of my soul.

"Detective Taite," I said. "This is Steve Dawes."

Quinn caught up to his partner. He nodded at Steve, taking in his face, his clothes, his stance, and who-knew-what-else in one sweeping glance. His eyes settled back on me. "This is getting to be a really bad habit with you."

I held up my hands in a warding gesture. "I know, I know. Twice in one week. But it's not my fault," I lied. Sort of. We'd come up with a story that bordered on the truth, so I plunged on. "Steve knew Greer Eastmore when he was a boy. When Steve was a boy, not Greer. Anyway, when Steve heard he'd come back to town after his father's death, he decided to stop by and pay his respects."

"Which explains nothing about why you're here," Quinn said with a hard look.

I shrugged. "He asked if I wanted to come along, and I said sure. Moral support, you know?"

"Right." Taite's nostrils flared.

"I did find his father, you know. I thought maybe he'd have questions."

"If he had questions he needed to ask us, not you," Quinn said.

Two more patrol cars arrived, and two of the officers herded the gathering crowd across the street. I turned my back to them. It would be just my luck if some of them recognized me from the bakery. The Honeybee had already been associated with one murder.

"Well, it doesn't matter anyway, because he's not going to be asking anyone any questions." My voice quavered, and a part of me was surprised to discover that I was on the verge of losing control. Steve's arm snaked around me, and I leaned into him.

Until six months ago, the only dead body I'd ever seen had been Nonna's. That had been in a fancy casket in a church, with my father holding my hand on one side and my mother holding my hand on the other. At nine years old, I'd been too young to really understand what death was all about. Now I'd seen three dead bodies since April, and I didn't like it at all.

And I still didn't understand what death was all about.

Steve said, "You know that Katie and I are dating. It only makes sense that she'd come with me." He gave me a squeeze.

I forced a smile up at him. *Dating* was inaccurate but vague enough.

Quinn raised his eyebrows. "What about Declan McCarthy, Katie?"

I didn't say anything. At least I had a valid reason to be here with Steve. I didn't know what I would have told the police if Declan had come along as originally planned. Still, remembering how Declan had stomped out of my house made my throat tighten.

"I was the one who discovered Greer dead," Steve said. "Katie was waiting outside. She didn't come inside until I called for her to." Again, dancing with the truth. I could tell he was trying to be gallant, though, to divert their immediate suspicion of me.

"Dawes," Taite said. "Any relation to Heinrich Dawes?"

"He's my father," Steve said easily.

"His name was among Lawrence Eastmore's effects."

Steve nodded. "I imagine a lot of names were. Dr. Eastmore knew a lot of people in Savannah. And didn't Katie just explain that we were here because I'm a family friend?"

Taite looked between us. "You're not telling us everything."

I pasted an innocent look on my face. "Like what?"

"I don't know, but you're coming down to the precinct with me, young lady, and we're going to find out."

Chapter 25

The blood drained from my face, and I felt light-headed. "What?" I said at the same time Steve said, "Now, look, Detective."

Quinn looked as surprised as I felt, but quickly recovered. "Detective, may I speak with you for a moment? Over here?" He led Taite around the side of the house.

I sighed. "I want to go home." Except now my carriage house felt tainted. "Or at least to the Honeybee," I amended. "I want to bake something delicious and feel in control of my life again."

"Baking does that for you, doesn't it?" Steve asked.

"In the kitchen I always know things will work out okay. Even if a recipe flops, I still feel that way."

He smiled. "I love that."

Which was a considerable way from *I love you*.

Quinn and Taite walked back around the corner. I was alarmed to see Taite glaring at me, licking his lips in a way that made me feel like prey.

"We'll contact you later for your formal statements," Quinn said. "But I think we have enough for now. You got here, the door was open, Dawes went inside looking for his friend, you stayed outside, the friend was discovered deceased, you went in to see if there was anything you could do, there wasn't, and you called us."

I stared at him, especially since he'd filled in a few more innocent "facts" for me. I quickly nodded. "Right. Yes. Exactly."

"The dispatcher said this guy might have died in his sleep?"

"I probably said something like that," Steve admitted. "I assumed since he was lying in bed . . . Well, you'll see."

"Right." Quinn glanced over at his companion. "Well, we have an investigation to start. Detective?"

Taite threw a fierce look at us and stomped up to the front door. A uniform let him inside. I let out a whoosh of breath when the door closed behind him.

"Okay, what the heck is going on between you and my new partner?" Quinn demanded. "I mean, you can be really irritating, Katie. I'd be the first to admit that."

"Hey!"

"But he wants to put you in a holding cell until you tell him—what?"

I swallowed audibly. "A . . . You're kidding." I considered how much to tell Quinn. "Did you know he came to see me at the Honeybee? He seemed to think I was involved in Dr. Eastmore's murder."

He gaped. "He never said anything like that to me. He thinks *you* killed him? Good God, why?"

"Oh, no, I don't believe he thinks I actually committed murder. Sheesh, at least I hope not. But he does think I know more than I do. He seems to be obsessed with some, uh, occult aspect of this whole thing." The best lies are full of truth. I stubbed my toe into the ground and shrugged. "At least that's what he said."

Beside me, Steve made a noise in the back of his throat that reminded me of Mungo.

Quinn didn't seem to notice. Instead, he glanced toward the house and sighed. "Yeah, he's got a thing about tracking down spirits or vampires or something."

"What?" Steve and I exclaimed at the same time.

"I don't know." He dismissed the notion with a wave of his hand. "I do my best not to pay attention. The guy has obviously watched too many horror movies."

I couldn't help the giggle that bubbled to the surface. It choked out of me, followed by another seconds later. Soon I was laughing so hard I had to gasp for breath.

Quinn cocked his head, watching me without breaking a smile. "Better take her home. She's hysterical."

"Am not!" I snorted. Another wave of giggles swamped me. I bent over, trying to catch my breath.

"Come on." Steve took my arm and guided me to his car. Feeling the accusing eyes of the crowd on me, I climbed in. Mungo stood on my lap, put his paws on my shoulders, and licked my chin. That should have made me laugh, but instead my outburst of laughter faded as Steve got in and we drove away.

"Sorry," I said after a while.

"It's all right. Been a long day—and night, for that matter."

"I'm not hysterical." At least not now.

"Okay." He turned toward the Honeybee rather than heading toward my house. Good.

"I just feel so relieved." I lowered the window and

hung my head out with Mungo, relishing the air moving through my hair.

I felt more than saw Steve looking at me. "Relieved?" he asked.

"Sure. Taite isn't a witch-hunter, not a real one. I mean, vampires? Really? He's just a harmless dork."

Steve drove in silence for a few moments. "A harmless dork who zeroed in on your coven and the Dragoh Society within a few weeks of arriving in town. A harmless dork with a detective's shield."

Well, when he put it like that I didn't feel like laughing at all.

By the time we got back to the Honeybee, it was late afternoon. I was glad to hear Lucy had sent Nel home early since she'd come in earlier than scheduled to cover for me. The bakery closed at five, and we found Ben checking supplies behind the espresso counter while Lucy wiped down the kitchen and readied ingredients for the next day's baking—including all the extra goodies we had planned for the party.

Leaving Steve to tell my uncle why we'd been delayed, I pulled Lucy back to the office to tell her that Greer Eastmore was dead. My gentle aunt listened with growing alarm as I related the events of the day, twisting a damp dish towel in her hands over and over until her fingers began to turn pink.

I eased the raveled fabric away from her. "Maybe you should sit down. There's more."

She sank into the desk chair with a resigned sigh. But when I went on to haltingly explain that Steve had spent the night at my house because I'd been magically assaulted and had been afraid of being attacked again, she responded like a trouper.

"We cannot allow anything like that to happen again," she said, leaping to her feet. "My goddess, your father would have my head if anything happened to you—not to mention my sister! I do want to hear more about how Mother was involved, of course. Imagine! Anyway, I'll call Mimsey, and she can tell everyone else what's going on, including Andersen Lane." She opened the door. "You're spending the night at our place tonight. Have Steve take you home, pack a bag, and drive immediately there. You know where the extra key is if you get there before we do."

It took a split second to decide. "Okay, I'll take you up on the offer." I cringed at the thought of spending the night alone at my carriage house, and I couldn't ask Steve to stay again.

Wouldn't ask Steve to stay again.

"Ask Mimsey to tell Andersen I couldn't get the book he wanted. That I'm sorry."

She froze in the doorway, then turned. "Was it for the counterspell he was working on?"

I nodded.

"Oh. Dear. All right. I'll tell her." Her jaw flexed in determination. "Don't worry, Katie. It's all going to be okay." She took three rapid steps and threw her arms around me.

I hugged her back. "Thanks. I really needed to hear that, you know."

She stood back and looked me in the eye. "Of course. We all need to hear that sometimes."

I began gathering files and paperwork.

"What are you doing?" she asked.

"Taking a few things with me to work on tonight. Orders, that kind of thing."

"Oh, Katie."

"Druids or no druids, dead bodies or not, we're running a business here, and I was no help at all today."

Shaking her head, she went back to the kitchen. I finished packing up and took my bulging tote bag out front to find Steve sitting at one of the bistro tables with Ben. His usual cappuccino steamed beside a plate of pumpkin spice cookies slathered with cream cheese frosting. I slid into a third chair and snagged a cookie, suddenly ravenous.

Ben frowned at me. "Steve told me what you found at this Lawrence Eastmore's place."

I nodded, mouth full.

"You okay?"

I nodded again.

"I don't like it."

Swallowing, I said, "Gosh, Uncle Ben. You think I like it?"

He opened his mouth, glanced at Steve, then closed it again and shook his head. "Of course not."

Steve drained his cup, grabbed another cookie, and stood. "You ready?"

"As can be. Mungo and I are going to stay with Ben and Lucy tonight."

"Good idea. I'll meet you out front." The bell above the door jingled as he left.

As I rose to follow, Ben put his hand on my arm. "Katie, what happened with Deck this morning?"

"Oh." I sat back down. "It was just a stupid misunderstanding. What did he tell you?"

"Nothing. Scott came in, though—you met him the other day?"

I nodded.

"He said Deck wasn't planning on coming in here for a while. Scott said he was pretty angry at you."

"He is." I passed my hand over my face. "But it's not my fault, and I can't deal with it right now, Ben. I'm sorry. I'll talk to Declan, I really will."

"When?"

I stood abruptly. "After the party."

It hadn't been my imagination. The carriage house really did feel different. When we walked in, I set Mungo down on the floor, but he didn't move any farther into the living room. Smudging with sage and juniper might have worked to get Heinrich's heebie-jeebie vibe out of the place, but it was going to take more than that to rid my home of the evil metallic aftertaste from the night before.

"Do you feel it?" I asked Steve.

He made a face. "I do. Did last night, too." Yet he'd stayed with me.

"I'm glad Lucy invited me over," I said. "I don't like it in here. And you know what? That really makes me mad. I've loved this place since the first time I laid eyes on it."

Steve looked at me with sympathy. "I know. You're sure you'll be okay driving yourself?"

"Sure." My fingers flew to my mouth. "Oh, Steve. You must have had other things to do today. Interviews. Your column. Deadlines at the *News*."

He put his hands on my shoulders and drew me toward him. "It's okay. You're more important."

Well, that made me feel good and bad at the same time. More good, though.

The kiss on the cheek he gave me then was nice, too. Not as exciting as our kiss the night before, but nicely . . . sane.

After Steve left, Mungo followed close at my heels as I quickly assembled clothes for the next day. I'd need my working clothes, plus my costume for the party. I began to throw another pair of sleep shorts and tank on the pile, then thought better of it and added an oversized T-shirt instead of the tank. Turning toward the armoire, I remembered my duffel was still out in the Bug. Grabbing the box with my unused wedding dress, I went out to the driveway and dumped it in the backseat, then reached for the bag.

With a sense of urgency, I rushed back inside to finish packing as quickly as I could. Mungo, who had followed me out to the Bug, stayed on the tiny front porch this time. I couldn't blame him. I fished sweatshirt, makeup, extra toothbrush, hose, and the heels I'd worn to the fund-raiser out of the duffel, replaced the toothbrush, and piled in my clothes. Then I added a pair of high-top tennis shoes with good arch support because this zombie bride wasn't inclined to wear high heels while working a party. Then I went into the bathroom to see what I'd missed.

It hit me then, hard enough that I had to sit down on the edge of the tub.

My hairbrush should have been in the duffel. It wasn't.

Steve had said whoever had breached my protections the night before would have needed a *piece* of me. Fingernails or *hair*.

And I hadn't locked my car.

Forcing myself to my feet, I went back into the bedroom, grabbed my things, and went out to where Mungo waited. As I locked the door I wondered whether I was locking something out or something in. "Come on, sweetie. I bet you're hungry. Lucy will have something for you."

"Katie! Wait!"

Margie hurried across her front yard to my driveway. I paused with the driver's-side door open, wondering what awkward questions I'd have to answer about the recent activity at my house. "Hi," I said.

"Oh, honey!" She flung her arms around me, almost knocking me over. "I've been so worried. But you're okay."

I bobbed my head. "I'm fine."

"Well, my heavens, girl." Taking a step back, she pressed her palm over her heart. "I was a little worried when your reporter arrived like his hair was on fire last night, but then when both your men were here at the same time this morning, and you didn't go to work . . ."

I could tell my smile was pretty lame.

Margie's forehead wrinkled. "And now you're leaving?"

"Only for the night." I hoped. "Staying with Aunt Lucy and Uncle Ben." I scrambled for a good reason and didn't come up with one. "The Halloween party tomorrow."

She stepped in, bless her heart. "Last-minute planning, eh? I get it." She leaned forward. "So what happened this morning? Did your fireman find out you've been seeing the reporter?"

"Oh, Margie, I haven't been keeping any secrets. But, yeah. Things did get a little dicey today."

Seeing my expression, she patted my shoulder. "Don't worry, honey. You had to make a decision sometime. I'm just so glad you're okay."

That lame smile flitted across my face again. We'd developed a close friendship in some ways, but as with Declan, there were huge parts of my life I couldn't share with Margie. It made for a special kind of loneliness sometimes.

"Thanks," I said. "Mind keeping an eye on the place tonight?" Not that anything would happen if Mungo and I weren't in it, but it seemed like a neighborly thing to ask.

"Of course, darlin'. I'll see you tomorrow night, okay?" She turned to go back home.

"Looking forward to those little costumes. And, Margie?"

She stopped, looking at me over her shoulder.

"Thanks for dinner last night. I had a great time."

A big grin split her face. "Me, too, hon. We'll do it again."

By the time I pulled out of the driveway, I was already wondering how I was going to get through the Halloween party while worrying the whole time about some crazy druid casting the Spell of Necretius.

All of them had alibis, except for Andersen, yet none of those alibis were what I'd call ironclad. Brandon Sikes could have left the Dawes home and then returned. Ditto Heinrich. Victor Powers' wife was his alibi, and wives were known to lie for their husbands. Especially high-profile husbands.

Then an idea occurred to me as I drove. Would the

Dragoh Society consent to a meeting on Samhain? A meeting at which they were all present? If only one was unwilling to stay with the other three for the duration of Samhain, then he'd give himself away.

I pulled into a parking space and called Andersen Lane. If he could get them to agree to a meeting, it might stop a murderous Dragoh from going through with the summoning spell.

Chapter 26

Lucy and Ben were already home by the time I made it to their town house. Mungo's head bobbed up and down in my tote as I walked up to their door. Of course I was juggling the tote, my duffel, and a bag of garden greens I'd plucked from the fridge so they wouldn't go to waste.

The sun had set while I broached my plan to Andersen Lane. Since he hadn't managed to come up with what he felt would be an adequate counterspell, he was open to the idea of having the Dragohs watch each other during the vital hours of Samhain. He said he'd make some calls and get back to me. His willingness to meet with the others helped assuage my suspicions about his motives.

Ben answered the door. "Thought you'd be here earlier. We were starting to get worried."

"Sorry. I would have called, but I was on the phone with Andersen Lane." I put Mungo down on the floor, and he ran to say hello to Honeybee, who was waiting in the doorway of the sunroom.

"Andersen Lane should go back to whatever rock he was under before he crawled out to bother you and the book club." My uncle's tone was acerbic.

I kissed him on the cheek. Ben was protective, and no matter how head over heels in love he was with my aunt or how readily he accepted her magical practices, he didn't have personal experience with magic. To him it was more of an eccentric hobby than actually working with the forces of nature.

Lucy stood by the stove, stirring a pot of butternut squash soup fragrant with the scent of smoky bacon. She greeted me by waving me into the room. "Would you mind scooping out the bread bowls?"

"Sure." I donned one of her aprons, sliced the top off a small sourdough boule from the Honeybee, and set about removing the soft interior crumb. I inhaled the smells of fresh bread and smoked pork that rode above the usual pungency of Lucy's herbal kitchen. Like me, she had a pot of basil on the counter, as well as one of parsley for easy snipping—and a little extra protection around the house.

Protection. What if my attacker came for me here?

I put the thought out of my mind. I had Mungo, and my aunt was no slouch when it came to spell casting. I refused to live every minute in fear.

Lucy ladled the soup into the bread bowls and garnished each with a generous sprinkle of freshly chopped chives. Leaving the formal dining room dark, we settled around the ancient wooden table in the kitchen. On the floor, Mungo licked delicately at the edges of his soup as it cooled. Honeybee the cat watched with an expression of amused disgust from across the room.

Winking at Honeybee, I popped a couple of antihistamines to battle my allergies and dug in. "This is delicious. What else is in it? Chicken stock? Cream?"

"Lucy tells me you had an attack last night," Ben interrupted.

My spoon paused halfway to my mouth. "Something like that."

"But you didn't go see a doctor." He sounded pretty upset.

I put my spoon down. "Why would I?"

He leaned forward. "Katie, you need to get a CAT scan as soon as possible." He looked at Lucy. "I can't believe you didn't suggest that."

"A CAT scan? What for?"

The skin tightened across Ben's face. "Honey, you smelled something funny, right? That can be a sign of something . . . serious."

"Ben," Lucy said.

"Serious," I said in a flat voice.

He took a deep breath. "I've heard it can be a sign of a brain tumor."

"Oh, for heaven's sake." I turned to my aunt. She looked away.

"I know you think it had something to do with some kind of magic, but it would make me feel a lot better if you went to a specialist," he said.

Stunned, I looked down at my soup. Brain tumor? But that was . . . Could he be right? What if what had happened last night was all in my head?

No. It *had* been in my head. But so had Mungo. And Nonna. The spell bottle had broken. And then I remembered the fused amulet. Steve had seen it. It had really happened.

Oddly enough, that made me feel better. "Okay," I said easily.

Lucy's shoulders seemed to relax a bit. As long as everybody got along she was happy.

Ben smiled his approval. "Good. Now finish up, because someone's coming over for dessert."

The doorbell rang.

"Come in!" Ben called.

I raised my eyebrows at Lucy, and she shrugged as if in apology. Before I had a chance to wonder what was going on, Declan walked into the kitchen.

He saw me and paused. "I didn't know you'd be here."

"That's because I didn't tell you," Ben said.

I gaped at my uncle. For a guy who seemed to sail happily through life since he'd retired as fire chief, he sure could stick his nose into things when he got the notion to.

"I understand you and Katie had a disagreement this morning. Some kind of misunderstanding. And we both know the best way to get over a misunderstanding is to come to an understanding. Talk it out. So I want you two to eat your ice cream sundaes and then go talk."

"But—," I said.

"No," Declan said.

"Yes," Ben said. "Go on. You'll figure it out."

Declan wouldn't meet my eyes. If it hadn't been for his close relationship with my uncle, I was sure he would have walked right out. "I'm not hungry," he said. "I'll meet you in the roof garden." I heard the sound of his receding footsteps on the floor and then the stairs.

"So much for ice cream sundaes," Lucy said. Ben frowned.

I was so tired I wanted to drop. The antihistamines made me even sleepier. But I wanted to make up with Declan, and this might be the only chance he gave me. He was my friend. I had to try.

"You two go on ahead," I said. "I'm going to grab some coffee."

Though the sun had been down for a couple of hours, the sky still glowed a lighter blue in the west. The moon hadn't risen yet, and the stars glimmered brightly against the cloudless cobalt above. Two candles flickered on the wrought-iron table, barely illuminating Declan on the far side. He still wore the FIRST IN, LAST OUT T-shirt he'd had on that morning. His muscular arms were folded across his chest.

"I brought you a beer," I said.

He took it in silence. I sat down across from him and took a sip of coffee.

The edge of the moon peeked over the horizon. Around us, Lucy's moon garden began to come to life. When the rest of the rooftop was dark, white petunias dripped from pots, moonflowers glowed like white saucers on their vine twining up a trellis, and tiny white jasmine flowers and night-blooming nicotiana lent their sweet aromas to the humid evening air. The sound of car tires on the pavement below drifted up to us.

It felt very peaceful. Except, of course, that in the last three days I'd found two bodies, someone had tried to kill me, and now a man I adored was so mad at me that he couldn't even meet my eyes.

I wished I knew how to start.

"That coffee will keep you up tonight," he said.

"Fat chance. Not after the twenty-four hours I've had."

He gave me a look. Even in the dim light I could see the disapproval.

"I'm sorry," I said.

He was quiet for a minute. I lit another candle on the table.

"What, exactly, are you sorry for?"

I thought for a moment. "Well, I'm sorry that you're mad at me. I'm sorry you worried about me being sick and now you think I lied. I'm sorry you came to my house to help me and instead ran into Steve Dawes. I'm sorry you think I've been playing games with you when I haven't, and I'm sorry Ben tricked you into coming here tonight." My words were coming faster now, and louder.

He held up a hand, "Whoa."

I rubbed my tired eyes.

He took a deep breath. "Okay, okay." He sipped his beer, watching me over the candle flames. "So why did Steve Dawes spend the night?"

Oh, boy. My guilt must have shown on my face, because he shifted in his chair and said, "Don't lie. That's all I ask."

Suddenly I was overcome with weariness. I didn't have any fight left. "You really want to know? You really want to know *me*?"

His eyes shone blue in the flickering yellow light. "That's what I've always wanted. Since the day I met you."

Never mind that when I'd met Declan, Detective Quinn had been questioning Uncle Ben as a murder suspect.

"But you've always sidestepped, always changed the subject. What are you so afraid of?" He took another sip and licked his lips. "What is it about Dawes that draws you to him?"

I couldn't look at him. He'd told me intimate details about his life, yet I'd skimmed along on the surface details of mine. It felt safe. Good. He felt normal, when the rest of my life might not be. I liked Declan McCarthy more than I could say.

I liked him well enough to tell him the truth.

"Declan, I'm a witch."

He looked at me, his face a mask. I'd bet he was great at poker. "And?" he said.

"*And?* Isn't that enough?"

He shrugged. "So, you're a witch. Like one of those Wiccans? Or just a run-of-the-mill pagan?"

"Somewhere in between. I'm a hedgewitch. It runs in the family."

His laugh was deep and rich and ran over me like caramel. "Hedgewitch. I don't know what that is, but I like the term."

"It's a green witch. Some people call us natural witches. We use nature, the four elements, plants— things like that—in our magic."

"Wow." Declan shook his head and took a swig of beer. "Magic. I always knew there was something a little different about Lucy. She's kind of, I don't know. Airy. Guess it makes sense. And you actually, like, cast spells and things?"

I nodded once, watching for the skepticism, the eye rolling. But Declan's grin seemed perfectly honest. Curious, even, if mildly amused. Was he taking me seriously?

"And you've been trying to keep this part of your

life from me because you thought I'd disapprove? Or think it was silly?"

"Well, mostly I figured you'd think I was a weirdo."

That laugh came again, different tonight from other times I'd heard him laugh. It was easy, full, rich with . . . relief.

My own relief made my shoulders slump. I'd told him. He'd not only taken it well, he'd apparently accepted it.

I didn't have to lie to Declan anymore.

My throat tightened and my eyes stung. Sheesh, what was with all my weepiness lately? Of course, it had been a crazy twenty-four hours. I blinked back the tears and managed to get out, "Oh, Declan. You don't think I'm crazy?"

"No crazier than I did before."

My laugh came out more like a snort.

"It explains all the time you spend with Dawes, too."

I raised my eyebrows.

"Remember, I went to school with his little brother, and we were roommates as well as working together until . . . the accident. You think I don't know a little about what goes on in that family?"

"Uh . . . like what?" Did Declan already know about the Dragoh Society?

"Oh, Arnie didn't talk about it much, and it was clear I wasn't supposed to ask. But I knew his family had some rather unusual beliefs." One side of his mouth quirked up. "I guess you and Steve have a lot more to talk about than you and me."

"Not . . . more. But different. At least so far."

He drained his beer. "And last night?"

I remembered how I'd taken the news that magic really existed. If Lucy had led with information about a magical attack I might never have believed her.

But I didn't want to lie. Not now. I chose my words with care. "There was some kind of black magic directed at me," I said. "I felt it." Then I laughed. "Of course Ben wants me to go to a doctor. Thinks I have a brain tumor." All true.

Declan's eyes widened. The candle flame echoed within his wide pupils. "I don't like the sound of that."

"I called Steve afterward, and he came over. He fed me and Mungo, put us to bed, and then slept on the couch to make sure I'd be okay."

"But you believe it was black magic," he said.

I put my hand over my eyes and shook my head. What had I been thinking? This guy was a firefighter. Mr. Practical. Handy around the house. Able to work on car engines. Not even Uncle Ben fully believed me, and he'd been madly in love with a witch for years.

"So-o-o-o," Declan said, drawing the word out, thinking. "Dawes wasn't there for any romantic reasons."

Now I laughed. "You have a one-track mind." But I wasn't going to mention my near capitulation. Things could have ended quite differently last night.

Declan pointed a finger at me. "Yes, ma'am. I sure do when it comes to you."

I grinned at him. Things had just gotten complicated all over again, but I didn't care. "I take it back," I said.

"What?"

"I'm not at all sorry that Ben tricked you into coming tonight."

Chapter 27

After Declan left I settled into Lucy and Ben's guest bedroom with my laptop and the door closed to keep Honeybee out. In general, she respected my allergies and walked a wide berth around me, but she loved hanging out with Mungo and sometimes broke the rules. As for my familiar, he lay draped across my shins, lazily watching me work.

I felt almost transparent with weariness and giddy with relief that I no longer had to keep secrets from Declan. I mean, I hadn't told him all about the Dragohs, or the spellbook club, but those weren't just my secrets. Hopefully, the Dragohs wouldn't be an issue for much longer, and in time I was sure I'd get permission to tell him about our coven.

Well. Maybe Dragohs wouldn't be an issue, but a future member of the society might be.

Guilt stabbed through me. Steve had been so sweet and open lately. He'd taken care of me and stopped me from making a fool of myself during a moment of weakness.

Steve, Declan, Steve, Declan. I wanted them both in

my life, I really did. But I wasn't ready to settle down with either of them. Not yet. I still needed to find out more about who—and what—Katie Lightfoot was.

Additional guilt about neglecting my duties at the bakery lately impelled me to do a few things before calling it an early night and recharging for the next day. First, I pulled out the list of supplies we were running low on at the bakery. The local grocery warehouse allowed us to place orders online and then pick them up the next day. I added the items we needed, billed it to our account, and made a mental note to ask Ben to pick up the order the next morning. There were a few items I'd need for the special spread we were putting together for the Halloween party—a case of pumpkin puree for the pumpkin gingerbreads shaped like tiny squash, crispy apples to cover in salted caramel, extra eggs, and lots of sprinkles to decorate cookies and cupcakes.

Maybe I should make Margie's Coca-Cola cupcakes for the party.

I shook my head. This order was already late. Just stick with the plan. Tomorrow was going to be another really long, really busy day. Thank goodness we'd have the professional help of Nel Sandstrom to lighten the load.

Speaking of Nel, I fished her file out and got going on her W-2 paperwork and the tax forms we had to fill out for the Honeybee's accountant. Glancing at her application, I saw her address was in a rather upscale neighborhood. Probably living in her father's house after his death, as Greer had planned to do . . .

I grabbed the application and ran my finger down to the bottom. Mungo's head snapped up. Nel had listed three references. I'd called only one of them—the bakery in Athens where she'd worked the last nine years. I'd used my cell to call David Talbot, owner of the Halcyon Bakery, so Nel wouldn't inadvertently pick up the Honeybee phone and hear me checking with her old boss. That call was the only one I'd made in the last week to a number I wasn't familiar with.

I picked up my phone and scrolled to my own recent calls. There it was. The number matched the one on the application. I began to dial it again.

Yip!

I ended the call before it rang. "Right. Thanks, Mungo." If this was the number for the phone I'd found on Greer Eastmore's dresser, the police would know if I called it now.

But was it Greer's phone? Or was it David Talbot's?

I thought about calling the number from a pay phone, or blocking the caller ID on my own phone. But I didn't trust the latter, and I'd have to leave the town house to call from a public phone. A better idea came to mind.

The Halcyon Bakery's Web site was fancier than ours, but they focused more on specialty breads and decorated cakes. The phone number was different, but the man I'd talked to had told me that I'd reached his cell phone. The site said the owner's name was indeed David Talbot, the name Nel had listed on the application.

Was it even possible that Greer Eastmore was in possession of the phone of a guy who owned a bakery in Athens?

I scrolled down to the bottom of the homepage and caught my breath. Mungo padded up to look at the screen with me. I clicked over to the STAFF page.

"Oh, no," I said.

Mungo made a questioning sound.

"It says here that David Talbot is originally from Ireland. The man I spoke with had a strong Southern accent. And not only that, but Nel isn't in this group photo. She should be."

He tipped his head to the side.

"It was taken two years ago, when she was supposedly employed there."

Yip!

Sure enough, a little more digging revealed how much Nel had lied in order to get a job at the Honeybee. First, I called the other two numbers she'd listed as references, figuring that even if Emily Post would have disapproved of the late hour I'd probably just get voice mail anyway. I was wrong. One number was a pizza place, and the other was a very confused teenager in Seattle.

At least it was earlier there.

Giving two blatantly fake references was a rookie mistake. Though, come to think of it, as potential employers we'd more interested in her most recent job, especially since that was supposed to cover nine whole years of her baking experience. The others were short-term positions. Perhaps Nel had thought it worth the gamble. And, in fact, it had worked for a while.

Then I searched online for "lily airbrush cake" and bingo!—the exact same photo of the cake Lucy had loved so much from Nel's portfolio filled the screen. The name of the person credited with the cake was definitely *not* Nel Sandstrom. A few more minutes of searching netted me two more fake photos of award-winning cake decoration—also not Nel's work.

I slumped against the pillows. Looked at Mungo, who waited expectantly.

"Yeah, yeah. I guess I have to go tell Lucy and Ben now."

The door to their bedroom was open. Lucy was propped against a mountain of blue-paisley-patterned pillows on the bed, legs tucked under her as she read a section of the newspaper from that morning. She wore white pajamas and had woven her wavy gray-blond hair into a thick braid, which fell over one shoulder. Purple-framed half-glasses perched on her nose, and Honeybee the cat curled in the crook of her legs, orange tabby stripes vivid in the light from the bedside lamp.

Ben, still in slacks and a polo shirt, sat in the over-stuffed reading chair with another section of the *News*. He looked up when he saw me in the doorway. "What's up?"

Lucy put down the paper, peering at me over the tops of her reading glasses and smiling. But her smile faded and her eyes grew wide as she listened to what I'd found out about our new employee. Ben's jaw set and his eyes narrowed as he heard the catalog of Nel's deceit.

When I finished, Lucy took off her glasses and pinched the bridge of her nose. "She lied about every-thing? Her experience, those beautiful cakes? How could we not know?"

Honeybee rose and stretched, then rubbed her head against Lucy's arm. My aunt distractedly stroked her familiar, who purred encouragement.

"She's a very good liar," I said.

Lucy looked up at me. "And I wanted to believe her. I convinced Ben, too."

He stood and walked over to the bed. "Don't even try to take on the blame for this, Luce. I liked her, too."

"Sometimes I think I'm intentionally naive," she insisted.

He pushed a stray strand of hair from her forehead. "No, my darling wife. You have managed to retain the ability to look for the best in people. Do you know how rare that is?"

"He's right," I said. "Rare and valuable. Don't ever get cynical on us, Aunt Lucy."

A tentative smile tugged at her lips. "I'll do my best. Sometimes it's hard to stay optimistic, though."

I looked at Ben and nodded. "That's why we need you to stay just the way you are."

Questions had swirled through my mind as I'd fallen asleep the night before. They were still there to greet me when I awoke, and stayed with me as I rushed around the Honeybee kitchen trying to get the regular day's baking out of the way so we could get cracking on the food for the Halloween party that night. Why had Nel wanted to work at the Honeybee so badly? Other than being childhood friends, what was Nel's recent connection with Greer Eastmore? Dead men tell no tales, but I was sure as heck going to get the answers out of Nel.

I realized I was gripping the edge of the counter, staring into space with my jaw clenched. I deliberately loosened it, did a few shoulder rolls, and began gathering ingredients for miniature ginger pecan Bundt cakes.

The woman we'd hired was really Nel Sandstrom— Steve knew her. But who the heck was the *real* Nel Sandstrom? She'd seemed so *nice*, and had totally fooled Cookie, Lucy, Ben . . . and me.

The more I thought about it, the angrier I got. And the angrier I got, the more things I wanted to say to her. I glanced at the clock. Almost six. She'd be coming in the door any minute.

Except she never did. By the time we opened at seven it was pretty obvious that Nel wasn't going to show up for work. I tried the number she'd provided on her application and was immediately shunted over to voice mail. At least it was her voice inviting me to leave a message.

"Hi, Nel. It's Katie. It's after seven, and we were wondering where you are. Give me a call, okay?" It was difficult to keep my tone light.

Then I called the Halcyon Bakery—the real one—using the number I'd found on their Web site. Sure enough, David Talbot himself answered with a charming Irish lilt. He'd never heard of Nel Sandstrom. He wished me luck and we hung up.

"I'm calling Cookie," Lucy said from the office doorway.

"Good," I said. "In a few hours maybe you could call the other ladies, too," I said. "They were going to help with the last-minute decorations, anyway. Maybe they could come a little early?"

She pointed her finger at me. "Good idea."

The morning rush kept us busy for the next hour. Cookie showed up then, and responded to the news about Nel with more puzzlement than anger. When things slowed down a little, I left her and Lucy out front and got back to work in the kitchen. As my hands sifted and mixed, my mind went back to work on Nel.

Why on earth would anyone lie so she could work

at a bakery? It had to be related to the murders some-how. But what did we have that she wanted?

She'd filled out the job application the very same day Declan and I found Lawrence Eastmore in Johnson Square. Now I wondered about that timing. The next night she'd been at Brandon Sikes' art opening and convinced Cookie that she would make a great Honey-bee employee. Then she'd shown up the day after that and charmed Ben and Lucy before I got back from the fund-raiser. The topper had been when she told us she was a practicing Wiccan—but who knew if that was even true? She'd known we were witches, though. Then Greer, posing as David Talbot, had given her a glowing recommendation.

I paused in kneading blueberries into a mound of scone dough, mulling over what I knew. So Nel had been working with Greer. I'd heard that murderers sometimes tried to involve themselves in the investigation, and in this case the real center of that investigation was defi-nitely at the Honeybee, not the police precinct. Greer wasn't even supposed to be in town when his father died, and he couldn't fake bakery experience like Nel could. But if they were working together . . . how? Greer had been in Europe for years. I thought of the Parthe-non wallpaper on his laptop. Nel's application had listed addresses and employment in Athens, Georgia.

However, it had already been established that Nel was a liar.

Steve had mentioned Nel living in Athens. So had Andersen. They could have meant Athens, Greece.

Go, Bulldogs.

No, that had been Carolyn Powers, talking about her husband.

But Nel had definitely led us to believe she'd been in Athens, Georgia, before moving back to Savannah. My bet was she'd been living in Athens, Greece, all along. And in some kind of contact with Greer Eastmore.

I remembered the click on the office phone when Andersen Lane had called to ask me to find *The 33 Curses*. Had Nel listened in? The more I thought about it, the more it made a creepy kind of sense. Between that phone call and the next day I had been attacked. By Greer, as I'd first thought?

Or . . . could it have been Nel who had invaded my mind? She'd looked a bit tired when I saw her at the bakery the next day, but nothing like I'd expect if she'd worked that kind of magic against me.

I shook my head and reached for the butter. I needed more information about our absent employee, and I needed it soon.

Declan came in around noon with Scott and Randy. This time they were all out of uniform, though with all the logo T-shirts those guys wore there was no question that they were firefighters all the time, on duty or not.

"Coming to the party tonight?" I asked.

"You bet," Declan said.

"How would you feel about helping me a little sooner than that? I feel kind of bad, asking after the whole, well, you know . . ."

Amusement played across his face. "You don't have to feel bad. I thought I made that clear last night."

Scott and Randy exchanged knowing looks.

"Thanks," I said. "In twenty minutes? Half an hour?"

Declan nodded and took a bite of molasses oatmeal cookie.

Fifteen minutes later, Mimsey came in decked from head to toe in black in a skirt-and-tunic combination. Along with the black hose and black shoes, she might have looked downright witchy. The black satin bow in her hair kind of ruined that effect, though. But I knew she'd picked the color not only because it was Halloween, but because black was a deeply elemental color, representing the earth itself, and powerful in protection.

"Is everyone ready for tonight?" she crowed, her eyes shining.

Customers turned toward her, smiling and nodding. Ben waved from the reading area, where he was adding another loop of candy corn garland to the Halloween tree. I greeted her from behind the espresso machine, and Lucy hurried out of the kitchen. "Thanks for coming early," she said. "We're nearly ready, but Katie has to leave for a little while."

Mimsey shot a look at me.

"Lucy will explain," I said. No need to air anything about a Honeybee employee in public.

"Jaida was looking for a parking space. She'll be here in a few minutes," Mimsey said, emanating curiosity as she bustled into the kitchen and donned a royal blue apron covered with ruffles.

"Perfect." I raised my eyebrows at Declan across the room.

He nodded and pushed back from the table. "Duty calls, guys."

"Duty." Randy snorted around another maple cardamom scone. "Right."

I wrinkled my nose at him and took off my apron. In the office, Mungo happily jumped into my tote, and I smuggled him out to the sidewalk. Declan looked surprised to see that my dog had been in the bakery, but no way was I going to confront Nel without my little wolf. Maybe she was just a rotten liar, but evidence pointed to her being something worse.

Outside, I headed for my Bug, but Declan put his hand on my shoulder. "We're going someplace?"

"To Nel Sandstrom's."

"Really? Well, what do you say I drive?"

It was true that he always looked a bit uncomfortable folded into the seat of my little car. "Okay, sure."

We crossed Broughton Street to where he'd parked his big king cab pickup. He opened the door and lifted me in with one hand on my elbow. As we pulled into traffic, I told him about discovering Nel's lies the night before and that I wanted to talk to her.

He frowned. "That's pretty rotten. The Honeybee is too busy to have someone flake out on you like that."

"She told us she was Wiccan," I said, trying out our newfound honesty. How would Declan react to talk of magic sans alcohol and moonlight to soften the whole idea?

Unfortunately, he had such a good poker face I couldn't tell what he thought. "Did that influence you?" he asked, the words measured.

"Probably," I admitted. "But not as much as her fake portfolio of fancy cakes. She counted on my checking only one reference, too, if any."

"Hmm."

"There's more, though. See, the guy who lied for her? Who said he owned the Halcyon Bakery? It was Greer Eastmore. The guy I wanted you to go with me to talk to yesterday."

Declan looked over at me so fast I thought he'd pull

a muscle. I hadn't wanted to spoil last night, so I'd kind of conveniently forgotten to fill him in on the events of the previous afternoon.

"Keep your eyes on the road. Yes. The son of the man we found. And Declan? Um, he's dead now, too."

This time Declan didn't mess around. He pulled to the side of the road and threw the truck into park. "Dead, how?" His voice held foreboding.

"Well, I'm not sure. There weren't any wounds that I could see. He was simply . . . no longer alive. Maybe a heart attack, or something else. But there was something that reminded me of what happened to me the night before. The, er, attack I mentioned."

He was staring at me. "Something reminded you— you saw him?"

"Oh. Yeah. After you ran out of my house, Steve offered to go with me."

"I did not run out."

I let that pass. "We were the ones who found him."

"Katie! What the heck is going on with you?"

"Well, that whole witch thing might have something to do with it. Lucy seems to think I'm some kind of catalyst. I don't know for sure how that works, but stuff seems to . . . happen around me sometimes."

He grimaced. "I'll say."

"Anyway, Nel was connected to Greer, and I'm afraid she might have had something to do with Lawrence Eastmore as well."

"Like she was involved in his death?"

I shrugged. "I don't know. But there's some connection. And she lied. A lot. And I don't know why. So, I'm going to ask her."

"Shouldn't you call the police?"

"And tell them what? That we didn't properly vet our new employee, and that she happened to know the dead son of a dead man you and I found in Johnson Square?"

We looked at each other for a long moment. Then he sighed and pulled back into the street.

Chapter 28

The Sandstrom house was on Waters Avenue, on the edge of the Baldwin Park neighborhood. It was all chunky lines, painted in varying shades of dull mushroom and surrounded by a sprawling lawn. We parked smack-dab in front of the overblown portico, and I hopped out of the truck with Mungo and marched to the door. I rang the doorbell, then knocked, then rang the doorbell again.

Declan joined me. "If she's in there she might not answer—"

"Oh, no," I interrupted.

He looked puzzled.

"You don't smell that?"

My familiar's head popped up from my tote bag.

Yip!

Declan glanced down at Mungo and sniffed. Shook his head.

Darn it. "Something's burning."

The effect of saying the word *burning* to a fireman hadn't occurred to me. Declan pushed past me and pounded on the door. Hard. The sound reverberated through the wall. Anyone inside would have to hear it.

He sniffed again. "Now I smell it, too."

"You do?" I asked, surprised. Though I had to admit this wasn't the same nostril-curling stench as burning hair.

His elbow crashed through the glass beside the door. I watched with wide eyes as he reached inside and unlocked the front door. "Stay here," he said.

"Like heck." I followed right behind him. The smell was stronger, but I didn't see any smoke. The atmosphere in the house gave me the creeps. The memory of the ice-cold finger running down my back outside Lawrence Eastmore's potting shed flickered through my mind. There was something like that here.

Yes, Nel looked like she belonged in Mayberry, but under the surface you wouldn't find fried chicken and apple pie. There was something cold and dark—and scary.

"Hello?" Declan called. "*Hello?!* Anyone home?" His baritone echoed through the rooms. There was no response.

It was a big house. We checked room after room on the first floor, jogging from one to the next. A fuzz of dust covered brocade and dark wood furniture, knick-knacks, and tabletops. It rose into the air from the carpet in the family room and den, and we left hazy footprints on the wooden floors of the hallway and the dining room. A grand piano dominated the expansive living room, its shiny dark surface grayed with dirt. In contrast, the kitchen counters were sticky with old food stains and the sink was piled with dirty dishes. Some had started to mold, and a whole new smell mingled with the smoky odor that had first caught my attention.

I gagged and followed Declan to the glassed-in sunroom that opened off the kitchen. He ducked his head inside quickly before retracing his steps to the main entryway. I went inside the enclosure, stunned by the graveyard of dead plants. A banana tree, enormous trailing vines that had taken years to grow so large, three tiny bonsai trees perched around a dry fountain, and pot after pot of ornamentals, all shriveled and dry. My throat worked. All that life, gone.

Mungo whined.

Rapid footsteps sounded on the wooden treads of the sweeping staircase, and I hurried back out to the entryway in time so see the bottoms of Declan's shoes as he turned the corner at the top of the landing.

"Hello!" he called again.

I ran up the stairs, Mungo bobbing beside me. Declan was opening doors off the hallway, one after another.

"Deck—"

He opened the last door, glanced inside, and hurried past me back to the stairs.

I spun to follow him. Nel obviously wasn't home. Maybe didn't even live here. Except . . . that kitchen. Despite the mold, some of the food on the dishes had looked relatively fresh.

Good goddess, I'd let that woman in my kitchen. Yuck.

Mungo made a conversation noise, and I paused at the top of the stairs. His eyes cut to the interior door nearest us.

I peered into the last room Deck had opened up.

"Oh. Dear." Mungo's snort echoed my sentiments exactly. Slowly, I ventured into the room. It was the master bedroom. An elaborate altar stretched along the back wall, eight feet long at least. A plain black cloth covered the top. After a couple of slow steps, I scurried over to see what was on it.

A brass goblet, a fancy wrapped athame, a heavy silver pentacle, and a red pillar candle clustered in the middle. Pretty typical Wiccan altar fare. The sculptures that took up the rest of the space were a bit out of the ordinary, though. I recognized Venus, Artemis, and Daphne. Various three-dimensional dryads and naiads reached toward me, and beyond me to the bed. A simple stylized woman made of dark wood with an opening in the middle looked like an African fertility statue.

In fact, all of the statues represented women—powerful ones. I could sense the female energy just by standing there.

The dowdy woman who looked like Opie's great-aunt was quite the fervent goddess worshipper. I wondered how that had played with her father. If he even knew.

I looked around the rest of the room. The open closet showcased a lot of denim, and what I thought of as hippie shoes lay in mismatched piles on the floor. The bedclothes were pulled up to the pillows but the bed wasn't really made. Dirty clothes spilled out of the hamper. Papers were scattered across the dresser top.

No, not papers, I saw upon closer examination. Brochures.

Brochures for Savannah cemeteries.

And tucked between them, an empty envelope with a return address in Greece.

"Katie!"

I grabbed the pile and pushed it in beside Mungo.
He panted up at me.

I turned and went back downstairs. "Where are
you?" I called.

"In the den."

Following the sound of his voice, I found Declan
standing with his hands on his hips in front of a smoking fireplace. He looked up. "Whatever she tried to
burn in here didn't ignite very well."

I stooped and peered at the contents. It looked like
Nel had tried to burn three or four books, and there were
other indefinable papers curled black and ashy. Nudg-
ing at the pages with the fireplace poker revealed a title
on one of the books that gave me pause. *The 33 Curses.*
But then I saw something that made me catch my breath.

"It's okay," Declan said, putting his arm around my
shoulders. "I'll have to call the department and report
this, though."

I tore my gaze away from my half-burned hairbrush
lying crookedly across the grate as a chill snaked up my
spine. "You have to report a fire in a fireplace?"

"An unattended fire . . . and I broke in, if you recall.
I have to report it so we can officially contact the owner
and secure the home."

"Good luck," I muttered, looking at my watch. "I'm
sorry I got you into this."

He grinned and gave me another squeeze, then
reached into his pocket. "No worries, lassie. Here—
take my truck. I know you're pressed for time. I'll get a
ride back."

I took the keys and kissed him on the cheek. "Thanks."

As I left I heard him talking on the phone.

*   *   *

I tried to call Andersen Lane, but he didn't answer. I dialed Steve next, breaking all my own rules about not talking on the phone while driving.

"Nel was behind the attack the other night, either alone or with Greer's help," I said as soon as he answered. "I need to talk to your father."

"Oh, I don't—"

"She had my hairbrush."

A couple of beats while he digested that and then he recited a number. I repeated it back a couple of times to make sure I had it right, then said good-bye. At a red light, I punched it into my cell phone and waited while the line rang on the other end.

When Heinrich answered, he didn't sound all that happy to hear from me.

I couldn't help that, though. I explained that the spellbook club knew all about the Dragohs, and that we'd been trying to find Lawrence Eastmore's killer in order to prevent him from casting the Spell of Necretius.

"Do you think my son hasn't already told me all that?"

"Oh." Actually, on the one hand I was surprised, but on the other it seemed that this horrible situation had managed to bring Steve and his father closer together. It was hard to argue that that was a bad thing. "Well, there's more," I said, and I told him about all of Nel's lies, about the altar in her bedroom, about the envelope with Greer's name on it, and about how she'd accessed my hair in order to psychically attack me.

"I think she killed Dr. Eastmore, Heinrich. She knew about the Spell of Necretius, and she killed him for it."

"Impossible," he scoffed.

"Not once you remove the assumption that none of the Dragohs' wives or daughters know about the society. Whoever bashed your friend over the head with a clay pot didn't hit him hard enough to kill him. Not to be sexist myself, but most women really aren't as strong as men. If you or any other of the Dragohs—even Andersen—swung a pot at someone's head, it's hard to imagine him getting back up." He was silent.

"I think she stole the spell and killed your friend. Possibly killed his son, too."

"How would she even know about the Spell of Necretius?"

"Maybe her father told her." I pulled into an empty spot a block down from the Honeybee and turned the truck's engine off.

"That's . . ." His voice trailed off. A long silence ensued on the other end of the phone line. "She was his only child. It's possible he told her about us."

"You think Judge Sandstrom wanted his daughter to take over his position since he didn't have a son?" I asked.

"Oh, I simply can't imagine that," Heinrich said. "It's never been done. Never. And even if he hoped to go against centuries of tradition, he would have told us. He'd have to, in order to get the rest of the members to agree. Not that we'd ever accept such a thing."

I wanted to reach through the phone line and shake some sense into this chauvinist druid. Instead, I took a deep breath in order to focus on the matter at hand. "What if he didn't get a chance to tell the rest of you?"

"Lars had a heart condition. Had it for years. His death wasn't exactly out of the blue. He had plenty of chances to bring it up with us." I heard a door close and imagined Heinrich going outside to talk in private. "No, I'm sure he didn't plan for Nel to join our ranks, but he loved her very much. And I know there were occasions when they cast spells together. I could possibly imagine Lars telling his daughter about us, just so she'd know who to go to if she got into trouble. So she'd know why her cousin is suddenly moving to Savannah. But that would still be unprecedented." He was speaking slowly now, thoughtfully.

"Then she might have known about the spell to summon . . . the Spell of Necretius. All the society members know of it, right?" I asked.

". . . Yes, that's true. But even if Lars told Nel about us, why on earth would he tell her about the spell? Even if she was capable of completing such a spell— and she's simply not that powerful—why would her father endanger her with that knowledge in the first place? The Spell of Necretius is the last thing I'd want a loved one to know about."

He had a good point.

"If she's not the killer, then it's one of you. I'm going to ask you this once: Would Brandon or Victor or Andersen have murdered Dr. Eastmore?" It was a risk, asking him that, because if I was completely wrong about Nel, then Heinrich could lie to me and I wouldn't know. After what I'd learned about Nel and what I'd seen at her house, though, I knew I wasn't wrong.

"No," he said.

"Did Andersen talk to you about all the Dragohs gathering to keep an eye on each other during Samhain?"

"Yes . . . Was that your idea?"

"It was."

"Figures. But yes, we are convening. I'll expedite our meeting so we can find Nel and deal with her."

That sounded ominous.

"Good luck with that, but I imagine she's laying low. Trust me—she's very powerful, and she can hide her true self. Listen, at her house I found a bunch of brochures about cemeteries in the area. Would a graveyard be a good place for Nel to perform the summoning?"

"Of course, that would be ideal for the spell," he said. "But it's Halloween. They'll be full. They'll be giving *tours*. She can't do this spell with other people around. Tell me the names of the cemeteries."

Mungo jumped out of my tote so I could grab the pamphlets. I read off the places they advertised: Bonaventure, Colonial Park, Laurel Grove, and several modern "resting places." "Wait a minute—she scribbled a note on the back of one of these. Drayton Hills."

"That's it. It's small, it's been closed down for years, it's not open to the public, and it's barely maintained if at all. Good work, Katie. We'll handle it from here."

"We'll meet you there," I said.

"No need. She's only one woman, and there are four of us."

"A woman who has likely already killed two of your number. A woman who nearly killed me. You need all the help you can get. All the power you can get."

There was a long silence. "All right. We'll meet you there at nine thirty."

"What are you planning?"

"To bind her before she can cast the spell. We'll need a poppet."

I'd never worked with a poppet, and tended to associate them with voodoo curses despite the spellbook club's explanation that while all voodoo dolls were poppets, not all poppet magic involved voodoo. I didn't care, though. The Dragohs could bring out as many poppets as they wanted if it would stop Nel.

"I know just who to give that task to," I said, thinking of Cookie. "You bring whatever else you need for the binding."

Staring into the mirror, I fingered the lace at the neckline of my wedding dress. What had I been thinking when I'd bought it last year? Fluffy and pure white, with a fitted bodice, thin straps, and a long, swirly skirt, it wasn't my style at all. It was traditional to the nth degree. Of course, Mama had pushed for it. Even though she didn't particularly like my choice of groom, she was happy to offer her opinion about all things wedding related.

Not that the planning got very far.

Traditional had seemed like a good idea to me then. The whole idea of getting married and moving into a cute starter home, getting a dog, and having kids had seemed like what normal people did. What people who belonged did. I'd felt like an outsider my whole life, and I'd thought that getting married would change that.

Now I knew better. And now, thanks to Aunt Lucy and the spellbook club, I knew other people who were like me. I belonged. The thought made me smile as I drew dark circles around my eyes. Then I smudged dark makeup on my face and arms to look like grave dirt and added a scar to my neck. Some gel in my hair to make it stick up funny, and I was good to go.

But when I emerged from the restroom, Ben took

one look and shook his head. The gesture made the
bells on the tips of his bright red jester hat jingle mer-
rily.

"What's wrong?" I asked, eyeing his purple leggings
and curly-toed shoes.

"The dress. It's too perfect."

"I'm not done yet," I said, heading toward the door
that led to the alley behind the Honeybee. Lucy had
given me a small bag of potting soil from her garden.
Now, with a twinge of regret, I rubbed it into the white
fabric, staining the lace and leaving a dark streak along
the bodice.

Back inside, Ben jingled his approval. "Better."

Lucy swirled by, a gypsy vision of layered skirts,
smocked blouse, and kerchief. Bangles piled up on her
arms, rings flashed from her fingers, and three-inch
hoops hung from her earlobes. "You look lovely,
Katie."

"I don't want to look lovely!"

She waved her hand at me. "You know what I
mean."

Ben went next door to check in with Croft Barrow at
the bookstore. Moments later, Bianca came in, dressed
in a long white flowing robe. I'd seen her wear it for
spell work—she liked to dress the part—but now it was
transformed into a Princess Leia costume by the wig
with the huge buns over her ears. Apparently some
things never grow old.

Jaida and Cookie followed behind her. Jaida was a
musketeer, complete with feathered three-corner hat and
sexy thigh-high boots. Cookie had gone with Cleopatra: straight dark wig, glittering makeup, thick eyeliner,
and exposed midsection.

"Wow!" I said.

"Thank you," Cookie said, twirling once.

Jaida grinned at me. "Nice dress. For a dead bride, I mean."

I curtsied. "Thanks. Now how about helping me set out the food for the living?"

All over the Honeybee, we put out bowls of sticky popcorn balls individually wrapped in cellophane next to plates of frosted sugar cookies in the shapes of orange jack-o'-lanterns, autumn leaves, and black cats. I set a platter of salted caramel apples in the display case, figuring they'd go quickly. We'd baked the ginger pecan cakes in miniature Bundt pans, then used icing to stick them together at the bottom to form little pumpkins. Lucy had decorated each with a marzipan stem and leaf, and they looked too pretty to eat. Somehow, I didn't think that would stop people. There were bowls of chocolate eyeballs and brightly colored gummy worms for the kids, and another of chocolate-covered espresso beans for the adults.

Black paper streamers dripped from the ceiling, and orange crepe paper covered the bistro tables. On top of each one was a small vase of black carnations that Mimsey had supplied and a battery-operated candle held upright in a bowl of candy corn. I wondered how long it would take for the candles to start tipping over as partiers sampled the decor. Lucy had brought her black cast-iron Dutch oven—which she also used as a cauldron on occasion—and we filled it with dry ice and set it high on the display case where little hands couldn't reach it and adults wouldn't knock it off. Wisps of vapor trailed up as the ice began to melt.

Mimsey breezed in the front door. "Hello-o-o-o-o!"

She'd replaced her black ensemble with a multicolored floor-length caftan . . . and a towering hat topped with fake fruit. A parrot perched in the middle of it.

"Carmen Miranda?" I asked, peering at the bird to make sure she hadn't actually brought Heckle along.

Her head bobbed in confirmation, and I braced for oranges and bananas to go flying. Everything stayed put, though. "My version, at least," she said.

Now that the last member of the spellbook club had arrived, I waved them all into the reading area. First I told them what Declan and I had found at Nel's house. "I spoke with Heinrich Dawes on my way back here."

Everyone moved a little closer.

"He said a cemetery would be the ideal place for her to perform the summoning spell, but that tonight there would be too many people roaming around. But on the corner of one of the cemetery brochures Nel had made a notation about a place called Drayton Hills."

"I know that place. It's been closed down for decades, as a cemetery at least. The city took it over for back taxes, and now they're stuck with it unless they relocate the graves," Mimsey said.

"It's little known, isolated, and not at all a tourist attraction. Heinrich feels it would be the ideal place for Nel to summon"—I swallowed—"Zesh tonight. I told him we'd meet the Dragohs there at nine thirty to stop her."

Mimsey's lips pressed into a thin line.

I held up a hand. "If any—or all—of you don't want to go, that's fine. I don't blame you. But as I told Heinrich, I think the more power we have in place to stop Nel, the better. And for whatever reason, I've been dragged into this from the beginning. I'm going to see it through."

Silent, we all exchanged glances. Then Cookie stepped forward. "I'll go."

"Me, too," Jaida said.

Lucy took my hand and squeezed it. "You can count on me."

Bianca looked at the floor and shook her head. "I can't believe I'm saying this, but I'll come with you."

Mimsey threw up her hands. "Fine."

I smiled. "Thanks. I mean it. Lucy, the little kids will be thinning out by then, but we advertised that the Honeybee would be open until eleven. I hate the idea of shutting down in the middle of the party."

"Don't you worry. I'll talk to Ben."

Chapter 29

We opened the doors again at six, and a few people trickled in for cider and goodies. Then came the families with very little ones—wee bunnies and princesses, a ladybug with wildly waving antennae, a frog and a fairy, and a lion growling *Arrrrrrr* at anyone who came near. Wide-eyed, they accepted candy from the jolly jester behind the register and wandered around the bakery snagging more goodies. Most paused at the Halloween tree, blinking up at the fairy lights and occasionally sucking a thumb.

"Oh, my Lord. Will you just look at this place?" a familiar voice drawled behind me. "Y'all have done a wonderful job, Katie!"

I turned to find Margie had arrived. "Glad you could make it! Oh, my, you two are adorable." I knelt in front of the JJs. They were dressed as Raggedy Ann and Andy. Red yarn wigs, a pinafore for Julia, and a sailor suit for Jonathan.

"Thank you," they said in unison. "Where's the candy?" Julia asked, and Jonathan pointed. Off they scampered to see Ben, who greeted them each with a pat on the head.

"Did you make those costumes?" I asked Margie, whose eyes followed them with watchful affection.

"Oh, sure. I think this is the last year they'll let me pick their costumes, though. Boy, they grow up fast."

"At least you can dictate to this little bumblebee for a few more Halloweens," I said, leaning over and making funny faces at Bart in the baby pack on Margie's back. His eyes grew large, and he started to cry.

"Oh, Barty," I said.

"He probably doesn't recognize you," Jaida said in passing.

My hands flew to my face. Of course. Poor kid, having a zombie make faces at him.

Margie bounced on the balls of her feet a few times, which distracted him. In seconds he was back to his usual happy self. She laughed. "You look great. Really. Shame about that dress, though."

I looked down and shrugged.

Soon the age of the kids increased, bringing in a baseball player and a commando, Catwoman and a witch. This was the group who dressed as characters from popular movies. They also ate a lot more.

About eight thirty, Detectives Taite and Quinn pushed through the door. Margie had already left, and more costumed adults had joined the crowd. "Monster Mash" boomed from the stereo, and the atmosphere was thick with the dry-ice fog that had been drifting out of Lucy's cauldron all evening.

Lucy hurried to greet the detectives at the door. "Welcome to the Honeybee Halloween Extravaganza."

"Ms. Eagel," Quinn greeted her. "Just thought we'd stop by and see how it's going." He folded his arms over his chest and leaned against the wall by the window.

I carried a plate of cookies over to them. "It's going well. Detective Taite, this is my aunt, Lucy Eagel. That's my uncle Ben over there."

"Ma'am," Taite said, inclining his head toward Lucy.

A quick glance at me, then my aunt said, "Pleased to know you. May I pour you some cider?"

"No, thank you," Taite said. "We're just checking in. Thought you might like to know that Greer Eastmore had a coronary. Just like your boyfriend thought." He met my eyes as he spoke, searching my face.

Lucy blinked.

Taite's expression held more puzzlement than threat. Had he found my number on Greer's cell phone?

I glanced around to make sure none of our customers had heard. "Thank you for letting me know. He seemed a bit young to die that way."

Taite said, "He was." His gaze flicked around the room. "Doesn't Nel Sandstrom work here?"

"Not anymore." My words were clipped.

An awkward silence descended. Finally Taite said, "We'll be on our way, then. Have a good night." He turned to go. Quinn, who had been watching his partner with curiosity, pushed away from the wall and raised his eyebrows at me.

The door flew open and Declan, Scott, Randy, and two other firefighters in full gear came in, carrying their helmets. Scott and Randy nodded to me as they passed by on their way to the register. "We're here, Ben. As promised."

My uncle laughed. "And in full costume, I see."

"Hey, we can't all be as original as *that*." Randy pointed to Ben's hat. "But at least we're here to help hand out candy, whatever."

Declan met my eyes and smiled, then gave a little nod toward the detectives Lucy and I were talking to. I shrugged.

Taite's head tipped to the side as he looked around the room. "You seem to have plenty of help."

"Can't ever have too much," I said, all bright and smiling.

His eyes narrowed at me. "Detective Quinn, what do you say we try some of that cider on offer?"

Quinn shrugged, but the curiosity was back on his face. "Fine by me."

Lucy shot me a look of alarm, and I glanced down at my watch as she poured out hot cider for the detectives. We had an hour to get to Drayton Hills, and Mimsey had said it was on the very edge of town, but if we started changing out of our costumes now, Franklin Taite would know something was up.

It was ten minutes after nine when Taite and Quinn finally left. Jaida and Lucy quickly gathered supplies in the kitchen while I ran into the office to grab my tote. Mungo put his paws on the arm of the chair, ready to go.

"I'm sorry, little one. I need you to stay here."

He glared at me.

"All the ladies are coming, and those druids will be there, too. I'll be fine."

He growled in the back of his throat.

I put the bag down and lifted him into my arms. "I want you to keep an eye on things here." I nuzzled his head. "I know what you truly are, a wolf in terrier clothing. On Samhain, all sorts of things can happen. I need you to protect Ben and Declan and the others."

When I put him back on the chair, he sighed and seemed to nod.

The spellbook club waited for me outside. Lucy pulled the Thunderbird up to the curb, and, still fully costumed, we piled in. With six of us, it was a tight fit. I wedged myself, gown and all, into the backseat, and off we went. Every time we turned a corner, Bianca's Leia wig bumped my head, and I couldn't see over Mimsey's hat o' fruit. At least it was warm enough to have the top down, so I could see the sidewalks of Savannah.

It was the middle of the week, so many locals had already headed home, but the out-of-towners were still going strong. Hearses carried paying passengers on the ghost tours all over the historic district, and I could hear the guides' voices blaring through speakers clear down by the river. Heinrich was right: The tourists would be all over most of the cemeteries in town, especially Bonaventure, since it was featured in that wildly popular book set in Savannah.

Lucy drove quickly, following Mimsey's directions, and soon we reached the edge of town. She turned left onto a gravel road. After about half a mile, she pulled over to the side and turned off the Thunderbird's engine. I could hear it ticking in the cooling night and Bianca breathing beside me. A night bird called from the top of a tree.

I craned my neck but couldn't see what lay ahead. "Mimsey," I hissed, "can you take that contraption off your head?"

She opened the passenger door and got out. I crawled forward from the backseat, hauling my heavy skirt out. At least I had on sneakers. Mimsey removed her headdress and shook out her white pageboy.

"Much better," she proclaimed in a low voice.

Something flew by. Cookie squeaked. "What was that?"

I whispered, "A bat, I think."

She giggled nervously. I looked around at the others now standing by the car. Bianca looked like one very worried Princess Leia. Jaida's expression was serious and determined as she took off the three-cornered hat and tossed it on the front seat. Lucy, however, appeared almost placid.

Ahead of us, a tall spiked gate blocked the road. It guarded a fenced-in area, heavily wooded and over-grown. Even in the bright light of the waning gibbous moon I couldn't make out where the iron fencing ended.

The sound of tires on gravel made us turn our heads. A black Cadillac Escalade crunched slowly down the road, then pulled in behind the Thunderbird. Victor Powers got out from behind the wheel. He wore dark slacks and a zippered Windbreaker. Steve's father stepped to the ground from the passenger seat, also clad in dark clothing. The rear doors opened to reveal Andersen Lane and Brandon Sikes.

Andersen shut the car door behind him and approached, peering at me through his plastic-framed glasses and tugging at the collar of his pin-striped oxford-cloth shirt. "I knew I was right to enlist your help." He glanced around at the others. "I never would have suspected our erstwhile member's progeny."

"I just hope we can stop her."

Victor Powers held out his hand. "We've never actually met, though I believe I did see you at my fund-raiser?"

After a second's hesitation, I shook his hand. No comment on the fund-raiser.

Brandon's eyes lit up when he saw Cookie's Cleopatra costume. He kissed her on the cheek. "You look gorgeous."

"So do you," she said.

He did, actually, in a dark T-shirt and jeans, but everyone except the lovebirds exchanged disapproving looks.

As Heinrich's gaze continued to take in the rest of the spellbook club, his disapproval deepened. "What on earth are you people wearing?"

I held up my palms. "We were at a party at the Honeybee. We had to dress up, and then there wasn't time enough to change our clothes."

He sniffed. "Well, you look ridiculous."

Mimsey took a step forward. "And you look pompous. The Samhain spirits couldn't care less what we look like, Heinrich. We have a job to do. Now let's go do it."

The Dragohs exchanged looks in the moonlight and turned as one to face the iron gate that blocked the road into the cemetery. They moved toward it, and the spellbook club followed. Two live oaks loomed on either side of the entrance, long shreds of moss hanging from the branches like clumps of trailing hair. Jaida fumbled a flashlight out of her knapsack and shone it on the lock. Rust encrusted the old-fashioned keyhole. Victor shook the gate, and the decayed metal sifted to the ground like so much red dust.

"It's not locked," Jaida said, and pushed against it. A brief shriek of metal on metal tore through the night, and the sky above filled with a rush of flapping wings.

Victor and Brandon helped push the gate open a few more feet. Jaida shone the light through the opening to reveal a mass of overgrown vines.

"Is there another way in?" I asked. "Because I don't think Nel came this way."

"The road circles the fence," Heinrich said. "There's another gate on the opposite side."

Andersen harrumphed. "I hope this hasn't turned into a snipe hunt."

No one responded, but I felt the same way.

Tires sounded on the road behind us again. My heart leaped in my chest as I watched the headlights barreling toward us. The vehicle suddenly swerved in behind the Cadillac. The driver cut the engine and lights, and then the sound of the door opening and closing reached our ears. I squinted at the approaching figure, recognizing his walk before I could make out his face.

Steve had joined the fray.

He stopped five feet away from where we'd gathered at the gate. The moonlight glinted off his hair. "Father."

Heinrich nodded at his son in silence.

Steve looked at my face, then down at the dress, and again met my eyes. Something passed between us. I remembered months before when we'd linked together to heal a wounded man. The power we'd shared then had convinced me once and for all that I was a witch—and had saved the man's life. Now it made me feel better that he'd come to help us. To help me. We worked well together magically.

Perhaps that was what he'd been referring to when he'd talked about our destiny. Perhaps we'd be awfully

good together in other ways, too. Perhaps I should re-
think our relationship. Give it a try. I thought of Declan,
back at the Honeybee. My good friend. But even if he
was willing to roll with my being a witch, there could
never be that bond of magic between us.

Steve walked right past me and stopped by his father's side.

"Steve?" I tried to keep the hurt out of my voice.

He shook his head. "This is my place." No apology,
no explanation. Apparently, he'd rethought a few
things himself.

I took a deep breath. Now was not the time to take
umbrage. Now was the time to focus. "Since we don't
have a counter for the actual Spell of Necretius, we
have to find Nel before midnight and bind her so she
can't summon Zesh in the first place," I said.

"Did you bring the poppet?" Heinrich asked.

I nodded. "Cookie?"

She looked at Jaida, who extracted a small figure
from the knapsack. It was about seven inches long and
off-white. It was the stick figure of rag dolls—no
clothes, no features, no anatomy other than torso, head,
arms, and legs. It did, however, have a gray braid
stitched to the scalp. Looking closer, I realized the
whole thing was made of fiber rather than cloth.

"Where . . . ?"

"It's lightly felted wool," Cookie said. "Annette already had the form and helped me . . . personalize it
this afternoon. She thinks it's for a Halloween gag."

"Nice," I said.

"How shall we do this?" Mimsey asked. "Y'all bind
her while we protect you?"

The Dragohs looked at each other and appeared to

reach a silent agreement. Victor nodded. "A circle within a circle."

"All right." Jaida patted the bag of magical goodies she carried. "We're loaded for bear."

"I hope you're ready for considerably more than that," Steve said, looking at me again. "Nel is willing to kill."

"Well, now, I don't know about that," Heinrich said. "It's unlikely she could even complete the summoning."

"No, Father. Her attack on Katie was viciously strong. Don't make the mistake of discounting her because she's female."

Heinrich began to bristle as the other men looked to him. Of course: The Dragohs were not a democracy. They had a leader, and it was Steve's father. How had I not realized that before?

Would that role pass to Steve as well?

Then Heinrich looked at his son and nodded. "Understood." He inclined his head toward me.

Slowly, I returned the gesture. "Where would Nel choose to cast the summoning spell?"

"I would choose the northern part of the cemetery," Heinrich said. The other men murmured agreement.

Mimsey's head bobbed. "Of course. Uriel's side, near the edge where the veil will thin at midnight and the souls can cross."

Chapter 30

"Let's go, then." I started pulling at the vines that clung to the gate, but they seemed to twine into the folds of my lacy skirt. I tried to tear it, but the fabric was too tough. "Darn it. I wish I'd had a chance to change out of this thing!" Frustration blew through my words.

Victor elbowed his way to my side. He leaned down, pulled up his pant leg, and extracted a ten-inch dagger from an ankle sheath. The metal blade gleamed wickedly. My breath caught as he plunged it into the edge of my skirt. Unless accompanied by food and a cutting board, knives gave me the heebie-jeebies, but I had to admit Victor's athame was effective. Within moments the wedding dress had been modified into a mini, the skirt raggedly falling halfway down my thighs.

"Thanks," I said.

"No problem." Victor shouldered through the gate, now using the dagger to hack at the kudzu.

"Those high-tops are a nice touch," Brandon said.

Cookie pushed him playfully.

Ignoring them both, I peered into the cemetery again.

A weight rustled against my shoulders, and I turned to find that Steve had put his jacket around me.

"Thank you, but I'm not cold."

His gaze held affection and amusement. "Maybe not, but that white dress is bright enough to see from space. Zombie dirt or no zombie dirt."

"Oh." I tugged the navy blue fabric closer. "Good point."

Heinrich fell into step behind Victor, and one by one the rest of us followed. The vines thinned enough within a few yards that we could move through them, albeit with care. They crawled over the graves, a green blanket to never warm the dead. Celtic crosses dotted what had once been a lawn to our left. Ivy and moss covered most of them to the point that only their vague shapes defined them as grave markers. To the right, a section was so overgrown with kudzu that no human could have gotten through it.

At least that narrowed the options.

The air grew cooler under the canopy of branches, and I was thankful for Steve's jacket. The humid breeze caressed the back of my neck like fond fingers, and I shivered.

As the path widened, I saw it was a road broad enough for vehicles to drive down. None had for a long time, though. The Dragohs had taken point, Heinrich and Steve side by side in front, followed by Victor and Brandon. Andersen trailed behind them, and the spellbook club members followed, our jaws clenched. Around us, crumbling gravestones tilted, their lettering faded nearly smooth. It was like something out of a haunted house, the reality of it adding another level to the terror. My shoulders hunched against the possibility of something springing out from the darkness.

A bird flushed from a cluster of azaleas ahead. Cookie shrieked, then ducked her head in embarrassment. The men turned to glare at her, but Brandon broke rank and rushed to her side to put his arm around her.

"Sikes," Heinrich admonished. Brandon moved back to his posse. Steve wouldn't look at me.

We reached the northern edge of the cemetery without seeing any sign of Nel. The group paused. In the silence I heard Mimsey breathing. It had been a bit of a hike for a seventy-eight-year-old.

"Are you okay?" Lucy asked. Jaida took a bottle of water out of her supply bag.

Mimsey nodded at my aunt but took the water with a grateful smile.

"Maybe you were wrong about Nel after all," Andersen said to me.

I curled my fingers around the iron fence and leaned my forehead against the back of my hand. "I don't think so. Maybe she's planning to summon Zesh from some other place altogether."

I opened my eyes. "Wait. Do you guys see that?" I pointed at a bright red MINI Cooper—just like the one Nel had driven away from the gallery the night of Brandon Sikes' art show. "She's here. Somewhere."

"Maybe we should break into pairs and search separately," Cookie said, flashing a look at Brandon.

"Are you crazy?" I asked at the same time that Heinrich said, "Absolutely not."

She shrugged, chastised.

"Hang on." I sniffed the air. A thin wisp of something familiar.

Of something burning. Not hair this time, thank goodness. But something nasty nonetheless.

With everyone's curious eyes watching, I took another deep breath and oh so carefully cast out with my mind. Gently, gently—there. A trace of that cold slipperiness I'd felt by Lawrence Eastmore's shed.

"This way," I said, turning to the west. A narrow path led through the wreckage of gravestones. I began to move down it. Heinrich followed me without a word. Victor fell in next, and the others followed.

"Are you sure—" I heard Andersen begin before Bianca shushed him.

The nature of the underbrush changed. Less dense, more dry. The ivy and even much of the kudzu had been beaten back. It appeared someone maintained this part of the cemetery, at least to a minor degree. The air smelled green, but I could still detect the burning smell under the lushness.

The ground suddenly collapsed beneath my foot. I gasped, stumbled, and managed to catch myself on a headstone. It crumbled under my hand as I pushed myself upright. Heinrich grabbed my other elbow. I leaned on him, extricating my foot from the loamy earth. I had gone in to my ankle, but my high-top had helped protect the joint.

"You okay?" he asked in a low voice.

I took a tentative step. "I think so. Nothing's broken or sprained."

The others gathered around, concern on their faces. "Be careful," I whispered. "The ground is uneven, and there are sinkholes."

Everyone nodded.

We continued on. It took me four more steps to realize that sinkholes in a cemetery had to be because the plots had been caving toward the center of the earth for many years. I hid a shudder from Heinrich, who had remained by my side, and moved on with great care.

The silver light of the moon shone at an angle through the branches of the trees. I was glad it was past full. A full moon on Samhain would add another factor to the mix, and there were plenty of things to think about already.

The teasing odor became infinitesimally stronger. We were getting closer; I could feel it. Did she know we were coming?

Had she enticed me closer on purpose?

Well, that thought certainly slowed my steps. The others rustled behind me. I craned my neck. There was no sign of Nel. The brilliance of the moonlight shone in the sky, and the trees and underbrush had become thicker again. Only spots of illumination fell all the way to the ground now.

I stopped altogether. We all stood perfectly still. Quiet descended, enveloped us. A bird flapped its wings, breaking the silence. I heard a slither in the bushes and tensed until the sound grew fainter.

Great: snakes. I *hated* snakes.

I turned in a circle, taking in the bare space around us. How much farther? What direction? From what I could tell, we were smack-dab in the middle of the cemetery. Bare dirt ran from my feet to a square stone structure in the middle of the clearing. A building, really, at least twenty-five feet square. A tapered dome roof reached toward the sky. Four marble steps led to a landing and a recessed entry. I squinted at the name carved under the roofline.

DRAYTON.

A hand on my shoulder made me jump. Mimsey leaned close, barely whispering in my ear. "Above-ground burial for the Drayton family."

I nodded. Probably the only part of Drayton Hills that was still fully maintained.

A long scraping noise issued from inside the mausoleum. Eleven people stopped breathing. We tiptoed closer until we could see the faint strip of vertical light that shone from the partially open door.

We'd found Nel Sandstrom.

Heinrich gestured for everyone to retrace their footsteps. We gathered at the edge of the clearing for a quick, whispered huddle.

"Where's the poppet?" Mimsey breathed. Jaida handed it to her. She held it up for everyone to see. Andersen put out his hand, and she gave it to him.

"Okay," she said. "First we'll set the protective circle around the burial chamber as quietly as we can."

"And then you maintain it while we go inside," Andersen said.

"No. The quarters will be too tight for us all to work," Victor said, peering over his shoulder at the poppet. "We have to call her out."

"Oh, for heaven's sake," Mimsey said. "That's just like a man. 'Call her out.' You don't have to call her out for a binding spell, boys. Just bind her using the poppet. It's not high noon at the OK Corral."

But it wasn't far from that. High midnight at the Drayton mausoleum.

"You're close enough to direct the spell, and you don't have any doubt it's Nel in there, do you?"

We all shook our heads.

I checked my watch. "It's already eleven thirty. We don't have time to argue. Cast the circle."

Jaida handed Bianca four white candles. She lit one and placed it on top of a nearby stone pillar. I saw Mimsey mouthing words and knew she was appealing to the element of air and the archangel of the east, Raphael. Jaida took out a two-pound bag of salt she must have lifted from the Honeybee kitchen.

"You hauled that all the way in here?" I asked.

"Good thing I did," she said. "We'll need it for a space this large." Cookie and I stood with the druids, watching as Bianca and Mimsey moved deosil around the clearing to the south. There they lit another candle and placed it on top of a large rock. Jaida and Lucy tiptoed behind them with the salt, stopping at each compass point as they lit another candle.

The salt created a white line on the ground. The four women joined us again at the eastern edge of the clearing, closing the circle around us all. Mimsey and Jaida finished by inscribing a protective dome above us— Mimsey with two sweeping gestures of her arms and Jaida with an honest-to-goddess wand.

The men moved toward the marble steps leading into the mausoleum, on the south side of the structure. We all made our way to where we could see them. Lucy took hold of one of my hands and Bianca took the other one. Cookie took Bianca's hand, then Jaida and Mimsey linked with her. I felt the power surge among us as Mimsey and Lucy joined hands to complete the circuit.

The druids had reached the bottom step when Andersen tripped. His cry lashed through the humid night as the poppet flew out of his hand and he fell sprawling to the ground. Lucy's hand gripped mine so

tightly I thought she'd fracture my fingers. Beside me
Bianca tensed in fear and readiness. The sudden silence
after Andersen's outburst was broken by subtle rustling in the undergrowth around the clearing. A black
snake, long and ropy, slid out of the bushes. It stopped
at the line of white salt, watching us.

I licked my lips and willed myself to stop shaking.

It didn't work.

The partially open door of the mausoleum swung all
the way open. Nel strode out onto the marble landing
carrying a small flaming torch. She wore a long black
cloak with a hood—pretty standard witch garb for outdoor work, really. The hood was thrown back to reveal
her long gray hair falling unfettered to her waist. I blinked
as the tendrils seemed to move of their own accord, curl-
ing and flexing against the dark fabric. Her face was and
yet was not Nel's. Easily recognizable, but so . . . altered.
Her wrinkles, so seemingly friendly before, carved deeply
into her flesh now. Her cheekbones and chin appeared
elongated, and her eyes—oh, her eyes! They blazed with
hatred—and they were focused on mine.

"You!" She pointed at me. As if there was a question
about who she was talking to. "You think you can defeat me twice? You cannot. This time I'm ready. I didn't
know how strong you were before."

As Andersen scrambled to his feet, Steve lunged for
the poppet lying on the ground. It had fallen just inside
the salt circle. Bending, he closed his fingers around it.
He spun on his heel and tossed it to his father.

"But are you ready for them, too?" I asked.

Victor snapped his fingers at Andersen. The younger
druid had lost his glasses when he fell, and now blinked
myopically at the other men.

"Cord!" Victor barked.

Andersen nodded vigorously, reached into a pocket, and withdrew a length of fine silver chain. Victor grabbed it and handed it to Heinrich, who began winding it around the woolen figurine.

"No!" Nel screamed and sketched a symbol in the air.

"Concentrate, girls," Mimsey said. The spellbook club bowed our heads. I centered my attention on protecting ourselves and the druids, silently calling on the elements all around us. At the periphery of my consciousness I felt a presence join us. Without ever having met him, I knew it was Lawrence Eastmore, adding a little extra oomph to the proceedings from the other side of the veil. I had to wonder whether his son would join us, too. Or if he'd join Nel.

"By air and fire," the Dragohs chanted in one voice. I looked up.

"Water and earth: We bind you."

Heinrich nodded to the spellbook club. "By six, and"—he looked at Steve, hesitated, then said—"and by five: We bind you."

Nel continued to draw figures in the air, muttering in a language I didn't recognize. Her torch had fallen to the ground. The flame sputtered and went out.

Brandon produced a small iron bowl, and set it on the ground. Heinrich continued to wind the chain around the poppet. I could hear the ragged breathing of the other ladies, but then the rustling around the clearing grew louder. Snakes began pouring toward us. I quelled my panic, throwing as much power as I could to maintaining the protection of the circle. The serpents slowed, then stopped outside the line of salt as the first one had.

Motion above alerted me that not all the snakes were

on the ground. They were looping down from the trees above us. But that part of the circle held as well, and along with my awareness of the creepy crawlies up there I sensed something else.

Souls. Souls of the dead, come to watch the show.

A whiff of gardenia reached my nose, and despite everything, I smiled.

"By sun and moon," the druids chanted, "stars and sea: We bind you."

Nonsense syllables tumbled from Nel's lips. Her voice grew weaker as Heinrich finished wrapping the figure in his hand. Her hands went to her head. But still she spoke, still she glared at me.

I felt my eyes go wide as the candle flames at the compass points winked out: one, two, three, four. The snakes slithered back and forth along the salt line.

Heinrich put the poppet in the iron bowl. Without my noticing, Victor had removed the dagger from his ankle sheath. He bent over the bowl, ready to plunge it into the poppet.

"No!" I shouted. "No killing!"

Victor paused. Steve reached for the long-handled lighter Mimsey used to light the candles around the circle and held it up for me to see. I nodded. Burning magic I understood. The intention would be to burn away Nel's power, not Nel herself. Too bad the doll was made of wool, though. That was going to smell pretty awful, and frankly I was ready to smell a whole lot more sugar and spice and a whole lot less burning hair.

Victor stepped forward with his knife again, and I realized he'd never intended to impale the figure in the bowl. He cut his finger and allowed a drop of blood to drip into the bowl.

Beside me, Bianca began to shudder.

"It's all right," I whispered, though in truth I was pretty grossed out, too.

Steve stooped to light the figure in the bowl.

"By sky and lava, beyond and within: We bind you."

The lighter went out. Steve flicked it again. The flame steadied.

"We bind your intent. We bind your darkness."

Victor lifted his knife again.

"We bind your power," they chanted. "We bind you. We bind your power. We bind your darkness."

I squeezed my eyes shut, focusing with everything I had. In my mind's eye, I could see the iron bowl, the poppet, the lighter. The sweet smell of gardenia increased, made my head swim. Something began to glow in the clearing, but I ignored it, instead concentrating on the fire burning away Nel's evil intentions, hoping that anything I could do as a catalyst would help the others. Then a flash of bright light and a scream made me open my eyes.

The poppet burned, bright flames licking up from the bowl. Nel slumped on the steps of the burial chamber, looking disoriented. And everyone was staring at me.

I realized I wasn't holding Lucy and Jaida's hands anymore. Steve's jacket had slipped to the ground. All the snakes had vanished from the edges of the clearing and the tree limbs above. And the light, the light in the clearing, was fading.

I looked around. "Nonna?"

Mimsey shook her head, staring at my dress. I looked down. It was glowing.

No. It wasn't.

I was.

It faded so quickly I wondered if I'd really seen it. Because how could I, you know, *glow*? No, I had to have imagined it, all caught up in the magic of the moment.

Literally.

The poppet suddenly went out, and the clearing became dark except for the moonlight now streaming from straight overhead. A stunned silence fell over the group; then Jaida clicked the flashlight on. Heinrich seemed to shake himself. He and Steve went to Nel and helped her sit up.

"She's all right, but we were successful in stripping her power," Steve said. "Katie, can you bring my jacket?"

Jaida handed me the light. I picked up the jacket from the ground and carried it to him. Nel looked up at me wearily, and I opened my mouth to speak. But then Steve reached for his coat, and I saw something in the beam of the flashlight that made my jaw snap shut again.

On the inside of his upper arm, small and inflamed but recognizable: a new tattoo of a wreath with six spokes radiating from the center.

He saw me staring and met my eyes. "It's my place, Katie."

Clap. Clap.

I spun toward the sound at the edge of the clearing, squinting into the shadows.

Clap. Clap. Clap.

The thick undergrowth rustled. Druids and witches alike tensed. Steve and his father both raised their arms in a warding gesture.

Franklin Taite's pale round face seemed to float out of the darkness. He walked toward us, revealing the dark clothing that covered him from head to toe like some kind of SWAT commando uniform.

He continued to applaud slowly. "Bravo!" He stopped outside the salt circle and raised one eyebrow.

Chapter 31

"Who are you?" Victor Powers rumbled.

Taite looked at me.

I sighed. "Everyone, meet Detective Franklin Taite. He's a witch-hunter. Detective Taite, meet . . . everyone."

"Oh, I know you all by now, by reputation if not in person." He peered at Nel blinking with bleary eyes from the steps of the burial chamber. Steve closed his hand around one of her wrists, but she didn't seem inclined to run. "And I'm not just a witch-hunter, Ms. Lightfoot. I hunt black magic of all kinds."

I remembered the word Lucy had used: *discerning*. So did that mean Detective Taite was on our side?

"What are you going to do?" Jaida asked. "Arrest us for trespassing in the cemetery? Because nothing else we've done here is illegal."

His attention turned to her. "Ah. Even the lawyer is a witch. Actually, I'm not in the least interested in punishing you. Um, mind if I come in?" He gestured at the salt at his feet. "I have a murderer to arrest."

Mimsey clasped her hands. "Excellent. Lucy? Shall we?"

Together they circled the clearing widdershins, sweeping aside the salt with a tree branch and remembering to thank the elements and archangels as they gathered the cold candles along the way. As they worked, Franklin Taite kept staring at me.

"Will you stop that?" I asked. "You make me feel like a bug under a microscope."

"Oh, but you fascinate me. I knew this group was involved with Lawrence Eastmore's murder somehow, and you in particular, but I had no idea what you were."

"Could have fooled me," I scoffed.

"No, I knew you were a witch. Just not what type."

I shrugged. "Hedgewitchery is pretty tame. We don't garner the attention of the police much."

His face went slack for a moment, and then he laughed. "Oh, my. You don't know?" He looked around at the others. "None of you know what she is?"

Lucy finished opening the circle and gestured Taite into the clearing. "She's a catalyst." There was pride in her voice.

"Oh, I bet she is, yes indeed," he said without moving. "But I'm talking about the fact that your niece is a *candela*. A lightwitch."

"Detective Taite, of course I'm a light witch. I don't have any desire to practice dark magic."

"Well, that's good, because you *can't* practice dark magic. You are incapable of it."

Cookie's head tipped to the side. Brandon put his arm around her, but she was much more interested in what the good detective was saying than in her new boyfriend's attentions. Out of the corner of my eye I saw Heinrich slowly nodding. I glanced over at him and was disconcerted to see deep respect on his face.

"How could you be unaware of your calling?" Taite stepped into the circle.

"Calling?" Surely I'd know if I had a calling by now.

"You are here to battle black magic. As a candela you can never be tempted by the darkness, only work for the good. A tricky business, that, given all the gray magic out there. But your power comes from the whitest of magic. And my dear, you do indeed seem to possess a great deal of it."

Oh, brother. This guy was really something. At least he didn't want to burn us at the stake or something equally melodramatic.

Still, all eyes turned toward me as if he weren't talking nonsense. I turned my palms up. "I'm just glad we stopped the summoning of Zesh."

Detective Taite froze. "Zesh?" He strode the last few steps to Nel. "You were going to summon Zesh? That's why you killed Eastmore?"

"For the Spell of Necretius," I explained.

"Do you have any idea what could have happened if you'd been successful?" he demanded, inches from her face. "To you? To everyone?"

"I would have proved that I'm powerful enough to be a Dragoh," she replied, glaring at me again. "I would have broken the patriarchal ranks and taken my rightful inheritance as a member of the society." She distributed a sneer among the druids. "I'm more powerful than any of you individually. More powerful than my father, even. When he told me about the society, I mocked the idea that you wouldn't let me in. At first. But he was convinced it could never happen. I was determined to prove him wrong."

Andersen, cowed after almost losing the poppet, had found his glasses and put them back on. Now he moved to the steps and leaned in beside Taite. Nel flinched. He said, "You killed my friend because you wanted to prove you were good enough to be a Dragoh? You would have risked the summoning spell not because you actually wanted to summon the spirit, but because you wanted to prove something?"

She nodded, uncertainty crossing her features for the first time.

His hand drew back as if to strike her, but Taite caught it. "You stripped her power," the detective said. "Secular justice is my department. Back off."

Taite pulled what looked like an oversized plastic zip tie out of his pocket and gestured Nel to her feet. "You are under arrest for the murder of Lawrence Eastmore. Anything you say can and will be used against you in a court of law." As he turned her around I saw a flash.

"Knife!" I yelled.

He dodged as she feinted right, but the blade she had pulled from the wide sleeve of her cloak was in her left hand. He caught her wrist, and the knife dropped to the stone below with a metallic clang. His eyes bored into hers. "Take the cloak off."

Nel was tired, and the battle of wills was short. With a sigh, she unclasped the robe and let it fall to the ground. I'd been afraid she might be au naturel underneath, but she wore the same red caftan she'd worn at the gallery. Taite continued with her Miranda rights as he cuffed her. She didn't struggle again, and when he asked if she understood she said she did. He began to march her toward the path that led from the northern entrance.

"Detective?" I asked. He paused. Turned. "Did you follow us here?"

He shook his head. "I took over the stakeout on this one, after she'd already arrived. We've had eyes on her all along."

I gaped. "You always knew she was the killer?"

"Not at all. But she's been in this since the beginning," he said. "First at the scene in Johnson Square, and then hanging around your bakery, and finally working there. Her background check turned out a little iffy."

"Tell me about it," I grumbled. "Greer Eastmore pretended to be her former employer. He fooled me, all right."

Taite's eyebrows arched. "Is that why you called him?"

Curious eyes turned my way, and I nodded, relieved to have an explanation.

Taite continued. "Then yesterday we matched her prints, which were in the system from decades back when she applied to be a substitute teacher, to some we found in Lawrence Eastmore's home."

Hard evidence that she'd murdered Dr. Eastmore. My attention returned to something Taite had said. "Wait. Nel, you were in Johnson Square?"

She lifted her chin in one last show of defiance. "I went back to Lawrence's the night after I'd hit him. I needed one more book, to make sure no one could create a counterspell."

"*The 33 Curses,*" I said, glancing at Andersen.

She nodded. "Yes. I thought I'd killed him, but there he was, staggering down the street at midnight. I saw him heading for the square, but there were people around. I couldn't do anything. I saw him fall. So I waited."

I gaped. "You could have saved him."

"Why would I do that?" she asked.

I ran my hand over my face. Evidently, Nel's need to be in the Dragoh Society had driven her far beyond the edge of sanity. I could only hope she wasn't beyond help altogether. My hand dropped as I remembered. "You were on the bench. Reading the paper. In front of the bank on Bryan Street," I said.

She smiled.

"Why did you want to work at the Honeybee so badly?" I asked. "You went to a lot of trouble, and you had to know we'd find out you lied sooner or later."

Her head ticked to the side. "You found him. You saw the tattoo. I could tell what you were—magically, I mean—even from across the street. I wanted to keep an eye on you." Her laugh held no humor. "I sure didn't expect a whole coven working out of that silly bakery."

Taite took a step, tugging at her arm.

"Just one more thing."

He stopped and turned halfway back.

"Greer, Nel. What happened to Greer?" The spellbook club and druids gathered around me.

"He died," Nel said, looking around at all of us. "He was the one who told me about the summoning spell in the first place, when we were together in Greece."

I shot a questioning look at Taite. He nodded in response. "We found out about their connection just this evening."

"Oh, don't look so surprised," Nel said to me. "I'm a little older than he is, but we had a good time for a few years. Then after he came back for the funeral and saw me, he guessed that I'd killed his father. Poor man wasn't very interested in magic, but I needed a power source, and he fit the bill."

I was afraid to ask. "Power source."

"When I attacked you. I couldn't afford to use my power for that. I had to be ready for tonight. Heck, I had to be ready to come into the Honeybee and cover for *you*. We had an old connection, Greer and I, and so I used him."

Steve took a step forward. "You *used* him?"

I put my hand on his shoulder. "I'm afraid she used him up. It killed him."

"He always was weak," she said.

"Detective," Steve growled, "you'd better get this woman out of here before she says another word."

Taite took her by the arm. "Done."

"I'll go with you," Victor said, looking around at all of us. "So she doesn't try anything stupid."

I looked around at the clearing. "We'll clean up here."

The ladies sat in the mismatched chairs in the gazebo, sipping sweet tea and keeping me company while I dug a hole on the north side of the structure. It was early evening; after a long day at the bakery, I'd met the spellbook club back at my carriage house for some heavy smudging. Once again it stank to high heaven of sage and juniper. They'd also helped me cast a deep cleansing spell and re-up the standard protections around the place. A new spell bottle sat on the bookshelf, courtesy of Lucy. Even Mungo was content with the work we'd done.

Steve's ring still hung from the chain around my neck. While the others packed up our magical paraphernalia the night before and swept away what salt they could, Steve and I went into the Drayton mausoleum to see what Nel had left there. We made a grisly discovery.

Nel had created an altar on a stone sarcophagus on the north side of the room. We lit a couple of the candles there so we could see, and found that her working space held a lot of familiar items as well as a few oddities: a jar containing a black sticky substance that smelled like Limburger cheese, a perfectly preserved skin of a copperhead snake, and . . . human finger bones.

She'd broken into one of the burial vaults and removed them for the summoning spell. I'd called the police precinct and asked them to track down Detective Taite. He'd called Quinn back in, and they were both interviewing Nel—I had to wonder how that conversation went. When he came on the line I told him about the bones, and he said he'd add a charge of grave robbing to the list. But he couldn't charge her with Greer's death, which appeared to be a straightforward heart attack.

On the altar, Steve and I also found the Spell of Necretius, the actual volume Nel had stolen from Dr. Eastmore. It was much smaller than I'd expected, a quarter of the size of *The 33 Curses*. Thin—maybe ten pages, bound in leather and gilded with gold. It smelled ancient. I couldn't resist flipping it open. The ink on the yellowed pages had faded so it was hard to read, and from what I could see the language was barely recognizable as English. More like something Chaucer might have written.

"You take it, Katie."

"I don't want it!" I shoved it at him.

He ignored my outstretched hand. "If what Taite says is true, you won't be tempted. Anyone else might be."

"Pfft. That lightwitch stuff? Please. I'm just as bad as anyone else."

"Maybe. But not when it comes to magic. Katie, *you glowed in the dark*. I believe him."

You glowed in the dark.

But my mind shunted away from the thought. I didn't want to have a calling, be a lightwitch or a candela or whatever. To suffer the onus of always having to be good. Darn it, I wanted to try a new recipe for lavender vanilla biscotti and grow my little spells in the backyard.

"Fine," I grumped and stuffed the little book into my bra. He grinned. "I don't have any pockets," I said defensively.

"Okay."

"And while I'm thinking about it—" I reached behind my neck to unclasp the chain. "Here's your ring."

He held up his hand. "Keep it. I can get another one."

I paused, then lowered my arms. Eyed the tattoo on the inside of his arm. "Are you an actual member of the society now?"

He nodded slowly. "They decided to make an exception. Greer had no children, and Lawrence's sister didn't, either. At least I'm here, and . . . ready. We need six."

I didn't ask why.

"Nel's cousin is joining us from Kentucky," he said.

"So they made an exception for you, but not for Nel, even after her father's death. That's pretty crappy, you know."

"I know. But I'm glad she didn't become our first female member."

"Yeah." I had to agree with that. "You have a point there."

Now as I shoveled dirt out of the hole by the gazebo, I thought about Lawrence Eastmore planting the Savannah holly tree in his backyard. About how there were six of them, just as there were six members in the Dragoh Society. And I knew about them. Enough about them, in fact, that I didn't like the idea of being involved with one of them, no matter how he made me feel.

"I think I found someone who can help out at the Honeybee," Cookie said, breaking into my reverie.

I leaned on the handle of the shovel and looked at Lucy. Her response was a serene smile. I tugged at my gardening gloves and knelt by the hole. "No, thank you."

"Seriously, you're going to love her."

"Uh-huh."

Mimsey laughed. "You might want to give her a chance. Cookie is good at what I've begun to think of as 'job magic.'"

I looked up at her. The twinkle was back in her blue eyes. I hadn't realized how much I'd missed it the last few days. "Okay." I capitulated.

Bianca rose. "I need to pick up Colette." She looked around. "It really is lovely here."

"Inside and out now," Jaida said, standing. "I have to get going, too."

Lucy nodded, eyeing my planting efforts. "I think we should all give Katie a chance to settle back in." She gave me a knowing smile. A smile that said she understood that I needed to be alone for what I was about to do.

Hugs all around, and I walked them out front, Mungo trotting at my heels. "Thanks, everyone. I can't tell you how much I'm looking forward to sleeping in my own house tonight."

More hugs, and then the ladies climbed into their respective vehicles and drove off to their own lives. When Lucy's Thunderbird had vanished around the corner, I turned back to the house. Margie waved from her front porch, and I waved back.

Back by the gazebo, Mungo sat and watched with interest as I lifted the gardenia plant out of the plastic pot and settled it into the hole.

Recipes

Cinnamon Raisin Biscotti

Makes 12 biscotti

1 cup raisins
2 teaspoons cinnamon
¼ teaspoon nutmeg
2 cups all-purpose flour
2 eggs
½ teaspoon baking powder
⅔ cup sugar
½ teaspoon salt
1 teaspoon vanilla extract

Preheat oven to 350°F. Line a cookie sheet with parchment paper or nonstick aluminum foil.

Combine the raisins, cinnamon, nutmeg, and flour and set aside. Combine the eggs, baking powder, sugar, salt, and vanilla extract and beat on medium speed until mixture is light and the sugar is mostly dissolved. Mixing on low speed, add the flour mixture in gradually until it is just incorporated. Do not overmix.

Shape dough into a 3 x 12–inch loaf and transfer to the cookie sheet (or form the loaf on the cookie sheet). Bake for 25 minutes. Remove loaf from oven and reduce the temperature to 325°F. Allow the loaf to cool for 15–20 minutes on a cutting board, then use a serrated knife to slice it into 12 pieces. Slice either straight across or diagonally, depending on the desired shape and size of the biscotti. Lightly mist the loaf with water first to help prevent crumbling.

Place the slices back on the cookie sheet and bake for another 20 minutes until crispy but not browned. Cool biscotti completely before storing in an airtight container.

If you like nuts in your biscotti, replace half the raisins with slivered almonds or chopped pecans. These are wonderful dipped into coffee drinks or a glass of dessert wine, and are something special with a cup of hot apple cider in the fall!

Margie's Coca-Cola Cake

Makes one 9 x 13–inch sheet cake

1 cup Coca-Cola
½ cup buttermilk
2 cups all-purpose flour
¼ cup cocoa powder
1 teaspoon baking soda
1 cup butter
1¾ cups sugar
2 large eggs, slightly beaten
1½ teaspoons vanilla extract

Preheat the oven to 350° F. Butter and flour a 9 x 13–inch baking pan.

Mix the Coca-Cola and the buttermilk together and set aside. Sift together the flour, cocoa, and baking soda and set aside.

Cream the butter and sugar together on low speed with an electric mixer. Add the eggs and vanilla extract and beat together until thoroughly combined. Add half the flour mixture and combine well. Mix in the Coca-Cola and buttermilk, then add the rest of the flour, mixing until just blended.

Pour the cake batter into the prepared pan and bake at 350° F for 30 to 35 minutes until a cake tester inserted in the middle comes out clean. Allow to cool for a few minutes while you make the frosting.

Coca-Cola Frosting

½ cup butter
¼ cup Coca-Cola
3 tablespoons cocoa powder
1 teaspoon vanilla extract
1 pound confectioners' sugar
1 cup chopped dried cherries (optional)

Melt the butter in a saucepan. Add the Coca-Cola and cocoa powder and bring the mixture to a boil. Remove from heat and whisk in the confectioners' sugar and vanilla. Stir in the chopped cherries if you like. The cherries can also be replaced with the same amount of more traditional chopped pecans. Pour the warm frosting over the warm cake and allow to cool completely before slicing.

ABOUT THE AUTHOR

Bailey Cates believes magic is all around us if we only look for it. She's held a variety of positions ranging from driver's license examiner to soapmaker, which fulfills her mother's warning that she'd never have a "regular" job if she insisted on studying philosophy, English, and history in college. She traveled the world as a localization program manager but now sticks closer to home, where she writes two mystery series, tends to a dozen garden beds, bakes up a storm, and plays the occasional round of golf. Bailey resides in Colorado with her guy and an orange cat that looks an awful lot like the one in her Magical Bakery Mysteries.

CONNECT ONLINE

www.baileycates.com